Rourke activated the jaw profile radio at the side of his mouth. "This is Rourke! Get back. All bets are off. We're going in, getting what we came for. Meet us out front!" And he ran toward the tunnel mouth, the casing around the tunnel collapsing now, as was the lip above it.

The shaking of the ground was unlike anything John Rourke had ever experienced, could ever have imagined. With each step, it was necessary to fight to keep his balance. And now, as he neared the tunnel mouth, the roadway surface beneath his combat-booted feet was cracking, splitting into massive chunks, debris exploding upward, pieces of the tunnel casing flying everywhere around him. A piece of synthe-concrete struck at his left arm, tearing the snow smock. Rourke kept running.

The tunnel mouth was just ahead of him, Natalia and Paul, Danzig and his three men near one of the trucks. There were other SS uniformed personnel around them, but all of them apparently with Danzig, loyal to Helmut Anton Griem and disloyal to Deitrich Zimmer.

As Rourke raced toward them, he shouted, "Zimmer will release the virus if he thinks this is it, the end! Into the trucks!"

THE SURVIVALIST

#27 DEATH WATCH

BY JERRY AHERN

ZEBRA BOOKS
KENSINGTON PUBLISHING CORP.

ZEBRA BOOKS are published by

Kensington Publishing Corp.
475 Park Avenue South
New York NY 10016

First Printing: December, 1993

Printed in the United States of America

To the people who have read the adventures of the Rourke Family, in some cases named their children after the Rourke children, who have, for more than twelve years, made the Rourke Family, and by that, the Ahern Family, a part of their lives—sincerest thanks and affection . . .

One

John Thomas Rourke raised the two pistols in his hands, bringing them to eye level. They were the Lancer copies of the SIG-Sauer P-228 from the days Before the Night of the War. He wore not his customary dark-lensed aviator-style sunglasses, but grey-lensed shooting glasses instead, "earmuffs" as well. This was an indoor range within the very bowels of the submersible carrier *Paladin,* the facility for the use of the *Paladin's* security forces and whatever Navy SEAL detachments might, from time to time, be stationed aboard.

As he began firing the matching 9mm Parabellums, a bizarre parallel crossed Rourke's mind. The guns were so identical to the originals that they were like clones. And he lived because of a clone, the clone's heart beating now within his chest.

That was nineteen days ago, when the heart was placed within him. Even Before the Night of the War, he would have been up and around, capable of limited activity by now. But, with the fantastic strides made by modern medicine 625 years in the objective future from the date of the Great Conflagration, he was fully restored. Indeed, the heart which had been given him was stronger, newer than his own, albeit an identical tissue match.

People lived considerably longer these days, and he had spent more than six centuries in cryogenic sleep, which also lent itself to heightened longevity. The new heart, his surgeon had told him, would add years to his lifespan.

That was ironic. There was, in process, a limited nuclear war between the Trans-Global Alliance and the nation of Eden and its ally, the Nazis under the leadership of Deitrich Zimmer. And, according to the best scientific data available, the suboceanic rift in the Pacific Basin was still progressing inexorably toward the North American Continental Plate. Once it reached that plate, there existed the almost certain likelihood that the rift would split along the edge of the plate and precipitate the eventual eruption of all major volcanoes comprising the Ring of Fire, forming a caldera of biblical proportions, eventually destroying the planet.

Life expectancy was all a matter of perspective.

If the war with the Nazis could be brought to a swift conclusion and the nuclear weapons in the Eden and Nazi arsenals, along with those of the new United States and New Germany could be utilized, it was theoretically possible to save the planet from destruction. The nuclear weapons, the preponderance of them in the tactical-yield range, could be used to relieve the pressure on the volcanic vent and avert catastrophic eruption.

It was the choice toward which the nuclear age had propelled itself since its very dawning: Would mankind use nuclear weapons to end the Earth? The irony was that mankind, if the option of self-destruction were not elected, might use nuclear weapons to save the Earth.

Rourke left the slides of the two 228s locked open, the electronic display beside him revealing the exact positioning of each of the hits on the target. He had blown out the center of mass kill zone. He set down the pistols, picking up the little Detonics CombatMasters which he had used since Before the Night of the War. The actions were locked open. He inserted a loaded magazine into first one, then the other of the twin stainless steel .45s. He swept his left thumb round behind the pistol in his left hand and depressed the slide stop, more conveniently actuating the slide stop for the pistol in his right hand.

Both pistols cocked, actions closed, he brought them to eye level and began firing, emptying all twelve shots at the head of the electronically monitored silhouette. When he glanced at the display beside him, all twelve rounds had struck in the area analogous to the forehead. Satisfied that he had not lost his touch, John Rourke lowered both pistols to the counter in front of him.

At the next position, Annie was just finishing a ridiculously slow string with her Detonics ScoreMaster. As she lowered her pistol, its action locked open over the empty magazine, she turned toward him, smiling. Through the transparent divider, Rourke could see the electronic posting of her hit. "Very funny," he told her. She had shot a valentine heart shape over the heart of the silhouette . . .

Annie Rourke Rubenstein was pleased with her shooting, but even more pleased that her father seemed relaxed. Difficult times lay ahead of him; and, although the doctors were proclaiming that he was sounder than he had ever been, she still worried. Annie sometimes wondered if it was part of the job description which went with being a woman: Official Worrier.

Her father continued shooting, burning through previously loaded magazines with a vengeance. He had always enjoyed shooting as a means of relaxation. And she smiled bitterly, remembering. She retained the faintest memories of her mother and father arguing once—she imagined it had been more often than that—about her father taking Michael out to do some shooting. "Why would you put a gun in a little boy's hand, for God's sake?!"

"Because Michael won't always be a little boy, Sarah. As a man, he'll be well-served knowing how to use firearms. And it isn't any 'male' thing. As soon as Annie's a little older—"

"You're obsessed with guns, John."

Her mother still adamantly believed that her father was the man behind the gun that night at Eden when, in reality, Deitrich Zimmer had done the foul deed, shot Sarah Rourke in the head. It wasn't her mother's fault that she blamed her husband instead of the real culprit, but that didn't make living with the situation any easier . . .

9

Paul Rubenstein walked beside the gurney on which the stabilized body of John Rourke #11 rested.

Sedated.

About to die.

Natalia walked on the other side of the gurney, her eyes shifting from the body to the people surrounding the gurney.

They had not spoken about how the clone of John Rourke would die.

The *Paladin*'s chief medical officer had met them as soon as the primary landing bay in which they'd touched down was evacuated of water and pressure equalized.

"There is one very big problem, Major Tiemerovna," he'd told her.

"I know. Trust me," she told him. "It will not remain a problem."

They were on the medical level now, just clear of the elevators. Emma Shaw walked beside Natalia, Annie beside Paul, Michael behind the gurney, nearest to John Rourke #11's head.

The chief medical officer—Commander Tierney—had gone on ahead. From what Natalia understood, once the heart was available, the operation could get underway in a matter of minutes.

Natalia had her knife to hand. She would cut the femoral artery on the inside of the right thigh of John Rourke #11, completely severing it so that some misguided person could not somehow save John Rourke #11's life.

This was evil. This was murder. She was fully prepared to do the act.

She touched her fingertips to the butt of the Bali-Song in the pocket along her jumpsuit's right thigh.

She caught Annie's eyes. Then Paul's.

Paul still had her suppressed Walther PPK/S. Was his hand reaching for it under his sweater?

The pre-op area lay about twenty-five yards ahead, the

nearest thing to them a vacant intensive-care ward, the door open, the beds turned up and empty.

Natalia watched John Rourke #11's chest as it rose and fell.

John Rourke was a mind, not a body, the body merely the instrument by which the mind could function. She was not killing anything that was even a part of John Rourke.

She started to remove the knife from the pouch on her thigh.

There was a blur of motion from her right, through the doorway of the vacant intensive-care ward.

Sarah, some kind of knife in her hands.

Paul reached for Sarah.

Annie shrieked, "Momma, no!"

Natalia threw her body toward the gurney, trying to protect the heart of John Rourke #11 with her own body.

But the gurney was shoved forward.

Michael was reacting.

"No Michael!" Natalia screamed.

The knife hammered down in Sarah Rourke's hands, Paul and Annie were grabbing her, wrestling her back.

"I destroyed the heart!" Sarah screamed.

Annie clutched Sarah to her, half fighting to hold her.

Sarah looked over her shoulder, eyes wide, streaming tears. "I had to before he—"

"Shut up!" Natalie shrieked.

And she looked down at the body on the gurney.

John Rourke #11 was dead.

When Michael had moved the gurney so suddenly, Sarah missed. The knife had impaled the clone through the left eye on an upward angle into the brain.

Emma Shaw was already starting to shove the gurney toward the pre-op section, the uniformed nurses running after her, Emma shouting, "Doctor Tierney! We've got the heart!"

Whether Emma Shaw's eyes were opened or closed, she could still recall the image of the dead clone of John Rourke almost as vividly as the wild look in Sarah Rourke's eyes when Sarah had killed the clone in a vain attempt to kill John. Sarah had known full well that the clone was the clone,

11

not John, but also known full well that by killing the clone—she had tried to stab the heart—she would kill John.

The ship's psychiatrist, Commander Donald Blankenship, had requested that she come to see him, as a sort of "mental debriefing, let's call it, Commander Shaw."

She could have refused; but, on the plus side, talking about it with a disinterested party might do her some good. She had guilt feelings, as the "other woman," the "home wrecker," even though she knew that nothing she had done had precipitated what had happened.

The time was right for the "mental de-briefing," too, because tonight there would be dinner, then retiring early in order to be ready for the pre-dawn flight which would take them—John, his daughter Annie and herself—to Lydveldid Island where, if all went according to plan, there would be a neutral ground meeting with the one man in the world with whose help mankind might be able to save the planet from almost certain cataclysm. There would be no time, in either event—survival or death—for recriminations, nor time to waste in other ways. If she and John could somehow survive, they would marry after Sarah (if indeed Sarah really was Sarah) had divorced him. They both expected that to be an ordeal, considering Sarah's current mental state.

Lying beside her in her bunk on the first night after his release from the ship's sickbay, John told her, "I knew people who became embroiled in divorce. It was a common malady in the twentieth century. I suppose that's one reason I fought so hard to keep this from happening, because I believed that if I fought hard enough I could prevent it. The doctors say that Sarah's fine in every other respect, that on a rational basis she'll eventually accept as fact that it was Deitrich Zimmer who shot her, not me. But she can't forgive the death of Martin, or his clone. That she'll never forgive. But, it wasn't working anyway. And sometimes you get so tired that you can't endure any longer. She'll be happier with Wolfgang." Then, he folded his right arm around her and went to sleep. She hadn't wanted him to make love to her, just hold her; and, he understood that. It was several more days before she felt that he was well enough so that they could make love, even though the doctors had pronounced him 90 percent recovered. But she wondered now if she had merely been using his recovery as an excuse?

That for centuries John Rourke had been all but celibate (save for the obvious time with Sarah, making her pregnant with Martin, and doubtless other times with her after that and before Sarah was shot) would be unimaginable to someone who knew him only sexually; he was beyond terrific in bed, almost beyond human. But, John was born for monogamy. While there was a chance that his and Sarah's marriage might be saved—although she had wished it disolved even Before the Night of the War—John remained faithful to his wife. Emma Shaw knew that John had crossed a bridge on which he could never return when he made love to her that first time.

For the last three nights, they had been lovers again, John's stamina beyond question. But the guilt which she felt, however unjustified she knew it to be from a rational point of view, could someday interfere. She didn't want that; perhaps the *Paladin*'s shrink could help against that, perhaps not. She would wait and see.

Commander Blankenship entered his office, smiled, sat down behind his desk and apologized. "Even psychiatrists have emergencies now and again; should have been a dermatologist. They get them too, though."

"No problem, Commander."

"Don, please. May I call you Emma?"

"Sure," she nodded, crossing her legs, tugging at the hem of her skirt. For a psychiatrist, the man seemed to have something about him that was a little unsettling. She uncrossed her legs, slid back deeper into the chair and pulled her skirt down again, her knees tight together.

"You have a lot ahead of you, I understand. Isn't that so, Emma?"

Emma Shaw forced a smile "I hope so."

He laughed, amending his remark, saying, "What I meant was that you have a lot of responsibilities as a naval officer and as a woman. It hasn't been easy for you, I imagine, this whole thing with Dr. Rourke's near death, your own encounter with the would-be assassin, and then—"

"I'm holding off, Don, on whether I want psychoanalysis or not. But, no, it hasn't been easy. Let me settle a few things," Emma Shaw told him, opening her purse as she spoke, and looking for her cigarettes and her lighter. "I'm the 'other woman' in this whole thing, and even if I didn't think of myself that way, everyone else probably does. Sarah Rourke's a living legend, a role model to women everywhere. As a little girl, when you read about Sarah Rourke in the history books, you don't picture her trying to stab to death a clone of her husband so that she can ensure his death. So, yeah, it was a little unsettling to say the least."

She lit a cigarette, dropped the pack and lighter back into her purse and closed it. Why was she telling this guy Don all of this? Maybe he was a better shrink than she'd thought. "When I was a little girl," she told him, exhaling smoke from between her lips, "I read about Sarah Rourke and thought, 'Wow, what a courageous woman to do all that stuff!' You know? And none of that's lost; she's still one of the finest women in history for my money. But, then here I am, the home wrecker. I know on a rational basis that I'm not responsible, that John and his wife would have broken up anyway. But her trying to kill him because Deitrich Zimmer implanted a memory in her brain that never took place is tough to deal with. Why don't you answer a question for me?"

"If I can, Emma," Don responded, smiling that same smile.

"What can be done for Sarah Rourke? I know that you've spoken with her several times over the last two and a half weeks, but does it look like she'll be able to be convinced about the memory Zimmer put into her head?"

"I don't suppose I'm betraying the doctor-patient confidentiality by telling you; Sarah Rourke knows now on a rational basis that her husband never attempted to kill her. If you feel some guilt in your self-described role as the perceived home wrecker, you can imagine the guilt she feels—considerably more genuine, more reality based, about killing the clone of Dr. Rourke in an attempt to prevent the heart transplant which saved Dr. Rourke's life. Mrs. Rourke will have a tough time dealing with that, and for a lot longer than your misgivings should endure.

"But," Don went on, "the memory is still there, however false that memory is, coloring her perceptions. There's nothing we can do to eradicate that memory entirely. I can bury it through hypnosis, so it's much less close to the surface, but that won't rid her of it. And she still blames Dr. Rourke for the death of their son Martin, even if in fact the man Dr. Rourke thought was Martin was really a clone.

"And she knows that's an irrational position," he continued, "but that doesn't alter that fact that she perceives what Dr. Rourke did as wrong. Actually, you were quite right in what you said a moment ago, that you're not responible for the dissolution of their marriage. It's obvious that their marriage ceased functioning as anything more than something to be tolerated years ago, long Before the Night of the War, I'd say.

"She needs to start over again, just like Dr. Rourke himself needs to. She told me yesterday, Mrs. Rourke did, that she hopes things work out for you and Dr. Rourke. That's the real reason I called you to this meeting. She asked if I'd tell you, because she doesn't want to see you at this juncture, nor see John Rourke."

Emma Shaw realized that her cigarette was burning down and she stubbed it out. "John feels the same, I mean about Sarah and Wolfgang Mann getting together. They still love each other, the Rourkes."

"Oh, I'd agree, Emma; maybe that's what makes the fact that their marriage is dead so sad."

Emma Shaw glanced at her wristwatch. Fortunately, she was running late and had to get out of there. If she talked about this much longer, she'd cry.

Two

James Darkwood sat behind the wheel of the electric car, all lights in the vehicle out. The road toward which Michael sometimes stared—he spent the rest of the time surveying the terrain around them—was little traveled, Croenberg had told them, perfect for their rendezvous.

Michael would allow its perfection only after Croenberg had joined them and they were under way, perhaps not even until they had reached the airfield.

This was the heart of Croenberg's operation, his own personal fiefdom within the Nazi empire. Once, Before the Night of the War when the then-existing West Coast disappeared into the sea, this had been Klamath Falls, Oregon. Now, it was disputed Eden territory and one of the principal North American seaports on the Pacific. Unlike New Reno, in Nevada, this was not an open port, but fully Nazi-dominated. It was called New Hamburg.

Before Darkwood had left with Paul Rubenstein, Natalia had imparted some advice. "Remember that any rendezvous in enemy territory—or, for that matter, any rendezvous at all—can be compromised. If the three of you wait just as you've been told, you will all run the risk of death or worse."

That, and common sense, was why James Darkwood waited alone in the car and Michael and Paul waited well away from it, both of them black clad against the darkness

16

and armed as heavily as they could be against whatever might happen. Michael looked at his watch.

Croenberg would be late in two minutes. The three of them had agreed that if Croenberg were more than one minute late, the rendezvous would be broken off and they would get out. If that happened, the meeting would have to be reset, because the chance which a temporary alliance with Croenberg presented could not be dismissed. It was, perhaps, the only chance for mankind's survival.

Croenberg wanted to depose Deitrich Zimmer and Martin Rourke Zimmer, thus enabling himself to seize command of Nazi forces and the country of Eden. Any alliance would, indeed, be temporary, because if Croenberg succeeded in attaining the power he sought, he would eventually have to be dealt with.

Perhaps that was the true lesson of history, that the world would never be a perfect place and that there would always be strife, at least as long as mankind survived.

Only a little over a minute remained before the rendezvous and, as yet, there were no signs of headlights coming down the road . . .

Paul Rubenstein shifted position slightly, his right leg starting to fall asleep. He moved very slowly, in case he was being watched. Available to him were night vision goggles, but he couldn't risk them now, so close to the time of the rendezvous. Even though they would automatically filter the headlights, his true night vision would be gone for several seconds afterward. Those could be deadly seconds.

Paul's position was on the far side of the road, almost directly opposite the automobile in which James Darkwood sat alone.

He glanced at his watch. About thirty seconds until Gruppenführer Otto Croenberg was due. Either Croenberg had precisely worked out the driving time to the last second, or Croenberg was late. That could mean betrayal by Croenberg himself, or that Croenberg's desire to depose Zimmer had

17

somehow been discovered and that Croenberg himself was compromised.

Waiting in pitch darkness—except for a too-bright moon—in the heart of enemy territory for a Nazi to arrive for a friendly chat was not Paul Rubenstein's idea of fun. Nazis had killed too many of his relatives during World War II, slaughtering them just because they were Jewish—Hitler had decided to blame everything which was wrong with Germany on the Jews and exterminating the Jews was an ultimate policy goal.

But, Otto Croenberg might, in an odd way, be mankind's salvation, if Croenberg's immediate goals to depose the current Nazi leadership sufficiently coincided with those of the Trans-Global Alliance. If Croenberg came to power and surrendered the nuclear weapons which would then come under his control, at least any conflict between the world's current superpowers would be non-nuclear.

Such was little consolation; but, at this stage, grasping at straws was better than despair.

Just as Paul Rubenstein was about to give up on the rendezvous, headlights appeared in the distance. Indeed, the road was little traveled, just as Croenberg had told James Darkwood that it would be. Odds were high that the car was Croenberg's, but nearly as high that this was the opening gambit of a trap.

Three

Aside from his chauffeur, Max, in the front seat and the girl who sat beside him in the back seat, Croenberg was alone, as he had promised. Max was expected, but Helga was not. It was doubtful that the Allied agents who awaited him out there in the darkness would kill Helga, but he would not be terribly dismayed if they did. Helga was a warm, very well put-together blond-headed body virtually poured into a pink minidress. Excellent in bed, she was, nonetheless, wholly expendable.

"Otto, just where are we going?"

"On a little trip, my dear," Croenberg answered, not lying. "You brought that nice warm coat that I gave you?"

"Uh-huh."

"Good! Now, be quiet for a moment, Helga."

She drew back into the far corner of the seat as Croenberg reached under the civilian jacket which he wore and touched the butt of his pistol. It was a Lancer copy of the Walther P-38, the most accurate pistol he had ever owned and wholly functionally reliable. He slipped the pistol free from its shoulder holster, his right thumb resting beneath the slide-mounted thumb safety, ready to flick it upward into the fire position.

The automobile's headlights, as they came out of the gentle curve along which the vehicle—a staff limousine—had driven for the last two or three kilometers, picked up the reflection of another, smaller car on the left side of the road. That would be the American Naval Intelligence Agent James Darkwood. It was too bad that Darkwood was so dedicated an anti-Nazi; Croenberg would have hired the fellow.

"Max?"

"Herr Gruppenführer?"

"Be prepared to stop the vehicle when I order. And, do nothing unless I say that you should."

"Yes, Herr Gruppenführer Croenberg!"

"Otto?"

"Not now, Helga. Just be silent."

Their vehicle was nearly even with the car at the side of the road. Croenberg ordered, "Now, Max. Stop the automobile now!"

"Yes, Herr Gruppenführer!"

The limousine came to a rapid but adequately even stop on the opposite side of the road.

"Now, Max, you will dim then raise your headlights, three times in rapid succession. This is understood?"

"Yes, Herr Gruppenführer!"

And, the headlights dimmed, brightened, dimmed, brightened, then dimmed and brightened for the third time.

The headlights of the smaller car came on, on high beam.

"Herr Gruppenführer?"

"It should be all right, Max. Wait in the car." He glanced toward the girl, feeling her unstated fear. "All is in order, Helga. Wait here and remain silent." Croenberg opened the door on the driver's side rear and stepped out, Max starting to get out to take the door. "I said that you should wait here, Max."

"Yes, Herr Gruppenführer. Forgive me."

"You only seek to serve me. Rest easily." And Croenberg stepped from the limousine onto the road. That the fate of the planet rested upon his shoulders did not escape him; and he meant to take advantage of it . . .

Paul Rubenstein lay in cover still, his eyes trained on Croenberg's tall, spare frame. Aside from the two Browning

High Powers—that old, battered one which he'd first selected from the Brigand biker weapons more than a half a millennium ago and the second, spare Browning which looked better but never felt quite as good in his hand—and his German MP-40 submachine gun, he also had an M-16. To use that rifle to kill Croenberg would have been absurdly easy.

Emotionally, he wanted to do that, kill the Nazi.

On a rational basis, he could not, of course.

As he watched Croenberg and considered his weapons, he suddenly smiled as an insane bit of irony crossed his mind. That battered old Browning High Power with the cone hammer and tangent rear sight, made in Belgium, was crafted there during World War II. After the Nazis overran Belgium. It bore the Nazi proofmarks.

Life was madness, indeed.

Croenberg was walking toward the car in which James Darkwood sat. In a moment, Darkwood would exit his vehicle, talk briefly with Croenberg and the Nazi would be driven away while his trusted chauffeur continued on, allaying suspicion of what might be transpiring.

And Paul Rubenstein thought of Sir Winston Churchill's remark concerning Joseph Stalin, that in order to defeat Hitler he—Churchill—would make a pact with the devil.

Croenberg. Devil. Little difference.

Four

Natalia Anastasia Tiemerovna raised her glass as John Rourke completed the toast: ". . . and, whatever happens, this glass is raised to us, all of us, those who are here seated around this table, those who are not."

Natalia drank down the wine, as did Annie, Emma Shaw and John Rourke himself. And her thoughts were shared, she knew, with the others. Except perhaps for Emma. Emma would think of Michael, of Paul, of Sarah, too. But Natalia remembered one other whom Emma had never met, who was gone from their company for a very long time. Her name was Madison Rourke, Michael's deceased first wife. She—Natalia—would be Michael's second wife. And, live or die, she knew that she and Michael would endure for eternity together.

Annie spoke. "I want to say that we're a family, just as we always have been. What has happened with my mother doesn't change any of that. So, I think we should each have another glass of wine, Daddy, and toast Emma, our newest member."

Natalia watched John Rourke's eyes and she realized that she was smiling. She said, "Hear, hear! To Emma, with love from her family!"

Emma Shaw was crying, and looking as though she felt so embarrassed that, were there a hole, she would have crawled inside of it.

John reached out and touched Emma's hand on the table beside him.

Natalia looked at Annie and winked. There was a lot to Annie Rourke Rubenstein, the woman Natalia most respected in the world. If men only realized, women were the truly stronger sex; but, men never would realize that because women didn't want them to—for very good reason.

John refilled the wine glasses for the other two women and herself. Annie raised her glass, saying, "To Emma, then."

"To Emma," Natalia echoed.

"To Emma," John barely whispered . . .

James Darkwood drove, Paul Rubenstein sitting beside him in the front passenger seat of the little electric car. Croenberg sat in back, Michael beside him. The chauffeur, Max, and a woman who looked like the perfect caricature of an airhead from a Hollywood movie—but a voluptuous one to be sure—were on their way again. Croenberg was to be gone for thirty-six hours, on a little weekend trip with the woman. Her name was never given. Paul Rubenstein secretly wondered if Max the chauffeur and the woman would have a good time together.

James Darkwood interrupted Paul's thoughts. "We've got somebody behind us, following with lights off."

"Shit," Michael observed.

"Indeed," Croenberg said, seeming to agree. "None of my personnel are to be anywhere near here, which means of course that the car is driven by some innocent who is too stupid to notice that his or her lights aren't on—there is a brilliant moon, after all—or that Herr Dr. Zimmer's intelligence agents are keeping a closer watch over me than I had supposed."

"We should assume the latter," Paul noted. "Would they merely follow, or would they report in at this stage?"

"They would not report in, for fear that any radio message might be intercepted by my own personnel. The structure of Herr Dr. Zimmer's empire is something all of you should

23

bear in mind. Dr. Zimmer is a leader without a country, and so we occupy little places, fiefdoms as it were, controlled by the local leadership. This area is mine. Being the Herr Doctor's enemy, I have taken certain steps to safeguard such things as communications security. And, he knows that I am his enemy, yet can do nothing at this juncture for fear of upsetting the delicate balance within his high command."

"Rather like Hitler's relationship with his General Staff, isn't it?" Paul suggested.

"In that case, I suppose that I would be best compared to Admiral Canaris."

Despite himself, Paul laughed at the man's ego.

Michael asked, "Okay, I've heard the name, but why was Canaris special?"

"He smuggled Jews out of Germany," Paul told him. "But I think Lieutenant-General Croenberg is referring to Canaris actively using German Intelligence to contravene Hitler's wishes."

"He fought against a less than able man in his own way, as do I," Croenberg announced.

"For more heroic reasons, though, I suspect," James Darkwood suggested. "Or, at least, less selfish ones."

"You will achieve your purpose, perhaps, and I will perhaps achieve mine. That is the essence of a bargain, James."

Darkwood didn't answer.

Paul, his eyes on the sideview mirror, said, "I think we're going to have to do something about these guys. If they don't get the idea that something's fishy when they see us rendezvous with an aircraft, they'd have to be too stupid even for Nazis—no offense, Croenberg."

"You detest my very existence, Herr Rubenstein, because I am a Nazi; I harbor the same animosity toward you because you are a Jew. How little the human species has improved in the last six centuries! Would you not agree, Herr Rubenstein?"

Paul answered him, saying, "I do indeed agree, Croenberg."

"James," Michael began, "why not speed up a little? If the car behind us should be innocent, we'll lose them. If not, we'll reach the rendezvous point for the aircraft a little early, early enough to nail these guys before the plane arrives."

"Good idea, Michael."

The engine of the electric car began to hum almost imperceptibly louder. Paul Rubenstein asked Croenberg, "Do you have a weapon?"

"Of course, Herr Rubenstein."

"Good. Maybe you'll need it. When we reach the rendezvous, James, you take the car on past, stop only long enough for us to get out without breaking an ankle. Michael, you ride with James for about a hundred yards or so and get out, find some cover and be ready. Croenberg and I'll stick together. Then James, you drive on for about another half mile, then double back. When the car that's following us comes in sight, we catch it between us. Got any objections to shooting other Nazis, Croenberg?"

"Only certain Nazis, my Jewish friend."

"One other thing," Paul cautioned, turning around in the seat to look at Croenberg. "I'm not your friend."

Five

The officers' lounge had sort of become their place, for a drink, a smoke, a little talk. Emma Shaw sat on the same bar stool that she'd occupied when John had first asked to make love to her. John Rourke would not remember that, of course, because men didn't remember things like that. But she remembered, and she always would.

John smoked a cigarette instead of a cigar, out of deference to her, she knew. But, she'd break him of that habit—not the smoking, but the unnecessary, almost exaggerated politeness toward her. She could take his cigar smoke because she loved him.

He lit her cigarette with his battered old Zippo. "I spoke with the psychiatrist. He told me to call him Don."

"What did Don say?"

"That Sarah wishes us the best, happiness. And that she knows on a rational basis that you never shot her, even though the memory Deitrich Zimmer implanted is still there."

"Don was the messenger. And did he say anything else, Emma?"

"He told me I shouldn't feel like a home wrecker. But I already knew that and it doesn't help," she said, exhaling smoke.

"And?"

"I love you and want to be with you forever, longer than that. I'll get used to that fact that none of this was anybody's

26

fault." Emma Shaw had never spoken so frankly with any other man, except her father. "You know what I mean? That I'll get used to the fact that there's nothing to feel guilty about?"

"I know what you mean."

"How are you feeling?"

"What? You mean my heart? It's still beating. I just wish there'd been another way."

Emma Shaw looked down at the hem of her skirt, tugged at it with the fingers of her left hand. "So, it does bother you, the death of the clone."

"Yes."

She inhaled, exhaled smoke, saying, "But if one of your Family or—"

"You? Remember what Annie and Natalia said? That you were part of the Family? They were right. What you're asking, though, is if one of the Family were dying and I could kill a clone in order to salvage a heart or whatever which could keep the original person, the real one, alive, would I do it?"

"Yes, John. I know the answer, so don't waste your breath telling me something different."

John Rourke smiled. He had a pretty smile, she thought, but everything about him was wonderful, even the way he breathed. "Would I murder someone to save my Family? Of course I would. But, that doesn't make it right. That clone of me, like the ones that Paul was forced to kill with Darkwood's help at Zimmer's base in the Himalayas. They were all living human beings, and being clones of us didn't change that. They could have experienced life, just like you, just like me, just like the originals. I'm alive because another man is dead."

"Uncomfortable feeling. Yeah," she told him, stubbing out her cigarette. "There was this girl in my squadron a couple of years ago. Her name was Angie. We were in a dogfight with some Eden fighter bombers over the Tuamotu Archipelago. About ten degrees south, below the Marquesas a little." John nodded. "One of my missiles malfunctioned and stayed half in the rack, throwing me out of trim and just

27

about to blow. The whole wing was going up in flames. I had to eject."

"And?"

"Well, Angie and the rest of the guys in the squadron took out the enemy aircraft, but Angie stayed around, overflying my position in the water, taking pot-shots at sharks, waiting there until a rescue chopper could get in and pick me up. It was two hours. We were in radio contact. I ordered her away, because I knew she was running low on fuel. She refused to obey my orders, though. She just stayed there. Finally, just about the time she was starting to run on vapor, the rescue chopper showed up.

"I radioed to Angie that she should ditch because the plane would never make it anywhere. Nearest carrier was about fifteen minutes past her maximum fuel time. She laughed, I remember, telling me that she wasn't any hero, that she was going to ditch even if I hadn't told her. They could take the plane out of her salary five bucks a week," Emma told him, laughing a little as she said it.

"She was a brave woman."

"Was. She hit the silk, but she was lower on fuel than she'd let on or than she realized. Just as she ejected, the plane's burners cut out and the aircraft intersected her trajectory and—"

John stubbed out his cigarette and their eyes met. "I love you," he told her.

Emma Shaw could only nod.

Six

The gun in Otto Croenberg's right hand was clearly visible beneath the bright moon, the classic lines of the Walther P-38 unmistakable. John Rourke had once said, "There are a lot of classic guns, but there are fewer with the classic looks to match. No two people would agree, but I've always thought there are really five handguns—if one confines the list to guns with an impressive service record, at least—that have the look. In chronological order, there's the Colt Single Action Army, especially in the seven-and-one-half-inch barrel, then the C-96 Mauser 'Broomhandle,' then the P'08 Luger, then the 1911 Colt .45 Auto and, finally, the Walther P-38. Some people would add the Beretta Model 1934, or the SIG P-210, or a host of others. But, that's my list."

The P-38 was adopted by Nazi forces in 1938, serving as military standard during World War II, and then redesignated the P-1 except for civilian sales and incorporating an alloy frame, it was used by West German forces until relatively few years Before the Night of the War.

"Alloy frame?" Paul Rubenstein asked Croenberg.

"Yes; most of the best 9mm Parabellums have alloy frames."

Paul Rubenstein felt himself smiling again, despite the nature of the man. Croenberg most probably knew that he— Paul Rubenstein—carried a Browning High Power, which had a steel frame. "Mine's more durable. John Rourke told me that the FBI—the United States Federal Bureau of Investigation—used High Powers for their Hostage Rescue Unit personnel for quite a long time, Before The Night of the War, getting upwards of forty thousand rounds out of each gun."

"Touché, Herr Rubenstein."

Michael had to be in position by now.

Paul heard the click as the safety on Croenberg's P-38 was flicked off.

And, the pursuit car was coming, slowing, tentatively.

The open field where the V-Stol would land for the rendezvous in under five minutes was to the left side of the road. Paul and Croenberg hid there in high brush, concealed but with minimal cover from low, sculpted pieces of concrete, the remnants of some pre-War structural foundation. On the far side of the road was where Michael would have taken up position.

The electric car, with James Darkwood behind the wheel, was out of sight now.

Paul Rubenstein drew back the bolt of the Schmiesser submachine gun.

The pursuit car was nearly even with their position.

Croenberg hissed in a low whisper, "I find it amusing that a Jew is using an MP-40 submachine gun, a staple of the heroic soldiers of the Reich who guarded the camps where your people were housed."

"Exterminated, you mean. But my using a Nazi-era subgun is just about as amusing as the neo-Nazis using Israeli Uzis Before the Night of the War."

"You are bitter, Jew."

"I have every right to be, Nazi. Your people murdered my father's aunt and uncle, my mother's parents, nieces, nephews, grandparents. Six million of us. When all this is over, you ever want to try your hand at killing a Jew one on one, I'm your man. Anytime, anywhere, guns, knives, bare hands. Yeah, I'm bitter. So bitter I'd kill your ass if we didn't need you alive right now. That clarify things, Gruppenführer?"

Croenberg laughed softly.

The pursuit car was dead even with them now. Paul ordered, "We shoot out the tires and see what happens."

"Agreed."

Paul rose from their meager cover, the MP-40's shoulder stock extended, the buttplate tight against him as he fired neat, three-round bursts into the driver's side tires, Croenberg's P-38 cracking double taps beside him. The car skidded across into the oncoming lane, shuddering to a halt.

Paul Rubenstein couldn't help thinking that his parents—if they'd had graves—would have been rolling over in them had they known that their son fought beside a Nazi.

Croenberg was up, in a low crouch, changing magazines in his pistol before he started forward, Paul Rubenstein fanning right, coming up on the car by staying just behind it, the Schmiesser trained on the driver's side doors. But, as he advanced, he could still see the passenger side. "Be ready!" Rubenstein cautioned Croenberg.

Michael would be closing in, but still staying to cover, his M-16 ready.

The driver's door opened and a man in a dark, high-collared jacket in the old Nehru look and a cap reminiscent of those worn by Greek fishermen Before the Night of the War stepped out.

"Bitte—"

"English!" Paul snapped.

"Please—what is this?"

"Keep your hands up."

"Yes!"

The man in the funny, stylish clothes threw himself down behind the door. "Look out!" Paul shouted, diving left and down as the rear window of the pursuit car shattered outward and bullets tore across the road surface, inches from where Paul had stood a second before. Paul returned fire, spraying a long, ragged burst through the door, trying for the driver.

Croenberg shouted, "Watch out behind you, Jew!"

Paul Rubenstein rolled left, as his eyes came on line with the road surface again seeing a second car, its bright lights cutting on, the car picking up speed, careening toward them.

There was rifle fire, sounding like Michael's M-16 opening up, but Paul Rubenstein couldn't be sure and there was no time to look toward the source of the sound. On his knees now and stabbing the nearly spent subgun toward the headlights, Paul fired from hip level. The passenger side lights went out. The car kept coming. The Schmiesser was empty.

Croenberg knelt beside him, firing his pistol toward the remaining lights.

Paul Rubenstein let the subgun fall to his side on its sling, grabbing for the High Powers from the double Tri-Speed shoulder holsters beneath his armpits, thumbing back the hammers, firing toward the windshield of the approaching car.

Croenberg got the other headlight. The car swerved, bouncing across the ditch at the side of the road and disappearing into the trees.

Paul threw himself down and into a roll, coming up to face the original car still behind him. Michael Rourke's assault rifle was spitting flame in the darkness, into the first pursuit car, one of the tires blowing out, the windshield shattering, whoever remained inside no longer answering fire.

Paul shouted to Croenberg. "Help Michael!"

"I'm on my last magazine, Jew!"

Paul Rubenstein fired out the last three rounds in the newer of the two High Powers, the slide locked open, then shouted to Croenberg, "Empty! Catch!" The Nazi caught the piston on the fly, Paul already reaching for one of his spare magazines, then tossing it to Croenberg. As Croenberg caught it, Paul was ramming a fresh magazine into the Schmiesser, working back the bolt as Croenberg mated the High Power magazine to the pistol.

His submachine gun in his right fist, the battered old Browning High Power in his left, Paul advanced on the second car. "Get up after me as soon as you can!" Paul ordered.

"Of course," Croenberg responded.

Paul broke into a run, leaving the road, reaching the treeline, stopping beside a tall, thin-trunked pine. Taking what little cover there was, he swapped magazines in the High Power, replacing the mostly spent one with a full one. The car was in sight, but that was no reason to suppose that whoever had been in the car was nice enough to wait there for him.

The gunfire from near the first pursuit car had ceased seconds earlier.

Behind him now Paul heard running footsteps on pine needles and small bits of branch. Turning toward the sound, he saw Croenberg. Croenberg dropped to his knees beside another tree, loading loose rounds from his pockets into one of the magazines for his P-38. "Michael Rourke is guarding the road. There were two occupants of the first car, the driver and the one who fired through the window. You killed the driver. Michael Rourke killed the other one. May I continue to borrow your pistol, Jew?"

"Of course, Nazi," Rubenstein told him.

Croenberg volunteered, "I can move around to the far side of the car—"

"Bad idea. That works great in vid-movies and books, but if you get opposite me and I have to shoot I might hit you. No, we stay together. I'll lead, you cover my back."

"And what if I decide that the world could use one less Jew, right now?"

"My brother-in-law Michael would rip your lungs out. Satisfactory answer?"

"For the moment, Jew."

"Cover me and stay close," Paul ordered, then started moving slowly to his left. Since the vast majority of men were right-handed and would hold or control a pistol or rifle with the right hand, it was always wise to move to the left, the prospective shooter's right, since the body could more naturally turn in the direction away from the hand controlling the weapon, especially if one's enemy were in any position other than standing.

Croenberg behind him, Paul Rubenstein moved as silently as he could, still staying as close to what meager cover there was in case he needed it in a hurry. There was no sound of gunfire from the road, meaning that quite possibly there were only two cars—not a third one.

And, as best Paul Rubenstein could tell, the V-Stol should be arriving at any second. If the occupants of the second car were somehow able to fire at the V-Stol, damaging it or forcing it to flee, he and Michael and James Darkwood and Croenberg would be stuck here in territory growing more hostile by the second.

Seven

Annie Rourke Rubenstein and Natalia Anastasia Tiemerovna entered the officers' lounge as Annie's father and
Emma Shaw left, stopping with them for a moment and talking, watching them as they walked off together. To her cabin
or his, Annie wondered?

Annie and Natalia walked together to the bar. Natalia, as
usual, looked perfect and elegant, but in a way that was so
wonderfully natural. She wore heels, tailored black beltless
slacks and a grey silk blouses, open to her cleavage, with long,
full sleeves and high, button cuffs. Her only jewelry was a
simple gold chain, small gold earrings, each in the shape of
a just-blossomed rose and her Rolex with the Jubilee Band.

"How many weapons do you have?" Annie asked her, her
eyes on the black leather shoulder bag from which Natalia
took cigarettes and lighter as she sat down at the bar, Annie
beside her. Despite the ship's regulations, all of them were
armed.

"I must be getting old," Natalia said, laughing softly. "I
keep getting reminded of stories, things which happened
long ago. I remember meeting this charming man, once,"
Natalia began, "very handsome really. If I remember correctly, his name was Klon Newell. He had a positively elegant
white beard and there was a hint of laughter behind his eyes.
Vladmir and I were posing as private investigators. We were
trying to track down a rogue agent who had stolen a great

35

deal of money and murdered the female agent with whom he worked. Then the man went to the ground. Vladmir wanted to kill him personally. I don't think it had anything to do with righteous indignation. He might have been afraid that the fellow would eventually defect and damage some of our operations. Vladmir occasionally talked too much and may have talked too much to this man.

"Anyway, this fellow Klon Newell was very well connected in the field of science fiction, involved with various conventions and what have you. We had only one hope of finding this rogue agent Vladmir wanted to kill. The fellow was a fan of English-language science fiction. He'd always devoured every book and short story he could find.

"So," Natalia went on, lighting her cigarette, "we reasoned that the man we sought would attend some of these conventions if he could. We traveled all over the country and used the same story, basically, that the man we sought was responsible for some horrible crimes and the family of two of his victims had hired us to help in the investigation."

The bartender arrived, Annie ordered white wine, Natalia ordering a gin and tonic. Annie crossed her legs, rearranged her skirt, then leaned her elbows on the bar, listening as Natalia went on.

"I did most of the talking because my English was always more idiomatically correct than Vladmir's. What made me think of this man Klon was that before we left his office he promised to stop by our hotel and let us know if any of his friends might be able to identify the photo. Vladmir didn't like my leaving the picture, but I did it.

"Two days later, he called and said that he'd shown the photograph to some of his friends; they'd never seen the fellow we were looking for, but would keep an eye out for him. He wanted to bring back the picture. I agreed to meet this Klon Newell in the hotel bar. I bought him a drink for his being so nice; I mean, he didn't know who we were, and he thought he was helping us to track down some unspeakable villain. He wasn't far from right, because the man Vladmir and I were chasing had killed the female agent he worked with, then cut off her head and her hands so there would be

36

no means of identification through dental work or finger-prints."

"Yuck!"

"I saw the American police autopsy photos; 'yuck' indeed. So, I bought Klon Newell a drink in the hotel bar. It was just downstairs, so I didn't bother bringing a purse. He was very sweet about it, but he said, 'I don't mean to sound rude, but you said you're private detectives, you and your partner. I always think of private detectives carrying a gun.' And he laughed. All I had carried into the bar was my cigarettes and my lighter and my room key. Vladmir was out. I was wearing this little sundress and sandals. 'You couldn't possibly be wearing a gun, could you?' Klon asked me."

"Well?" Annie exclaimed. "Were you?"

"We were finished with our drinks and I did two things I've never done before or since. I kissed on the first date—and last one—and flashed a gun. But not in that order."

"What?"

"I looked around, then raised my dress so he could see my leg. I had my Walther PPK/S in a thigh holster. His eyes almost popped out of his head, and then he started laughing. He was so sweet, I leaned over and kissed him on the cheek. So, my rather long answer to your question as to how well I'm armed? A Lancer copy of the SIG-226 in my bag and a Lancer copy of the Seecamp DA .32 in the waistband of my pants, under my blouse. The Bali-Song is strapped to my right calf and there's an Executive Edge Grande pen knife—like your father always carries in his shirt pocket—clipped to the band of my bra. And, that's more or less it."

Their drinks arrived and Annie raised her glass. "It seems to be my night to propose toasts. Well, then, here's to pre-paredness. All I've got is the Beretta 92F in my purse."

Natalia sipped from her gin & tonic. "Too much tonic," she observed, smiling.

"It's funny seeing Daddy—" and then Annie thought better of what she was about to observe.

"Head over heels in love?" Natalia supplied. "I think it's rather sweet. Despite the relatively meager difference in your ages, you see your father as an older man. Even though you and I are about the same age, I see him as a contemporary. For you, he's a father; for me, well, you know how it was."

"Are you happy for him?"

"Especially now," Natalia told her. "If the world ends, with this volcanic vent or a nuclear war, well, I think it would be worse somehow if he were alone."

And Annie sipped her drink. Paul was off somewhere in what used to be the American Pacific Northwest risking his life, probably at this very minute. And the thing Natalia said about dying alone was hard to dismiss.

Eight

Paul Rubenstein could see the second pursuit car's passenger compartment with reasonable clarity under the bright moonlight, well aware that anyone in the woods through which he and Croenberg moved could likely see him just as clearly should he move from concealment. And, although the V-Stol had landed several minutes ago and each second lost merely increased the possibility of the V-Stol's detection by Nazi forces, Paul Rubenstein could do little but wait.

The moonlight was the critical factor. The pine trees here were particularly slender and the second pursuit car was the Eden equivalent of a full-sized American automobile from Before the Night of the War. Although the car was damaged beyond drivability, it appeared, the vehicle had effectively mowed a path into the woods as it went. Getting to the car in the moonlight would have necessitated full exposure to enemy fire. Moving any deeper into the woods would be dangerous because of the meager concealment provided by the trees and the almost nonexistent cover.

Croenberg was about five yards back, in the same predicament, Paul knew.

Paul Rubenstein searched his mind for an answer. John's knowledge of small unit tactics was second-to-none; over the time they worked together, Paul had picked up on a good bit of that knowledge and experience and, more importantly, on the logical parameters which allowed effective tactical thinking. But he was at a loss.

Croenberg, on the other hand, was a trained military thinker and, in his earlier days, according to his Allied Intelligence dossier, had been a commando of considerable ability.

Paul Rubenstein mentally shrugged. One of the greatest commandos of all time was the Nazi Otto Skorzeny and, had history taken a wrong turn and thrown him into a temporary alliance with Skorzeny, despite his contempt for any Nazi, he would have bowed to Skorzeny's tactical skills.

On knees and elbows, his submachine gun raised in front of him, Paul Rubenstein worked his away beneath the meager cover toward Croenberg's position. When he reached Croenberg, Paul pulled himself up into a crouch. "Croenberg" began, his voice a low whisper, "got any suggestions as to how we flush out these guys, assuming they're not dead in the car there, without getting ourselves killed in the process? And, don't forget, we're running on that V-Stol's clock. I'm tapped out in the tactical department."

In the moonlight, Paul Rubenstein could view the Nazi's skeletal countenance quite clearly. And Croenberg smiled. "I thought that you might never ask, Jew. We do, indeed, find ourselves faced with a dilemma. However, I think there is a way to circumvent our difficulties quite handily. Already having dismissed the idea of just riddling the car with bullets—because if the men are inside and dead, it will serve no purpose and it is dubious that they would remain inside were they not dead or incapacitated—and keeping in mind that firing would betray our positions, there is only one course of action. May I have your submachine gun please?"

Paul Rubenstein looked at Croenberg for a very long second, then removed the Schmiesser's magazine, closed the weapon's bolt, reinserted the magazine and handed the gun over.

Nine

Unraveling the V-necked sleeveless pullover sweater which Croenberg had worn beneath his tweed winter coat, they were able to get a long enough length of cord that Croenberg's plan would have a chance at being tried. Bracing the Schmiesser in the notch of a tree, padding it with Paul's own gloves and Croenberg's, then securing it with the extra pair of bootlaces Paul always carried (he had acquired the habit from John Rourke), the gun was locked down.

Working their way around the car while keeping some distance away from it, Paul Rubenstein and his unlikely ally were at a safely oblique angle to the submachine gun's cone of fire. And, should the gun go wild, only ten rounds were loaded in the magazine.

With both of his Browning High Power 9mms again, Paul covered one side of the wooded area and the impromptu clearing made by the automobile while Croenberg, with his P-38, covered the other. There were blind spots, of course; but, with any luck, if the personnel from the second pursuit car were still alive and able, there would be return fire when the Schmiesser opened up. Then there would be targets.

Croenberg, since the idea was his, had the honor of tugging on the multiple strands of yarn which had comprised his sweater and now served as the trip wire for the Schmiesser's trigger. Once the trigger was pulled, then held back, the submachine gun would continue firing (disallowing a jam,

41

always possible since there was no real resistance to the natural inertia developed during firing) until the ten rounds in the magazine were discharged. That would take approximately a second, the cyclic rate for the German MP-40 at 500 rounds per minute. Cyclic rates were always deceptive, which was why antigun crusaders in the latter decades of the twentieth century liked so much to quote them. "The such-and-such will fire two thousand rounds per minute," or something like that. But, there were no two-thousand-round magazines, the average submachine gun having a magazine ranging in capacity anywhere from twenty rounds to thirty-two rounds. The average assault rifle, whether a semiautomatic sporter or a selective-fire battle weapon, had a magazine capacity of twenty to thirty rounds.

This time, ten rounds would hopefully be enough.

Croenberg tapped Paul Rubenstein on the shoulder. Rubenstein nodded, waited.

The submachine gun burst fired ten rounds and, in the otherwise almost total silence, the discharges sounded like one long, ragged clap of thunder, their flash against the blackness of the night nearly as brilliant as lightning itself. Some of the glass in the driver's side of the automobile shattered inward.

Paul Rubenstein held his breath, a High Power in each hand as he waited for answering reports.

There was a shot from the darkness to his left.

Paul waited. So, he realized, did Croenberg.

After a few seconds, there was a long burst of automatic weapons fire, then the blue-white streak of an energy bolt, toward the position from which Paul's submachine gun had been fired.

"Now, Jew!" Croenberg shouted.

"Fuck you!" Paul snarled back, firing both pistols simultaneously, one to either side of the muzzle flash he'd first seen. There was a groan, a scream. Another energy burst was fired, toward Paul's position, but Paul Rubenstein was already moving, rolling right.

Croenberg's P-38 cracked twice, then twice again.

There was a long, ragged burst of automatic weapons fire, another scream, another burst of gunfire.

The energy weapon was fired again. Paul caught the flash the instant it came, firing both pistols toward it, zig-zagging the muzzles to right and left, up and down. The energy weapon fired again, but upward this time, the pine boughs immediately above it instantly aflame.

The flames raced upward along the tree's trunk.

A man ran from the trees, a pistol firing wildly toward them. Paul shouted, "Halt!"

The man fired.

Croenberg was beside Paul in the same instant. Both Paul and Croenberg fired, simultaneously, the man's body going down.

Croenberg shifted magazines for his Walther P-38. Paul's Brownings were nearly spent and he changed magazines as well.

"You circle from the right," Paul directed.

"Yes, of course," Croenberg rasped.

Paul Rubenstein started forward, toward the enemy position. The flickering flames from the burning tree illumined the ground in brilliant orange and yellow light. Croenberg, passing the man who had been running, called out, "This one is dead, Jew. I recognize him; one of Deitrich Zimmer's agents, a fellow named Heidler."

Paul Rubenstein saw three other bodies. If they weren't dead, they were making award-winning performances.

"Get Michael in here, or Darkwood. Bring a couple of fire extinguishers from the V-Stol and a shovel and an axe from the on-board foraging kit. We've gotta put this out before it spreads."

"Right away, Jew."

Paul Rubenstein's eyes cast about for a stout branch that he could use to dislodge some dirt. He shrugged his shoulders, belted his pistols and picked up the energy weapon that lay beside one of the three dead men. He fired the weapon into the dirt, then again and again, plowing up huge clumps.

The fire was spreading. He started hurling dirt onto the nearest of the flames, to smother them.

In a few moments, Michael was beside him, two fire extinguishers and a shovel with him. "Where's Croenberg?" Paul shouted, taking one of the extinguishers and starting to use it.

"He said he didn't give a damn whether the forest burned or not."

Paul Rubenstein, despite himself, started laughing.

The extinguishers were quite a bit better than ones Paul Rubenstein remembered from the twentieth century. He'd used a fire extinguisher once, then, to help a motorist put out the flames from a burning alternator. The foam these modern extinguishers sprayed smothered the flames almost instantly.

Within a few minutes, the fires were out. Paul and Michael checked the bodies for papers or other intelligence data, finding little of interest, then making a cursory examination of the automobile, too. The car was clean, except for supplies of ammunition, the modern equivalent of a thermos bottle (filled with coffee) and other odds and ends. Smelling of smoke, dirty, hauling their weapons (including Paul's retrieved Schmiesser) and the extinguishers and the shovel, Paul Rubenstein and Michael Rourke exited the woods, starting across the field toward the waiting V-Stol. They were nearly a half hour behind schedule, but the time could be made up. As they neared the aircraft, James Darkwood waited for them. "I checked out the first car and the guys near it. Not much of intell value, but maybe it'll help in piecing something together."

"Croenberg inside?" Michael asked.

Darkwood nodded.

Paul started up into the fuselage. Sitting on the starboard side on the long bench, Croenberg was smoking a cigarette and sipping from a hip flask. Other than his sweater being absent, Croenberg looked as if he'd done nothing more strenuous all evening.

Paul Rubenstein aimed the nozzle of the fire extinguisher toward Croenberg's cigarette, saying, "You tempt me, Nazi. You tempt me."

"And is this not half the fun, Jew? Hm?"

Ten

They left the adjoining door between their cabins open, and John was back in his own cabin, dressing. Emma Shaw, already into her flight suit, stood in the doorway, watching while John Rourke dressed. "Are you going to get fat or anything?"

"After we're married?" John countered. "No; at least I hope not. How about you?"

"Only if you want me to, in a special way." She realized that she was biting the first knuckle of her right index finger. She stopped that.

"But only for nine months at a time, hm?" And he looked over his naked right shoulder and smiled at her, then pulled on a black knit shirt.

He picked up his little .45s—she could recite what they were just as well now as when she'd written a report on the great hero John Rourke when she was a little girl in fifth grade, studying American History. The guns were twin stainless Detonics .45s, CombatMasters, carried in a double Alessi shoulder holster. He slipped into the shoulder holster as effortlessly as if it were nothing. "How long have you carried those guns that way, John?"

"About six hundred and thirty-two years. Why do you ask?"

"Just nosey, that's all."

John smiled as he continued arming himself. "Lew Alessi was a friend of mine, you know."

"The man who made the holster."

"Yes. He'd appreciate knowing that his product lasted better than six centuries and is still working."

Watching John arm was incredible. Anyone else would have been dwarfed by all the equipment. But not John Thomas Rourke (she loved the way the name sounded, especially with Mrs. in front of it). Tucked beneath his wide, black leather garrison belt, inside the black jeans he wore was the butt of his little revolver, carried on a Barami Hip-Grip (an original, not a Lancer copy, something a museum would have paid dearly for). It was a steel-framed stainless Smith & Wesson Centennial in .38 Special (again something for which any museum would have stood in line). At the small of his back was a knife sheath, carrying the little A. G. Russell Sting IA Black Chrome (also original, just as priceless to some museum curator). John buckled on his gunbelt. On the right side of the belt was a black, full-flap holster of gleaming leather, on the left side a long, black leather knife sheath, this connected to the belt loop by means of a bright stainless steel ring, almost the size of the sort of ring that was put into the nose of a bull. From the dresser top, John picked up a revolver. It was an original Smith & Wesson Model 629, so original that it had the old, partially lugged barrel. He holstered the .44 Magnum and picked up the knife. This was the Crain LS-X knife, its blade a full foot in length, the spine saw-toothed, a small portion of the blade polished mirror bright and drilled through in order to provide sighting for the polished portion of the blade to be used in heliograph signaling. He sheathed the knife, securing it with a snap-closured safety strap. He reached to the dresser top again, taking the two stainless steel Detonics CombatMasters. These he carried holsterless, thrust into the front of his gunbelt or his waistbelt, depending on circumstances. Affixed to his waistbelt was a single pouch, a black leather flap covered Milt Sparks Six-Pack, carrying six spare magazines for the little, shoulder-holstered .45s. On the gunbelt was the nearly identical unit, only large enough to accommodate full length magazines for the ScoreMasters. There was also a double dump pouch carrying extra ammunition for the .44 Magnum revolver.

It wasn't that John was particularly large. He stood over six feet, his chest (the scars from his surgery were nearly healed) and arms well developed, muscular, but not like those of a bodybuilder. It wasn't anything physical at all, although she thought he was incredibly handsome. But, it was something from within him which made him almost more than human.

He had two musette bags, and these he donned crossbody, from shoulder to opposing hip, the effect of the crossing straps reminiscent of the look of the old frontiersmen in the days of flintlock and caplock rifles, like the powder horn and the ditty bag. The bags carried various necessities, as well as spare magazines for his rifle.

John slipped into his battered brown leather bomber jacket, identical (except for age and wear) to the A-2 which was navy issue to pilots. His was made from goatskin, hers from synth-leather, the texture of the two substances identical. As he picked up his rifle—the HK-91—John turned to her, looked at her oddly. "You're staring at me."

"Uh-huh."

"Why?"

"You'd never understand," she told him, feeling herself starting to smile.

John Rourke picked up his little Executive Edge pen-shaped pocket knife and clipped it into his shirt.

Eleven

Trans-Global Alliance warplanes had, ever since the attack on the facility perpetrated by the Rourke Family nearly three weeks earlier, pounded at the Himalayan Redoubt, much of Deitrich Zimmer's air force destroyed (what remained of it after the Rourke Family's highly successful sabotage).

Ordering commando raids in Hawaii, attacks on United States and other Trans-Global Alliance personnel in every port to which he had access, Zimmer, Martin with him, flew to Eden City, where Martin would assume personal command (in name only) of the Eden Defense Forces.

All of the clones of the Rourke Family were destroyed in the attack on the Himalayan Redoubt. The only clones remaining were those of Martin and himself, in storage within Eden City. More clones could be made, but years would be required to grow them to useful age. John Rourke—whom no one had actually seen personally during the raid—had won the round, but not the fight. And Rourke would never win that.

Deep within the underground headquarters at the outskirts of Eden City itself, Deitrich Zimmer sat quietly and in relative darkness. Alone by choice in order that nothing should distract him from the task at hand, he weighed the many variables confronting him.

He and Martin, through the use of the remaining clones and the recording method he had perfected for downloading the brain onto the blank slate of a waiting clone's brain, could live for as long as the planet existed, and perhaps longer. As time progressed and his own wisdom grew, there was no way by which he could accurately gauge the potential for his mind. In centuries of learning, experimenting, growing, he could master what other men considered the prerogatives of a god. But none of this would be possible if he lost this war and were captured or killed.

With the racial stock of the Rourkes to draw upon—he still possessed the cells from which he could, again, make their clones in any number that he wished—he could create the true master race, the dream of the ages. He had extracted, as well, the raw material required from the remains which John Rourke had so kindly helped him to obtain, the remains of Hitler. Deitrich Zimmer wished not at all to grow clones of the Führer; any man who nurtured his own rival was madness incarnate. But, with the appropriate genetic material, he could alter Martin, make Martin a god.

All of this required time, and breeding. Many decades, perhaps centuries.

For the successful attainment of these goals, Deitrich Zimmer needed the opportunity to work, to experiment with human flesh and intelligence, something he could never do in a post-War environment in which he was the loser.

He must first vanquish his enemies, and he had prepared for this ultimate contingency.

While he had slept the Sleep, he had ordered constructed in utmost secrecy what, for lack of a better word, would be his Retreat, should all else fail. Humanity had survived the near-total destruction of the species, mankind's number decimated, only to be decimated again and again and again until the merest fragment of human population remained. Such could happen again, but under more controlled circumstances.

For the sake of human perfection, a true master race of supreme beauty and intelligence, he would engineer the deaths of the rest. From the Rourke racial stock and the genetic material of Adolf Hitler, Deitrich Zimmer would at last bring to flower the true glory of mankind.

He picked up the telephone receiver from the small table beside him. "This is Zimmer," he told the orderly. "Instruct the commander of my forces that I require his presence at once."

Zimmer hung up. From the table, he took up the CD Rom disc and inserted it into his laptop computer. He began calling up the data for Option Omega.

Twelve

Martin Zimmer was glad to be home in Eden.

His father otherwise preoccupied, he could exercise his own interests.

Vid surveillance devices were secreted everywhere about the city, allowing security personnel to randomly check for anything which might prove of a suspicious nature. The same monitoring allowed Martin Zimmer to indulge his dearest fantasy: sex was only satisfying to him when it was as a part of rape.

A handful of Land Pirates, all of them convicted killers and thieves and, themselves, rapists—so egregious in these endeavors that, despite his long-standing alliance with the Land Pirates, the men were prosecuted and sentenced to death—assisted him in his endeavors. The man he had appointed their leader was a big fellow with scars and a very ugly face. His name was Elder Watts.

It was Elder Watts who stood before him now.

Martin Zimmer asked, "Did you get her?"

"Yes, sir. She didn't live alone, though, so we took the one she lived with for ourselves."

Martin shrugged his shoulders. There was no need to ask what had been done to this other woman. She would be murdered in the usual way and he, Martin, would go on television and proclaim that Jewish Fifth Columnists, working for the Trans-Global Alliance, had once again perpetrated another terror raid in Eden City. These Jewish Fifth Columnists were doubtless the same ones responsible for the dozens of other deaths in recent months in which young women were kidnapped, their families and friends killed and their mutilated bodies later discovered in some field or by some roadside or in some alley.

Martin Zimmer cared nothing for mutilation, but loved rape. After he was through with one of the girls, he would give her over to Elder Watts and the other Land Pirates in his employ. They used the girl as they chose, killing her when they were through if she did not die during their adventures with her. Elder Watts came up with the idea of mutilating the bodies, making the potential for propaganda against Jews and the Trans-Global Alliance in general even greater.

There were no Jews, of course, living in Eden, unless they had so cleverly disguised their ethnic backgrounds that they had escaped all Eden's best efforts to locate them. But there were Jews in Mid-Wake, in Hawaii, in Australia and elsewhere. Easy enough to make a conspiracy theory believable.

Martin had spent the last three hours studying street video and made a selection for when he was through with this girl. "There is a blond-haired one on these discs," he told Elder Watts. "Locate her, be ready to take her in a few days. I will let you know when."

"What about this one, sir?"

"Have her brought to me in the usual way. I'll notify you when I am through with her."

Elder Watts smiled. "Right away."

Hunching his shoulders under the collar of his grey-black duster, Elder Watts started toward the door. Martin Zimmer closed his eyes, feeling the anticipation of the girl they would bring him, already stirred.

Thirteen

Lydveldid Island had changed.

However obvious it had been to him when he returned here for the first time after awakening from more than a century in Cryogenic Sleep, it was somehow more dramatic to him now.

Despite the death of his son's wife, Madison, and their unborn child, and despite too the cataclysmic vulcanism which had nearly destroyed the Hekla Community, John Rourke had always considered Iceland a happy place.

It was sad to come here with the death of all mankind imminent, and with a woman beside him—who had flown him here —with whom he would have liked to spend an eternity of life.

He looked at Emma Shaw, smiled at her.

She looked up at him. "Why are you looking at me like that, John?"

"For obvious reasons," Rourke told her.

The President of Lydveldid Island was a man these days, Mme Jokli dead these many years. The quaint houses, like that of old Jon the swordmaker, were all gone, the population here considerably increased. Neat, dormitorylike high-rise buildings replaced what had been here before.

The central square, the park and gardens, were all replaced. And, the V-Stol which Emma had flown (but let him fly for a little while) had landed there.

A second V-Stol U.S. fighter bomber had already landed, and John Rourke knew who had been aboard.

The head of Defense Forces of Lydveldid Island and his aide, a carrot-haired young man seemingly just past his teens, were the only ones to meet them as they walked from the V-Stol. Rourke glanced behind him once, Natalia and Annie walking a few paces behind them. Out of courtesy to the Icelandic Defense Forces, John Rourke had left his rifle in the V-Stol, the musette bags stripped away as well as the gunbelt. With his jacket zipped closed at the waist, he would appear unarmed. It was doubtful that anyone would think he was unarmed, but it was appearance that counted now.

"Dr. General Rourke, on behalf of the president and people of Lydveldid Island, I bid you welcome."

The commander of the defense forces—General Staat—saluted.

Despite his dislike for misplaced military courtesy, John Rourke returned the salute; to have done otherwise would have been insulting. "On behalf of the other members of the Trans-Global Alliance, sir, I heartily accept your welcome and offer my sincerest thanks for your hospitality as pertains to the forthcoming meeting."

"Follow me, sir."

"Certainly sir." And Rourke fell in beside the general, Emma dropping off to walk beside the carrot-haired aide.

"The anonymous visitor, your son, your son-in-law and Commander Darkwood wait in the conference center. Defense Force personnel are posted surrounding the building, but unobtrusively. Your discussions will not be disturbed. As prearranged, there are adequate sleeping quarters and appropriate facilities. Food and other refreshment are available should such be required. In short, all is as requested."

"Your cooperation, General, is most appreciated. Although, as you know, these are secret talks, I will confide that upon their outcome the eventual fate of the planet may well rest."

"That is my understanding, Dr. General Rourke. Those few among the people of Lydveldid Island privy to this meeting taking place pray for you all."

"That is always appreciated, sir," Rourke said sincerely.

They reached the low steps of the conference center. It was part of the university complex. Rourke saw no security, but didn't look hard for evidence of it. He took the general at his word that all was as it should be.

The general stopped at the base of the steps, nodding his head as he said, "It is appointed that I should leave you here, Dr. General. But, I am a call away. Should anything be required, merely lift one of the telephones located at various places within the conference center and you will be in touch with me instantly."

"Thank you again, sir."

The general saluted. John Rourke returned the salute.

Emma, Natalia and Annie flanking him, John Rourke walked up the steps, stopped at the entrance door—there was no lock—and opened it, letting the women pass through ahead of him.

Each of them carried a small bag, containing a change of clothes and whatever other necessities—toothbrush and the like—might be required for an overnight stay. Emma wore her flight suit and bomber jacket, her helmet left in the aircraft, her hair tousled from wearing it. Annie wore a near ankle-length charcoal grey skirt, the tops of her laced-up-the-front boots disappearing beneath its hem, the collar of a white blouse peeking above the neck of a dark grey, long-sleeved sweater. Natalia wore one of her black jumpsuits, a black leather hip-length jacket over it (hiding her shoulder holster). Both Natalia and Annie carried large shoulder bags, some of their weapons secured within these, he knew.

John Rourke closed the door.

They were in a low-ceilinged hallway or corridor, doors on either side—wide, double doors at the far end.

These doors were, unlike the others, open, and standing in the open doorway was James Darkwood. "We checked the building, Dr. Rourke. Everything is just as it should be.

"Croenberg's inside. He and Paul are developing an interesting relationship." Rourke and the three women walked the corridor's length as James Darkwood, still in the open doorway, elaborated. "Croenberg calls Paul 'Jew' all the time and

55

Paul calls him 'Nazi,' but they haven't tried killing each other yet."

Annie could be heard sucking in her breath just a little. Natalia laughed, saying, "He should like me."

Emma Shaw said, "What do you mean?"

"Croenberg would fail to appreciate my ancestry, I suspect. I'll explain it later," Natalia concluded.

"Any trouble?" Rourke asked as they stopped in the doorway.

"Croenberg even helped us. Some of Zimmer's Intell people followed us, two carloads. Must have been following Croenberg. Anyway, we neutralized them."

"Permanently, I suppose?"

"Permanently, Doctor."

Rourke nodded, shrugged his shoulders and looked past Darkwood. There was a long conference table at the center of the room. On either side of it lay a sofa and four easy chairs, these covered in synth-leather.

On the right side of the doorway, as they entered, Rourke noticed a bar and various microwave appliances. "You checked those? That they aren't disguised transmitters?"

"Yes, sir."

"Good," Rourke answered, nodding.

Croenberg sat on the couch to the right of the table. Paul and Michael, standing beside the conference table, began to walk across the room, Annie and Natalia going to meet them, Paul taking his wife into his arms, Michael embracing Natalia. John Rourke put his arm around Emma Shaw's waist and looked at James Darkwood as he said, "I guess you get Croenberg, James."

"Very funny, Doctor," Darkwood answered, smiling sheepishly.

Rourke touched his lips to Emma's hair, then walked toward Lieutenant General Otto Croenberg. Croenberg stood up, transferring a cigarette to his left hand. "Dr. Rourke! Whether you choose to believe me or not, I am honored to meet you, sir."

"You're too kind," Rourke responded, these words the only polite-seeming thing he could think of.

Fourteen

Although he often took direct charge of strategic planning, he respected the mind of Reichsführer Helmut Anton Griem. But Deitrich Zimmer had not called Griem to him for the purposes of eliciting either opinion or advice, merely to carry out the orders which were now the first phase in the modified Omega Option. "Helmut, I have called you here in order that you might supervise something quite important."

"Here" was Deitrich Zimmer's personal office suite within the underground command bunker. Not so elaborately appointed as his accommodations within the Himalayan Redoubt, the rooms were adequate. The fertile mind needed little of the creature comforts at any event.

"I await your orders, my Führer."

Zimmer only nodded, smiling. He knew that Griem would carry out whatever orders were given him, which was why Griem held the position in the first place. "You are aware, no doubt, that our scientists concur with those of the Trans-Global Alliance in assessment of the suboceanic rift and the threat which it represents to the survival of the planet."

"I am, my Führer."

Griem was a little man, portly, what meager hair remained to him terribly thin, of lesser volume than the neatly trimmed mustache which adorned Griem's upper lip. "I have determined, that for the good of all mankind, you will personally contact the commander of Trans-Global Alliance Forces and volunteer the use of our tactical nuclear arsenal for the cause of the salvation of the human species."

"My Führer?" Griem was visibly shaken, taking a step back, as if involuntarily.

Deitrich Zimmer inclined his head, smiled, then said, "I realize that you are charged with the defense of this regime and the defense of Eden, but I assure you that this act is in the final best interests of National Socialism."

"Yes, my Führer!"

Deitrich Zimmer began to outline what he wished Griem to do . . .

The girl had dark red hair, very pretty, as she was forced to her knees before him, her hands bound behind her, her ankles bound so that she could only take the very shortest of steps and it would be impossible for her to stand on her own.

"You may leave us now, Watts," Martin Zimmer said.

Elder Watts, grinning, his balding pate wrinkled at the brow, nodded, turned, started toward the door of the special, below ground-level suite where Martin Zimmer entertained. When the doors closed, Martin strode across the room and locked them, pocketing the key.

The girl whimpered, almost as if she knew what lay in store for her; but, of course, since her companions were killed when she was kidnapped, she likely suspected her eventual fate. Martin Zimmer walked over to the bed—that and a straight-backed chair were the only furnishings in the room—and sat down. "Tell me your name."

She didn't answer.

"Tell me your name."

"M-M-Mary."

"Well, M-M-Mary," Martin responded, laughing, "tell me what you think I am about to do to you. And, be honest with me, or it will go badly for you."

She was crying. That always added flavor.

"Tell me, Mary," Martin Zimmer repeated. He knew, and

he knew that she knew, but it was so good to hear it coming from the girl's lips.

"H-H-Hurt me."

"You're very bright, Mary." He stood up from the bed, walked over to where she knelt and unzipped his pants. The hurting would begin, but it would not end until well past dawn.

Fifteen

No one sat at the head of the conference table, but her father sat at the center of its length, Croenberg the Nazi seated directly across from him. There was no special order to the seating arrangement other than that. And Annie Rourke Rubenstein had nothing to do but listen; she could have done nothing else had she tried.

"I am empowered, Lieutenant General, to negotiate with you on behalf of the interests of the Trans-Global Alliance. As James Darkwood has told you," Annie's father began, "we are interested in your help in obtaining the tactical nuclear weapons under the control of the Nazi and Eden forces led by Deitrich Zimmer. In exchange, we will aid you in deposing Dr. Zimmer and establishing yourself in his stead. To that end, then, what do you suggest?"

Croenberg's face was truly skeletal, the eyes large, the cheekbones high, the cheeks themselves sunken, the jaw prominent. But the eyes sparkled with intelligence or wit, perhaps both, and the skin was tight. The skin was so tight that she could see the occasional pulsing of a vein. It was a little sickening, but that pulse and the eyes were the only signs that this was a living man and not some apparition. And, when he spoke, there was strength in his voice, and confidence. "Our interests are, indeed, parallel, Herr Doctor. We both believe that without the tactical nuclear warheads at Herr Dr. Zimmer's command, the entire world may well be doomed to destruction. I would rather not see that happen. Aspirations to power are always subject to death. No, it would be very stupid of me to willfully allow the destruction of this planet when I can assist in saving it. We will be enemies, Doctor, should we both succeed."

"We are enemies now, sir, but united in this moment in time by a common cause. When that cause is resolved, each of us will doubtless be interested in assuring the death of the other. That is to be expected."

"You are admirably candid, Dr. Rourke. And, I shall be candid as well. The one assurance I request—and I trust to your personal integrity that it will be honored—is that once the nuclear warheads your scientists require are transferred, neither these nor any other nuclear weapons will be utilized in the fight against me."

"You have my word, sir; and, though I'd be damning my soul, I would fight beside you if need be in order to make certain that the bargain is kept."

"Your word is all the assurance I need, Dr. Rourke. So, I will brief you and the others, hm?"

"Please," Annie's father said, nodding his head, taking a cigarette from the pack beside him, offering one to Croenberg. Croenberg accepted—and, although Rourke started to use his battered old Zippo, instead he allowed Croenberg to light the cigarette for him.

Croenberg leaned back from the table, drawing his hands together over his abdomen, the cigarette hanging from the left corner of his mouth, his left eye squinted slightly against the rising smoke. And, Croenberg looked at each of them in turn, at last saying, "And, this pledge of Dr. Rourke is something all of you will also honor?"

Natalia said, "Yes."

The others nodded. Annie caught Emma Shaw's eyes, a little look of panic in them as she nodded her agreement as well.

"Very well. I shall reveal something concerning Deitrich Zimmer about which Allied Intelligence has no knowledge." Croenberg looked quite pointedly at James Darkwood. "The

61

good Herr Doctor prides himself on being prepared for any contingency."

"An otherwise admirable trait," Annie's father said.

"Ah, indeed, Doctor Rourke, indeed! However, you shall find this contingency plan less than admirable, I think. Indeed, I know. You must realize, first, that Deitrich Zimmer is wholly dedicated to the classic Nazi ideal, that of the Master Race. For his purposes, however such can be achieved is a justification unto itself.

"His original plan, involving the clones of yourselves and of himself and Martin Rourke Zimmer, was to entrap you, Dr. Rourke, into serving his will. I learned of this plan only after the destruction of our base in the Himalayas and the concurrent deaths of the clones stored there. I was, I will admit, shocked by the plan's audacity.

"Your wife, Dr. Rourke. How is she? She is not with you, I see."

Annie's father never missed a beat, and she was proud of him. "Although it's a personal matter, suffice it to say that my wife and I have been experiencing marital difficulties since Before the Night of the War. We have each found someone else—" Her father paused. Croenberg looked at Emma Shaw. John Rourke went on, "—and my wife and I will soon divorce. The paperwork is already being accomplished. And, as you no doubt know, Sarah Rourke underwent a terrible ordeal, from which she is still recovering."

"I have unearthed information which may relieve your mind of some nagging doubts, Dr. Rourke, regardless of your situation with your wife. The woman whom you think is Sarah Rourke is, indeed, the genuine Sarah Rourke. Deitrich Zimmer had wished to use her to destroy you.

"He programmed her to believe that you were responsible for shooting her in the head that fateful night in what is now Eden City, but more than a century ago. He involved her with Martin; incidentally, you only killed the clone of that rather repugnant young man. The original is still alive. Deitrich Zimmer used Martin to further persuade your wife that you should die. With the memory of you attempting to

62

murder her—I believe Major Tiemerovna was suggested as the likely motive—"

Annie looked at Natalia.

Natalia lit a cigarette.

Croenberg went on. "With the memory, as the good Herr Dr. Zimmer altered it, and her living third child before her, in obvious jeopardy from you, since you were enemies, he may well have pushed her over the brink. You should be wary, Dr. Rourke."

Annie Rubenstein would be showing dirty Family linen in front of someone she held unfathomably far beneath contempt, yet felt that something needed to be said at any event. But her father spoke first, echoing her thoughts. "My wife attempted to murder the clone which the rest of my Family brought out of Zimmer's Himalayan Redoubt. She succeeded in the attempt, but not to the degree she had intended. The clone's heart was undamaged, and the heart was needed to replace my own which was irreparably damaged by a cyanide gas pistol."

Before Croenberg could say anything, Emma Shaw spoke. "You have to understand something, sir," she began. "John Rourke was unconscious, knew nothing about what was intended with his clone. All the rest of us—"

"That's enough, Emma," Annie's father said, his voice almost a whisper, his tone like that of a father, even though he spoke to the woman who would soon be his wife.

"No it isn't, John," Emma snapped, glaring at him for an instant, then telling Croenberg, "All of us took the responsibility. We were waiting in line to kill the clone, in order to save John." John Rourke's fingers splayed over the table. Annie could see the pulse beating in his neck. "And, we'd do it again," Emma Shaw continued. "You might care to remember that, sir, that all of us at this table—including Commander Darkwood, I believe as well, would do anything for John Rourke."

"Amen," James Darkwood intoned.

"Touching, and true, I am sure," Croenberg said after a moment. And then, Croenberg said something which stunned Annie Rubenstein, shocked her to the point that she reached out under the table and dug her nails into her husband's thigh. Croenberg told them, "In that one way, Dr. Rourke, I truly envy you. Truly."

Annie Rourke Rubenstein wanted to hate Otto Croenberg, and was frightened because she couldn't quite.

Sixteen

They had retired to one of the assemblies of couch and chairs, John Rourke sitting in one of the easy chairs, directly opposite Croenberg again, Emma Shaw sitting on the arm of the chair, beside him.

John and Croenberg and Natalia smoked. Emma lit up.

Paul Rubenstein promised himself that, if the world were indeed going to end, once he knew that there was no longer any hope for the planet's salvation, he would chain smoke his way through every day, except for the times that he was making love to Annie. Given the option, he'd prefer making love to smoking.

Croenberg told them, "Dr. Zimmer's plan was marvelously devious, but a trifle too complex, complexity in all of his dealings one of Deitrich Zimmer's greatest faults. He considers obfuscation a mark of his genius; I consider it only a mark of his ego. At any event, Deitrich Zimmer assumed that no matter how he programmed Sarah Rourke, it would be exceedingly unlikely that she would actually attempt murder, and vastly less likely that she would succeed. And, as you, Commander Shaw, and you, Dr. Rourke, indicated, she killed a clone, but did not attempt to kill the man Deitrich Zimmer so zealously tried to make her target.

"Deitrich Zimmer would certainly have been happy had she killed you, Dr. Rourke, but he was really hoping that she

65

would not. What he wanted was for her to attempt it and fail. That was his greatest goal."

"That doesn't make any sense," Paul announced.

"Ah, but it does, Jew," Croenberg told them.

Annie squeezed Paul's hand. He was glad she hadn't dug her nails into his thigh again.

"You see, Zimmer's true desire was that you, Dr. Rourke, realizing what had been done to Sarah Rourke, would go to him, demanding that she be put aright. I do not believe that even Zimmer can erase such a memory, without completely downloading the brain. You know, of course, that additional clones of Deitrich Zimmer and Martin Zimmer exist at Eden."

Paul murmured, "Shit."

John said, "I would have expected as such. Make your point, sir."

Croenberg shrugged his shoulders, stubbing out his cigarette. "My point is that Deitrich Zimmer wanted you alive and under his control. He wished to download your brain into a clone, adding certain memories when he did so. Then, he would have killed you, to be sure. Deitrich Zimmer wanted your mind, but altered in order to become an instrument of his will. You would triumph over him, as far as the world was concerned; and, a grateful world would make you its leader, if you desired."

"I have no political ambitions of any kind; just the opposite, in fact," John told Croenberg.

"You do not understand. It would not have been you, but a clone. A clone which was really a puppet. Your clone, controlled by Deitrich Zimmer, would have manipulated world politics to Deitrich Zimmer's ends. Eventually, Martin— whom Dr. Zimmer planned and perhaps still does plan to alter through something he can do with Adolph Hitler's remains—would have assumed control, appointed by your clone as rightful successor to world leadership.

"Deitrich Zimmer does not wish to rule over ashes, nor does Deitrich Zimmer wish to die. In fact, he is pathological in his desire for immortality, I think. Deitrich Zimmer's determination to live and rule is something which all of you must understand. You do not deal with some petty commissar, some Bolshevik madman—and I mean no offense to you, Fräulein Major Tiemerovna."

"None taken," Natalia said softly.

"All of you deal with an enemy whose madness I have only recently come to fully appreciate. Madness and genius, both in unlimited quality. Unbeknownst to the good Herr Dr. Zimmer, I have gained full knowledge of his ultimate contingency plan. It bears the rather colorful sounding code name of 'Operation Omega.' Some or all of you are religious; I am not. But, in the event that there is a real God, I might suggest that you pray to Him, pray that we are able to derail Deitrich Zimmer's ambition before Operation Omega is set in motion."

"Something worse to worry about," Paul queried, "than a nuclear war, or the planet blowing up under us if we can't divert the volcanic rift in the Pacific before it hits the North American Plate? What could possibly be more deadly than either of those options?"

Croenberg looked at Emma Shaw, but said, "I will tell you, Jew. But, first, a question. Commander Shaw?"

"Sir?"

"Did you participate in the raid on Eden Plant 234?"

"Tell him," John said.

"Yes, sir, I did. And, I'm proud that I did."

"That is of little importance. Trust me. But, is it the considered opinion of Allied Intelligence that the biological warfare effort under Deitrich Zimmer's control has been damaged?"

John spoke candidly. "Our assessment is that it has been set back, temporarily. Why is it that you ask, sir?"

"The conventional biological warfare effort was, indeed, seriously damaged, perhaps more seriously than your intelligence estimates would suggest. But this situation is another matter entirely. All that it requires to be put into motion is in readiness. And, Deitrich Zimmer will use that Omega Option."

"And, just what is this Omega Option?" John asked, stubbing out his cigarette in the ashtray on the low, marble-inset coffee table between them, then leaning back deeper into the chair.

"Deitrich Zimmer controls an airborne virus, capable of a wide range of mutations so that it cannot be countered by vaccines of any conventional nature. By the time a vaccine to counter the initial effects would be developed, let alone dissemination of the vaccine had begun, the virus would have mutated and the vaccine would be worthless. The virus, regardless of the mutated form it might take, remains equally deadly. The only vaccine effective against it Zimmer has administered to himself. It has been administered to young Martin. It has been administered to their clones, his and Martin's, and theirs only. It has been administered to no one else.

"Deitrich Zimmer intends, if his back is put to the wall, to kill by means of the Omega Option virus every living human being on the face of the planet. Higher animals might well be affected, too. And, once he unleashed this virus, it cannot be stopped.

"I learned of his plans only after I had arranged for this meeting. Had you not agreed, Dr. Rourke, to evenly trade for my assistance, I would have volunteered this information at any event. I cannot stop Deitrich Zimmer alone. And, if he is not stopped, only he and his son and their clones will survive. Once the virus has run its course, all mankind will be dead."

Paul Rubenstein closed his eyes. Annie still held his hand.

"Zimmer will then utilize the biological materials he controls—namely the cells from which he would be able to grow clones of all of you, with the exception of commanders Shaw and Darkwood, and whatever other cells he has decided to add to his bank of humanity over the years. He would grow a population, downloading into the brains of these hapless creatures the dogma, the philosophy which he considers the only acceptable way in which to think.

"Deitrich Zimmer would be the progenitor of the true Master Race, and from this breeding stock all of the population of the world would spring."

"There's a glaring flaw in his plan," John Rourke said, lighting a cigarette in the blue-yellow flame of his battered old Zippo windlighter as he spoke. "For a Master Race to exist, it must have other races to master, over which to feel superior. He would have none."

"The virus, Dr. Rourke, would remain virulent for centuries, until it had exhausted all mutations possible and there was no living host, even remotely qualified, within which it could live, thrive. While the Earth died around him," Croenberg said, his voice low, "Deitrich Zimmer's scientific research would go on. I have examined other data—"

"From what source did you obtain this data, Gruppenführer?" Natalia asked, interrupting him.

"Men loyal to me kidnapped one of Dr. Zimmer's chief technical assistants; the man was more interested in his life than his loyalty, shall we say. There was a charming term used during your twentieth century: hacking. He entered Dr. Zimmer's computer network. To have destroyed the data found there would have been inefficacious, however, since the same fellow advised that all files were backed up and saved on CD Rom disk, these stored independently of any computer."

"What were his other plans?" Paul asked Croenberg.

"Dr. Zimmer has worked in an area which might best be labeled 'degeneration of the human species.' The good Herr Doctor is well aware of the fact Dr. Rourke pointed out, that a Master Race needs an inferior race over which to rule. And, there will be great amounts of labor to be accomplished in a new world. There will be building to be done, roads to be built, menial tasks which must be accomplished for the advancement of the civilization which Dr. Zimmer foresees. Dr. Zimmer has lain the groundwork for the culturing of a race of humanlike creatures, but of subhuman intelligence, deprived of the ability to speak, to learn beyond simple tasks, expendable creatures who can be reproduced at will asexually by means of cloning alone. This is the world envisioned by Deitrich Zimmer.

"And," Croenberg concluded, "none of us at all has a place in it. Your bodies—Dr. Rourke, Fräulein Major, Frau Rubenstein, young Herr Rourke, and perhaps even yours, Jew, and of course the body of Sarah Rourke—would be the basis for the genetic material used in the development of both the Master Race and the Slave Race."

John Rourke stood up, stretching his arms above his head, rolling his neck and shoulders. He bent over the coffee table, stubbed out his cigarette and walked toward the bar nearest the closed doors of the conference center. He went around to the far side of the bar, took a decanter of whiskey from the shelves behind the bar, and a glass. He half filled the tumbler, took a swallow, set down the glass and leaned over the bar on his elbows. "We will have to confirm, of course, what you are saying, Lieutenant General; but, assuming that we are able to do so, I would take it that we should act very quickly. Were I a betting man, I'd say that relatively shortly we'll be hearing from Dr. Zimmer's people, offering us the use of the tactical nuclear warheads. As you say, Croenberg, Zimmer wouldn't wish to die and, if the volcanic rift beneath the Pacific isn't somehow prevented from reaching the North American Plate, the planet is almost certainly doomed. All of Zimmer's plans would be for naught. It's in his best interests that we prevent the rift from reaching the North American Plate.

"Once Zimmer learns we are onto his true plan, however, he'll release his virus. In fact, if we succeed in stopping the spread of the vent beneath the Pacific, that may well be Zimmer's signal to release the virus. We must somehow halt his plans and kill him and all the clones he possesses of himself and of Martin."

"And Martin, Herr Doctor?" Croenberg asked, his voice oddly without malice, or even sarcasm.

"Martin must die as well." John cleared his throat, then said, "Let's adjourn for two hours, then resume." He looked at James Darkwood, saying, "We can't trust a radio frequency of any sort; get Lieutenant General Croenberg—I assume he'll be willing—to assist you to speak with this technician of Zimmer's and get Allied Intelligence to hack into Zimmer's computer network and confirm what's been said here." John looked at Croenberg. "Is that all right with you?"

"Of course."

John nodded, then said, "James, after you and Lieutenant General Croenberg have conferred, take the V-Stol you came in, fly out of here, directly to Mid-Wake. All of us will join you there later, with the exception of Lieutenant General Croenberg, unless he wishes our protection."

"I think not, Herr Doctor," Croenberg told them.

"Your choice, sir. At any event, time is more truly of the essence than it has ever been in human history. There's work to do. Natalia, as soon as Michael's through getting the data he needs from Lieutenant General Croenberg, you and Paul get together and get every detail you can concerning where Deitrich Zimmer is headquartering now. Start working up the outline of a plan. Emma, get some sleep, because you'll have some flying ahead of you sooner than we expected. Annie, consult with General Staat and his people about security here. Get him to double whatever he has. If Zimmer suspects we're having this conference, he'll hit it."

John took another sip of his drink, then slid the glass away from him.

John picked up the telephone receiver from behind the bar. "Yes, General Staat, please." There was a moment's pause. "No, sir, everything is fine, just fine. My daughter has a matter she'll be working with you on in a few minutes, but I need a line to Allied Intelligence Headquarters in Hawaii at Pearl. Have your communications people reroute it as much as possible and scramble all transmissions from here. Get someone on that, if you would, then my daughter will meet you at the front doors as soon as you feel you'll be ready."

Paul Rubenstein stood up, still holding Annie's hand. "You be careful," he told her. "If Zimmer does know where we're at, he'd have nothing to lose—"

"I'm always careful," Annie answered, smiling at him.

Paul Rubenstein's eyes moved over the room. Already, Darkwood and Croenberg were conferring. Natalia was smoking a cigarette, sitting otherwise motionless, as if she were on pause, waiting.

Paul Rubenstein walked toward the bar.

71

Seventeen

James Darkwood was already en route to Mid-Wake, carrying with him the means by which he could gain access to Deitrich Zimmer's computer network, the pertinent data something Croenberg had committed to memory and subsequently divulged.

Croenberg looked tired.

Natalia and Paul had already begun organizing data Croenberg gave them concerning Deitrich Zimmer's current operational headquarters, in a well-fortified, all-but nuclear-bombproof bunker outside Eden City.

Annie had security for the conference upgraded, insisting that General Staat put the Icelandic Defense Forces on full alert. She ordered airborne, canceling Emma's sleep, the second V-Stol, so that if its landing at Lydveldid Island had been detected by the Nazi or Eden war machines, so would its take-off. The V-Stol would return for them at a predesignated time.

John Rourke himself had spent much of the two-hour period in direct telephone communication with Allied Intelligence Headquarters in Hawaii at Pearl Harbor, then in a three-way call including Thorn Rolvaag aboard the deep-sea exploration vessel, the *Dauntless*. The *Dauntless* was home base to the deep dive submersibles, many of them remotely driven, which prowled over the volcanic vent itself, monitoring its progress by every measurement method possible.

Indeed, Deitrich Zimmer's overall military commander, a

man named Helmut Anton Griem, had contacted Allied Headquarters, offering a temporary truce while this threat to all mankind was combatted, and committing the full complement of Nazi and Eden tactical nuclear warheads.

Martin Zimmer personally contacted the President of the United States, pledging Eden's full efforts for the good of mankind.

As John Rourke related this last, Natalia laughed.

"Indeed," Rourke almost whispered. "Yet, in a very real way, the surrender of the tactical nuclear warheads will achieve its effect, hopefully. By the same token, it would seem exceedingly likely that Deitrich Zimmer has given up on his other plans and is moving to execute his Omega Option." He looked at Croenberg, saying, "Tell us whatever you can recall concerning the method or methods by which Zimmer plans to disseminate the virus. Any jump we can get in preplanning before we access Zimmer's computer network will help us."

"I will tell you whatever I can, Doctor," Croenberg began. "As I said, it is an airborne virus. All I was able to see concerning it—I'm not particularly gifted in the field of epidemiology—was that he will release the contents of several hundred canisters of the gas which are already in place in major population centers throughout the world. There is likely at least one, perhaps several, right here, in Lydveldid Island. Eden's involvement with international shipping, by means of the Russian traders, has been quite significant and for better than two decades. I have no way of knowing how long Zimmer has had this plan in place. It would seem likely that canisters were shipped all over the world, to be detonated remotely when and if Zimmer required."

"And what about the nature of the virus?" Annie asked, hands knotting together in her lap as she leaned forward in her chair. Croenberg still sat alone on the couch.

"What does it do to the affected person? I have no idea, Frau Rubenstein. I consider myself quite literate in my native language, but the terminology was beyond me."

"You know Zimmer better than any of us, Croenberg. Give us your best guesstimate concerning his timetable for actual release of the virus. Would he wait," Natalia asked, "until the operation to combat the volcanic vent is completed? How long before the viral agent would take effect? Do you have any knowledge whatsoever of that?"

"Fräulein Major," Croenberg said, lighting a cigarette, then exhaling smoke as he continued, "as to his timetable, I will hazard a guess. As to the time required for the virus to begin its work, I have no way of knowing. Again, I have no skills in medicine and most of what I was able to read was beyond me, and since we stayed in Herr Dr. Zimmer's system for only a brief period of time, lest we should be discovered, there was no time to copy any of the material. Frankly, I was looking for intelligence data which might be of some assistance in deposing Dr. Zimmer. We came across this data by sheer accident and had no idea what to do with it. Yet, realizing its importance, we exited his system immediately and have not re-entered since.

"But, as to Dr. Zimmer's timetable, I would say that he will have all in readiness, waiting only for completion of the project to divert the volcanic vent. When he is certain that the world will, indeed, survive, then he will have no further use for the world's population."

John Rourke told his daughter, "Get Emma's plane back here. Have her make arrangements for another aircraft, destination not to be disclosed on the air, in order to get Lieutenant General Croenberg back to the Pacific Northwest safely." And, Rourke looked at Croenberg as Annie got up, leaving the room. "How will we stay in touch, Croenberg?"

"Commander Darkwood and I have a system for doing so."

"It makes sense, the system, John," Paul interjected. "It'll work."

Rourke nodded.

Croenberg said, "And now, Dr. Rourke, I would pose a question."

"And the question is?"

"You are a medical man, I know, and therefore more the man of science than I. A two-part question, really. Is it truly possible that Deitrich Zimmer's Omega Option virus could, in fact, kill everyone on the planet? and, what will happen

74

if the volcanic vent cannot be stopped, by your own best estimate?"

"I'll try to answer both questions," Rourke told him, standing, picking up the pistols he normally carried in his belt, securing them, then slipping into his bomber jacket. "The vent. Let's take that first. If we fail, the vent will stop against the North American Plate. Then, just as scientists have predicted, the force of the vent will have to go someplace. Force usually follows the line of least resistance, which will be the edge of the plate. This will lead northward and southward, more or less simultaneously, with each point in the ring of fire which circles the Pacific Basin the vent growing more powerful. Eventually, a giant caldera will be formed, perhaps larger than any in the universe, large enough at any event to dislodge the planet from its orbit. Depending on the time of day—in other words, which side of the planet is facing the sun—the planet will either be launched out of orbit and toward the boundary of the solar system, or toward the sun. The Caldera would act like a gigantic engine, driving the planet from orbit, expending its energy as it drove the planet away from the exploding gases, lava, etc., etc.

"And," Rourke went on, "as to your other question. To the best of my knowledge, medical science has never licked a virus. The common cold—that's what we called it in the twentieth century—was really an entire system of rhinoviruses. Flu virus was another example. The best we could do was soften the blow of the symptoms and build up an immunity, but only if we knew the character of the virus in time. But, with a virus designed to rapidly mutate, there would be no defense which could be devised in time to do any good. Perhaps a handful of persons might survive, naturally resistant by some fluke of nature; perhaps, too, the immunologists and some small group might be able to rapidly reimmunize so that they would survive.

"But, in essence," John Rourke said, taking one of his thin, dark tobacco cigars and placing it between his teeth, "Deitrich Zimmer would obliterate humanity for all time." Rourke started for the conference room doors, saying over his shoulder, "I suggest that we be on our way."

Eighteen

He had become accustomed to the constant darkness and the rain of ash which covered everything in sticky grey, but he would never become accustomed to the constant trembling of the ground beneath his feet.

The walls in Tim Shaw's office had become so badly cracked, along with the rest of the headquarters building and better than fifty percent of the buildings in Honolulu that people were conducting business from their cars.

He was conducting police business and business was too good.

His back was as good as new after his ordeal in the mountains with the Nazi saboteur, and he had more important things than ever before to worry about. But he was listening to an audio disk on the player in his car, a selection of George Gershwin pieces played by one of the world's leading pianists. The song was "Embraceable You." Gershwin music was something he'd shared with his wife, Emma's and Ed's late mother. For some reason, he found himself wanting to listen to it now even though he hadn't listened to it in years. Because the world was most likely ending.

The sabotage was all but ended, coinciding with the time that the ground began shaking.

When the tremors began, news—in a diluted form, in order to avoid wholesale panic—was released in the general media concerning the suboceanic vent. Nothing was said of the possible consequences for total destruction. Yet, somehow, it was as if people knew. The announcement was made a little over a week ago, when the earthquakes kept coming and coming and never stopping. Fortunately, none of them was powerful—yet.

This last weekend, attendance at churches, synagogues and other religious gathering places in the islands reached an all-time high. For everyone who had turned to his or her own personal idea of God, there was someone who had turned away from good entirely, it seemed.

Robberies, looting, killing, vandalism, arson—the litany was unending and, for cops, so was the work.

Quietly, Tim Shaw had told the men of Honolulu PD SWAT. "With what's happening, we don't have time to fuck around. We've only got twenty-four hours in a day, and everybody's working twelve-hour shifts or better as it is. Pretty soon, we'll be living in our cars and the SWAT vans. So, as if we didn't have enough to do, the chief's assigned us to assist the regular street cops in anything that amounts to a major crime. Essentially, when the artillery comes out, so do we. That being the case, although I've always told my son Eddie to make certain that a substantial part of your training was in how to act like gentlemen and shit like that—" Most of the guys laughed, except the ones who had guessed what he was about to say. "Anyway, if we're called in, we get the job done as fast as we can so we can be ready for the next one. If it means smoking a perp that after six hours of negotiation we might be able to talk into surrendering, but probably not, we smoke the perp so long as we can do it safely for any innocent civilians involved."

One of the guys, Gene Wells, raised his hand. "Gene, speak to me," Shaw said.

"Tim, you're tellin' us to kill people—"

"Nothing like that at all, Gene, so I'm glad you brought it up. I wouldn't order you guys to kill anybody. I'm saying, we don't have the time to futz around. If the opportunity is there, of course we talk it through. But, if it's a matter of being shorthanded on the next call and one of our guys maybe getting killed, damn straight we end it quick. We serve and protect; that doesn't mean we're supposed to be human sacrifices, all right?"

It was potentially human-sacrifice time again. Over the strains of "Rhapsody In Blue" Tim Shaw could hear the radio call. There were three, possibly four armed robbers holed up in a building which had already been vacated because of tremor damage, stealing computers. When they tried getting out the back door into the alley and were spotted, there was a fight, a security guard shot and killed and two civilians wounded. A third civilian was able to return fire, and had wounded one of the perpetrators, with blood to prove it all over the alley floor according to the dispatcher.

Tim Shaw shut off the Gershwin music. "This is Honolulu Kilo Lima twenty-one. En route, Ten-Four." And Tim Shaw thrust his left hand and arm out into the rain and volcanic ash and stuck the little light on top of his car and hit the siren switch as he turned into traffic.

Eddie would be there, exhausted as hell just like everyone else. Although it seemed that half the people in Honolulu had turned into bad guys overnight, in reality the criminal population hadn't soared. It was just that more crime was being committed in a shorter period of time. In a standoff this morning with two guys who'd robbed a bank two days ago, both perpetrators—now deceased—turned out to have records going back to juvenile.

Maybe the usual criminals were accelerating their activities because they wanted to live their idea of the good life in what might be the last few weeks or months anybody would be living at all. Or, maybe, they were scared, just like the people who went to church and the people who didn't change their lives at all. And, committing every crime they could think of was a way of crowding back reality, not having to think about what was going on under the ocean and why the island they lived on was trembling so badly and why the volcanic ash kept falling and the rains kept falling and the whole damn world seemed to be going crazier than ever before.

Maybe killing a perp was doing him a favor; he wouldn't

78

have to sit and wait around for death like everybody else. So, maybe, that was why crime was increasing exponentially.

Because Tim Shaw was privy to information that hadn't been given to the general public. Doctor Thorn Rolvaag and his colleagues were predicting that the Pacific vent would collide with the North American Plate in approximately fourteen days. It might be days or weeks or months after that, but if the vent reached the North American Plate and split, the world would end.

Eddie would be dead. Emma wouldn't get to marry John Rourke; or, even if she did, she wouldn't live long enough to have children.

Everybody would just be dead and gone.

Maybe that was why Tim Shaw didn't worry that he was driving a little fast.

Nineteen

People were working under awnings and improvised tents, their portable telephones in hand, laptop computers beside them, cold rain and grey volcanic ash blanketing everything around them. Cars, normally parallel parked on Lord Boulevard, were parked diagonally so that there would be more spaces. Inside almost every car there were people, sometimes three or four or five, doing as best they could what they would have done in the abandoned buildings flanking both sides of the boulevard. The park itself, which ran down the center strip, was a tent city.

Half blocking the northbound lanes of Lord Boulevard were three prowl cars and a SWAT van, most of Eddie's people rather than being deployed trying to get the area clear of civilians.

Grey mud was everywhere, covering everything, dripping off the tent roofs and awnings, clogging the sewers, puddling in every depression.

Eddie was in the doorway of the abandoned building, a high-rise office complex less than five years old. Tim Shaw remembered watching while it was being erected. But no building was made for constant earth tremors, maybe a dozen times a day, day after day.

Tim Shaw, his hat screwed down low on his forehead and the collar of his black raincoat turned up against the rain and ash, skipped over a puddle and edged in beneath the doorway beside his son. "Druggies, stealing the computers so they can peddle 'em and buy more shit," Eddie announced. "That's the way it looks. The descriptions of the men fit and the merch they were tryin' to boost wasn't anything special, worth maybe a couple hundred bucks tops hot."

"You try talkin' to 'em, Eddie?"

"Yeah; they won't talk. We know where they're at. Had a remote probe scan the building, got the thermal signatures on the fifth floor. Three men seem to be able to move around and a fourth one is lying on top of a desk or something. They're fuckin' idiots, Dad."

"Well, sure they're fuckin' idiots, Eddie. Whatchya expect? You need a rest, boy. How long you been on duty?"

"Not too long, Dad. I'm fine."

Eddie had been on duty for at least eighteen hours, Tim Shaw knew. "Okay, look, let's get this one over quick, then maybe grab some dinner and some Z's, huh? You up for that, Eddie?"

"Unless some other damn fool does—"

"Worry about that when it happens, Eddie. Remember what your mom used to say? 'Sufficient unto each day is the evil thereof.' Remember that? Burnin' yourself out isn't gonna make this volcanic vent shit go away."

"I'm, all right, Dad! For God's sake—"

"Hey, you're in such hot shape, fine. We give the rest of the guys a vacation and we go get those assholes ourselves, huh? Whadya say?"

"We could get ourselves killed!"

"So, you wanna stay alive? Good. Smart boy. Then cut out this no sleep and no food shit. That's a good way to get yourself killed. And, you got a right to do that. But you don't have any right to get your guys killed just 'cause you're too washed out to be sharp. Now, get me three guys that can still stand up. After this, we all go to La Vita's for pizza. SWAT gear and all—leastways it'll probably keep the place from bein' robbed."

"All right."

Tim Shaw slapped his son lightly on the cheek; Eddie was too old to kiss in public. "Good. Get me three guys."

"Hey?"

"Hey what?"

"How long you been up?"

Tim Shaw grinned. "I'm always up; that's why I'm such a killer with the babes, Eddie. Now, get your ass outa here."

His son laughed, then ran back into the rain and falling ash. Tim Shaw closed his eyes for a second, telling himself not to fall asleep . . .

With Eddie, Gene and two other guys from the SWAT Team, Tim Shaw at last got himself into position on the fifth floor. Eddie was monitoring the remote probe that was still circling the building. The positions of the three men who could still move around were pretty much the same, two by the windows and the front entrance to the office suite they occupied and one by the rear door and the stairs, where Tim Shaw, his son and the three SWAT Team members waited. The thermal signature of the fourth man was getting less intense, which could mean the fourth guy was dead. Judging from the blood on the stairs, there was a good chance of that.

Most people these days carried guns, which was good to keep crime down, and the civilian who'd shot the fourth man might have nicked the guy in an artery.

Eddie whispered, "The guy by the back door is walkin' around a little. Maybe he's bored."

"Him and me both," Tim Shaw cracked. "We gotta liven things up a little, fellas. Tell ya what. Gene, take Bob and Richie and cover us. Eddie, go lay an entry charge on the lock plate. Eddie and I go in and nail the guy by the back door. Gene, Bob, Richie, you guys cover us, then move in after us and get into position on the other two guys. And don't forget the wounded guy on the desk. Might still give us some action. Just before Eddie and I go in, Bob, you flip a sound-and-light grenade in there, but make sure we're clear 'cause these are new slacks I'm wearin'. Then throw in a tear gas." Tim Shaw took off his fedora and put it on the stair post. "Nobody do nothin' funny with the hat, right? This is a good hat."

Eddie moved toward the doorway, Tim Shaw covering his son as did Gene, Bob and Richie. Laying the entry charge—it would blow the lock plate off and maybe a hole in the door—took under forty-five seconds. Tim Shaw pulled on his gas mask, the goggles inserted into the mask self-adjusting and designed for use with sound and light grenades. He plugged one of his ears. Before the other men plugged theirs, he announced, "Signal the guys on the street to do their number, then gimme a hand signal, we count to ten and Eddie detonates the charge and we go. Ready!"

Tim Shaw plugged the other ear, checking too that the cheeks of the gas mask were popped.

He could watch Gene's lips move as Gene spoke into the radio. Gene gave a thumbs up.

Tim Shaw nodded his head as he counted, the others doing the same.

At ten, Eddie activated the electronic detonator for the entry charge and the door blew inward, the lock plate shattered, flying like shrapnel.

The .45 in Tim Shaw's right hand, the little snubby .38 revolver in his left, Tim Shaw started for the still-smoking doorway, Eddie already in motion, one of the Lancer copies of a Remington 870 12 gauge in both fists at high port.

Eddie was through first, Tim Shaw behind his son in the next second, his raincoat (made from an advanced form of bullet-resistant material) buttoned to the throat.

The sound-and-light grenade was already detonated, even with the goggles inset into the gas mask, Tim Shaw's eyes involuntarily squinting against the flash. The bang, like a thousand whistles all off key and louder than gunshots, was making his ears ring despite the ear protectors. The gas grenade rolled across the floor, there was a flash and the grenade detonated, a cloud of smoke mushrooming up, then dissipating along the line of the office suite's low ceiling, like fog, covering everything.

Probably messed up his slacks, Tim Shaw thought.

Eddie fired his shotgun.

Pistol shots from behind a desk. A lot of pistol shots.

Tim Shaw was still running.

With both pistols firing—the Colt .45 auto and the Smith & Wesson Centennial snubby .38—Tim Shaw ran toward the desk. No bullet had hit him yet. The top of the desk splintered away. There was another blast from Eddie's 12 gauge. The top of the desk split. Tim Shaw's .38 was empty. Two rounds remained in the .45.

The perp behind the desk was in motion. Tim Shaw fired a double tap, catching the man in the left cheek of his ass.

Eddie fired again and the perp, already falling, reeled toward the wall, down for the longest count there was.

Gene, Bob and Richie streaked past them.

Tim Shaw buttoned out the .45's magazine, making a tactical change, the .38 into his raincoat pocket.

Eddie was running full tilt, a few yards ahead of Gene, Bob and Richie, effectively blocking them from firing.

Tim Shaw started to shout.

There was a man, with a shotgun. He stood up from behind a desk, just as calmly as if he hadn't a care in the world. Drugs, Tim Shaw thought absently.

Eddie fired first, blowing out the guy's left shoulder with a blast from the 12 gauge. The bad guy stumbled back a pace, but didn't fall. Drugs. Definitely. The bad guy fired. Tim Shaw shouted, "Eddie! Look out, man!"

Eddie took the hit.

The bad guy was already bleeding to death, but Bob shot him with a long burst from his subgun, Gene putting a burst from his assault rifle into the guy—already dead—as he fell. Richie dropped to his knees beside Eddie. "Jesus! He's bleedin' bad, Tim!"

Tim Shaw, a fresh magazine in his .45, shouted as he ran past, "Get a medic, damn it! Fuckin' hurry, Richie!"

The man on the desk wasn't dead yet, proving it as he sat up like some corpse in a horror movie and sprayed a subgun at Gene, catching Gene in the thighs and bowling him over.

Bob shot the nearly dead guy in the face, rolling him off the desk and onto the floor.

It was all going bad, the bad guys armed better than Tim Shaw or anybody had thought, all wearing gas masks just like the cops, which protected them from the light and the gas, probably wearing ear protection, too. Gene and Eddie were more tired and out of it than Tim Shaw had ever imagined.

The last bad guy was standing by the main doors into the office suite, a subgun in each hand.

He shouted something that Tim Shaw couldn't hear.

Bob fired his assault rifle in the same instant that the fourth bad guy fired both subguns.

Tim Shaw stopped running, stood stock still and raised the .45, extending it nearly to his full arm's length as he shouted, "Fuck you, cocksucker!" and squeezed the trigger.

The bad guy took the slug in the right eye and crumpled, his subguns firing into the ceiling, debris from the ceiling tiles raining down around them all like the rain and the grey volcanic ash on the street. Bob was on his knees, not hit, but firing his rifle.

"The guy's dead, Bob!" Tim Shaw shouted.

Then he just closed his eyes, but only for a second. His son was bleeding to death at the other end of the office.

Twenty

Eddie wasn't going to die. Tim Shaw lit a cigarette, but he wanted to kiss the doctor instead.

There would be no pizza at La Vita's. With Eddie and the others who'd gone down—none fatally, thank God—no one was in the mood for anything even remotely like that, least of all Tim Shaw himself. And La Vita's roof caved in during a tremor which occurred about five minutes after the gunfight in the office building.

The hospital, like all public buildings, was built to stricter codes, and so was still habitable. But plaster walls were spider-webbed with cracks and the personnel in the hospital looked like they were about to crack a little as well.

Once Tim Shaw was certain that his son was all right, and the others as well, and that no one had sustained any crippling damage—except the bad guys and they were dead anyway—he excused himself and left. His car was parked back at the crime scene; he'd ridden in the ambulance with Eddie.

It was a lousy night for a walk, so he hailed a police car on its way back from the emergency room. He knew the cop behind the wheel, had known her father, too. "So, hear your SWAT guys had a bad time of it, Inspector."

"Pretty bad, Linda, coulda been worse, a lot worse."

"Ask me," she said, as he climbed into the front seat beside her, "it's gonna, get a lot worse I mean."

"Well, we get too many more earthquakes we'll just slide

86

off the friggin' island and we won't have to worry about it," Shaw told her, thumbing his fedora up off his forehead as he talked.

"Where to?"

"Over on Lord Boulevard, near the Stilton Building. Left my car there."

"Hope you locked it," she razzed, putting the car into gear and starting out of the parking slot, then into the driveway.

Tim Shaw leaned back, pulling his hat down low on his forehead, his eyes on the street as soon as she turned into it.

It was about time for the ground to start shaking again, almost as if Mother Earth were in labor and the tremors were her contractions. Gradually, the contractions were coming a little faster and a little faster. He remembered when Emma was born and he was racing her mother to the hospital and his wife was telling him, "The contractions are every two and a half minutes, Tim."

What would be born from these contractions wouldn't be life, only death. Even if Thorn Rolvaag got the nuclear warheads he wanted and got them planted just perfect, would it all work? Even if he'd been a more conscientious student in his high-school science classes, he wouldn't have understood a word of it.

Linda asked him, "We all gonna die, Inspector?"

"What? I look like some kinda prophet or somethin'? We just gotta hang in there. Don't be scared."

She was a pretty little girl, about Emma's age, reddish brown hair, a little upturned nose and the kind of pale skin that must have been hell to live with during the brief summers here. Before the Night of the War, when the climate in Hawaii had been tropical, she would've had to stay inside or burn. "I'm scared; I admit it."

There were people living in tents along the street here, the tents sometimes just blankets and tarps strung together, sometimes the tents the military had provided, but these few and far between. As they drove—she didn't seem to be in a hurry—he could see figures moving within the makeshift tents, silhouetted by the light against the fabric. People standing or sitting, looking like they were talking or sometimes maybe arguing. He saw a couple embracing, too.

His own apartment was holding up okay and he wasn't about to sleep out in the rain until the walls started falling down on him.

"Bein' scared doesn't help, kid," Tim Shaw said at last. "But, there's nothin' wrong with bein' scared. It's normal. You'd be an idiot not to be."

"You don't look scared, Inspector."

"Neither do you," he answered, grinning. But then, the ground began trembling, the streetlights flickering, sounds filling the night of things breaking. She pulled over to the curb, her little hands locked tight on the wheel. Tim Shaw put his arm around her. "You mind?"

"No—I'm sorry."

"Don't be sorry, kid," he told her.

The ground was still trembling, maybe for a little longer than it had shaken the last time. He couldn't be certain. Anyway, somewhere, some scientist would be monitoring it to the precise second. Not that that would do any good. Maybe nothing would do any good.

When the ground stopped trembling, Linda didn't.

Tim Shaw closed his eyes as he spoke. "You near the end of your shift?"

"In an hour."

"Call in, tell 'em you need the car. Tell 'em I relieved you, officially."

"Can you do that? Anyway—"

"Yeah, I can do it, and don't gimme any arguments. You eat any dinner?"

"No."

"Neither did I. Whatchya say we fix that?"

She looked at him strangely, a smile coming to her lips. "Are you asking me out to dinner, Inspector?"

"Yeah, yeah I guess I am. And, if you accept, you better start callin' me Tim."

"Tim," was all Linda said.

He moved his arm.

She sniffed.

"So, get on the radio and tell 'em you're off duty as of now."

She picked up the unit, but shook her head, saying, "Can you wait just a minute?" She was crying.

"Sure thing," he told her, lighting a cigarette.

If she were married, he would have known about it; a friend of the family before her father was killed in the line of duty and since, he would have been invited to the wedding. And, she had the same last name that she was born with. These days, unlike the twentieth century when some women made a big deal out of it, a woman took her husband's last name. At least any woman that counted. If she had some kind of professional career, she hyphenated her last name with her husband's.

Tim Shaw looked at Linda again. She seemed to be getting the tears under control, which was good. And, it was just going to be dinner because he was old enough to be her father . . .

They left her car at his place, taking his car as they searched for a restaurant. Every restaurant they tried was closed because of structural damage or a power outage. These days, almost all power was routed underground by a sophisticated fiber system and the loss of electrical power was so rare that a lot of people didn't even own flashlights. But the underground infrastructure of power, water, telephone and the like could only take so much battering and there were sporadic outages, most of these still caused by problems within the walls of the battered buildings, not by a failure of the system.

Finally, after driving around for better than an hour, Tim Shaw said, "My apartment's in good shape. If you can cook, there was a supermarket open a coupla blocks back. You up for it?"

"That'd be nicer than a restaurant, anyway."

"Look," he told her. "I just don't want you gettin' the wrong idea. I'm no dirty old man or anything."

"I know that," she told him.

She looked kind of cute, her uniform hat left in the squad car and her hair down like it was over the collar of her uniform rain gear.

He could tell that he was getting old . . .

The supermarket was out of a lot of things, like bread and milk and bottled water. Panic buying, he figured. But the real essentials—beer, pasta and things like that—were in good supply. His arms laden with two grocery bags, they took the stairs to his apartment. He'd given Linda the key so he wouldn't have to fumble with it.

"Was all the damage fixed up after those guys—"

"The saboteurs? Yeah. Got a new bathtub, walls fixed, the whole nine yards. Got some new furniture, too. Department even paid for some of the damage (but not much of it)."

She unlocked his door and hit the light switch. He followed her inside and she closed the door, setting his key on the table beside the door. "Kitchen's this way," he told her. "Ditch the raincoat and grab a beer."

"Sounds good."

She hung up the raincoat, her gunbelt on beneath it, and followed him into the kitchen. Having no idea whether or not she could cook—the absence of testicles didn't necessarily confirm the presence of culinary talents, as he'd learned a long time ago—he'd picked out stuff that was so hard to screw up even he could cook it.

Putting the bags down on the counter, he started packing beer into the refrigerator, leaving out two, twisting the bottle caps off and handing one to Linda. "You need a glass?"

"Whatever."

"Fine. Less to wash," he told her.

He took off his hat, his raincoat and his suitcoat, depositing all on a kitchen chair, retrieving his little .38 snubby from the raincoat pocket first and putting it on the counter. His .45 was still stuffed into his waistband, holsterless as always.

Linda unbuckled her gunbelt, setting it on the counter,

then took off her radio. It was already shut off. She sipped at her beer.

Tim Shaw offered her a cigarette.

"Don't smoke," she told him. "But it doesn't bother me when somebody else does."

He lit up. "So, place isn't so bad, huh?"

"Your apartment looks nice. You're lucky you're in a structurally sound building. I'm in a building like this, but one of my girlfriends—she works for the University, ya know—well, her place is almost in ruins. She moved in with me at the beginning of the week."

"You wanna give her a ring and let her know not to worry?"

"She never expects me. Ever since the tremors started, my hours have been worse than ever, just like everybody else."

Flicking ashes into the sink, he took a long pull from his beer. She went over to the kitchen sink and washed her hands. "Why don't I put your gun in the living room."

"Please."

He picked up her rig. He hadn't worn a duty rig for more years than he wanted to remember. It was heavy for a girl her size. "Carry a backup gun?"

"I remember the course you used to teach at the academy, Inspector—Tim, I mean. You gave us a list of the best backup guns. I bought from the list. Lancer copy of the Seecamp DA .32 in my side pocket."

"Good girl," he told her. He got rid of his raincoat, suitcoat, hat and the .38 along with her duty rig, then returned to the kitchen. The .45 was still in his waistband, just like it would have been if he'd been home alone. He didn't see any reason to behave any differently than he normally would have, except maybe to watch out for belching if he had too much beer too fast. Even though she was a cop, she was a lady.

Twenty-one

Part of his enjoyment was to make the woman do things which disgusted her, humiliated her. Mary had been sobbing uncontrollably for better than an hour and that was upsetting him. Martin Zimmer told her as much. "You're ruining everything, Mary. Stop crying or I'll hit you again."

"I—I—I—"

"Maybe this will help it then." With his gloved right hand, he slapped her hard across the back of the neck, so hard that she fell to the floor in a heap at his feet. She was really trying hard not to cry; he gave her that. But, evidently she wasn't trying hard enough. He kicked her, telling her as he began, "I will keep hitting you until you stop crying. Learn to control yourself. The longer you keep crying, the more I'll punish you and the longer this will go on. We could have been done almost an hour ago."

She kept crying. He kept kicking her, in her naked bottom, in her ribs, in her legs.

His father, Deitrich Zimmer, was right. People were weak, needed purpose, direction. This girl was the perfect example of that. She had no self-control, couldn't even put up a fight of any sort at all. She was ruining the whole thing. If she didn't stop crying pretty soon, he would call in Elder Watts and have her taken off, useless thing that she was proving to be. They could find him another girl, just grab one off the street for him so that he could finish. He didn't like starting something that he couldn't finish and, with her crying like she was, he was too distracted even to do anything to himself . . .

Deitrich Zimmer sat at one of the computer terminals.

He had acquired all of the data which was currently possible to obtain concerning the suboceanic rift which was crossing the Pacific, moving inexorably toward the North American Plate. The logic of the plan the Allies had, suggested by John Rourke, expanded upon by the scientist Thorn Rolvaag, was sound. But, application of theory was often a different case entirely. As a scientist himself, he knew that from bitter experience.

During a laboratory experiment, under controlled conditions, if something went wrong, one merely started over again. The laboratory here was the planet itself.

If the Rolvaag theory did not work, the planet would be doomed, just as doomed as it would have been had nothing been tried. No one could accurately judge, past the stage of computer models, what would be the result of detonating tactical-yield nuclear warheads along a volcanic rift. Would the detonation indeed vent off the pressure and prevent the spread of the suboceanic rift. Or, would it merely accelerate the linking of the areas of volcanic activity which comprised the Pacific Rim's 'Ring of Fire'? Were the latter to be the case, the planet would be destroyed all the faster.

If the planet were destroyed, he had lost. The fallacy in genius, however great, was that one was still dependent on outside forces. For once in his life, Deitrich Zimmer would exercise no control.

If the planet could be saved by means of the practical application of Rolvaag's theory, then he—Deitrich Zimmer—would institute the Omega Option and rule forever.

If not, like everyone else on the face of the Earth, he would die, although he held the key to immortality.

Twenty-two

Before sitting down to dinner, Tim Shaw checked with the hospital on the condition of his son and the others. Their conditions were unchanged, which meant that they were doing well.

Dinner was satisfying, Linda not the best cook in the world, but more than acceptable.

They talked cop talk for a while, then about the tremors and the volcanic vent which was probably causing the problems in the first place.

After a while, over another brace of beers, he realized that they were intentionally avoiding talking about themselves.

When dinner was over, they cleaned up together, stashing the unused pasta in the refrigerator, each taking another beer.

The time was getting late.

As they sat on the couch and talked some more—cop talk again—Linda paused, then said, "I guess I'm staying kind of late. Better get going."

"Yeah—gettin' kinda late." That sounded like he was trying to get rid of her. "I mean, hey, what's late for a cop? Look, want another beer? Maybe some coffee?"

She edged forward on the couch seat, perching there almost in thin air. And, she looked at him. "Do you want me to stay?"

"Yeah. I want you to stay. I'm too old for you."

"I don't care, Tim."

"Damn it, neither do I." And Tim Shaw folded Linda into his arms, just holding her for a moment, then touching his lips to her forehead.

Her fingers drifted along his chest, along his neck, touching at last at his face. "You need a shave, Tim Shaw."

"I need a lot of things, kid." And he kissed her, then kissed her again and again. And, the nice part about it was that she kissed back.

Twenty-three

Boris Jones, the son of an immigrant Russian girl and a college professor in Honolulu, may not have been the best American computer expert; but, if he wasn't, James Darkwood had no idea who could have been any better. Whenever there was something genuinely difficult involving computers, Boris—a civilian—was called in by the navy to handle it. Living and teaching at Mid-Wake, Boris was also convenient.

James Darkwood leaned over his shoulder now as Boris entered Deitrich Zimmer's network. "You guys are lucky that somebody gave you the entry keys for this."

"I never told you that," Darkwood told him.

"You didn't have to; even I'm not smart enough to have broken into this thing. Whoever put together the entry system is a genius, certifiable."

"He's certifiable, all right, but not necessarily the genius part."

"Shit, James, each pathway into the system has three ways to go. If you don't know which is the correct choice, you could follow a mazelike blind alley for minutes, maybe hours, and even if you had part of the entry key and didn't do the rest, you'd still be screwed. It's like a Chinese puzzle box. You can say what you want, but the guy who developed this is smart with a capital S and that's the truth. This is Deitrich Zimmer's system, isn't it?"

"What would make you think something like that, Boris?"

Boris Jones laughed. "Well, for one thing, you never told me whose system we were breaking into. That's a good indicator that it's a really high security level. And, I speak, read and write perfect German, which is another clue. I hope we can copy what we find that you want, because I don't command enough technical German to be able to understand what you might want to know, and neither do you, although your German's about as good as mine."

"Just get into the computer, huh, Boris?"

Boris Jones laughed, then kept splaying his chocolate brown fingers over the keyboard. Boris played piano, was rather good at it, and the way he attacked the computer keyboard was almost rhythmic to watch. James Darkwood had asked him once, "Why don't you give up this computer genius stuff and become a concert pianist? You'd make more money."

"I don't like playing the piano, really, anyway not as much as computers. For some of the stuff I do, I've gotta be fast and accurate and the piano was the best kind of training. Plus, all music is mathematical progressions, just like computers, really. So, it was easy to understand. I write music as a means of polishing my mathematical skills. But I'm glad you like my tunes."

The tune now was the near-silent clicking of the keys in the board, a myriad of images flashing across the screen, mathematical formulae mostly. "This guy is really good. You make one wrong step and the system kicks you out. I betchya that if you make enough wrong steps, the system shuts down. This is the ultimate burglar-proof entry system. If this is Deitrich Zimmer, he should quit being a dictator and just design stuff like this; he could make a fortune. Nobody would get through this without knowing how first. I guarantee it."

"Are you getting through it?"

"Yeah, but you have to be really careful with the protocols, because I bet that if you make a typing error, the system kicks you out. That's what I'd do with a system like this. Want to try it?"

"No! For God's sake, Boris! this is important, man!"

Boris only laughed. "Just pulling your leg, James, that's all. Only thing I hope is that there isn't a time limit on entry. You guys should have told me about this and given me the entry keys beforehand so that I could practice with them. But, we're in it now and there's no turning back. Onward and sideways!"

James Darkwood's eyes were starting to blur from the un-ending array of equations, line after line of them, which would flash onto the screen, have to be answered and then immediately flash off.

If Boris screwed up and they didn't get in, would the system automatically alert Deitrich Zimmer that someone had tried entering and failed? If that were the case, Zimmer could cancel all of his programs and entry into the system would be useless.

More and more, espionage was like this, playing computer games as opposed to clandestine meetings and forays into enemy territory, sterile, but still exciting somehow. When it all became this way, if it did so during the term of his naval career, he'd have to apply for sea duty. Although he'd passed all the required courses at the academy and all the other courses he'd had to take since, talking with computers was something he did poorly.

"Holy shit," Boris remarked, punctuating his words with a soft, low whistle. "My technical German notwithstanding, this is talking about some kind of virus with controlled mutations."

"Just copy it, Boris; if you read it, I might have to kill you."

Boris looked up from his console. "What?"

James Darkwood said, "Just kidding," but didn't know whether or not he was . . .

Professor Dr. Wilhelmina Krause, New Germany's pre-miere authority in medical German, was very quietly spirited away from her home in New Germany, with the help of the German authorities, in such a way that her disappearance would not—everyone hoped—attract attention. By trans-at-mospheric insertion flight, she would be arriving in Hawaii within the hour, James Darkwood was informed. She would then be flown by V-Stol to her undersea rendezvous at Mid-Wake.

The number of printouts of the data gleaned by Boris Jones from Deitrich Zimmer's computer network was strictly con-trolled, the data, the CD Rom disks to which it had been committed and the means by which Zimmer's network could be accessed locked in a special vault at Naval Intelligence Headquarters for Mid-Wake, six Marine Corps guards, rifles locked and loaded, were standing watch over the vault itself, security for the building doubled.

Poor Boris Jones was given access to every videotape he wanted, a piano, all the computer gear he wished and simi-larly guarded. Although Professor Krause did not know it yet, she would remain under guard once her work was fin-ished, and until the data she was able to provide them con-cerning the virus had been acted upon.

James Darkwood left word at the security desk that he should not be disturbed in his temporary office, and that he should be awakened in forty-five minutes. Sleep would be a progressively more scarce commodity and he would get what he could while he could.

Twenty-four

The V-Stol splashed down, plummeting beneath the wave crests, engulfed by the sea as John Rourke's breath involuntarily caught. This was an experience which could become addicting, the ultimate freedom of motion within the terrestrial environment, flying with equal ease in the air and in the water.

Below, growing from an infinitesimal-seeming dot of light deep within the sea, he could see Mid-Wake . . .

John Rourke, Emma Shaw beside him, Annie, Natalia, Michael and Paul around him, walked with the Naval escort toward the steps of Naval Intelligence Headquarters.

It was always spring at Mid-Wake, plants always in bloom, trees always green, something always new and fresh. Mid-Wake had begun as a Top Secret Project under joint control of NASA and the United States Navy in the years Before the Night of the War, as an attempt to develop beneath the sea the practical working environment for space, while at the same time providing a base for United States submarines which would be within convenient striking range of the then-Soviet submarine base at Cam Ranh Bay in Viet Nam.

When the Night of the War came, the people living and working at Mid-Wake, supplemented by the personnel from what submarines were able to reach the facility (and precious few submarine commanders knew of its existence between the islands of Midway and Wake), formed the racial stock from which the city beneath the sea had grown. That stock was as wonderfully diverse as the United States itself had been, a wide range of racial, ethnic and religious backgrounds represented there. Indeed, it was at Mid-Wake that Paul Rubenstein, more than a century ago, had discovered that he was not the only remaining person of the Hebrew faith to survive the Night of the War and the Great Conflagration.

Utilizing the same technology which was being developed for building a modular station in orbit over the Earth, Mid-Wake was able to expand on its own tenuous self-sufficiency in order to become the successor to the name, United States of America. A parallel program, begun by the Soviet Union, was discovered, and beneath the sea, World War III raged for five centuries, submarine warfare unlike any ever conceptualized by William Bourne, a British mathematician and writer on naval subjects who in 1578 published *Inventions or Devises,* describing a completely enclosed boat that could be submerged and rowed underwater. Bourne never actually constructed this boat but Dutch inventor Cornelis Brebbel is usually credited with building the first submarine. Between 1620 and 1624 he successfully navigated crafts designed after Bourne's creation beneath the surface of the Thames River. It is said that King James I took a short ride in one.

Mid-Wake survived. Its Communist counterpart was conquered and, with peace at last—however short-lived—the population of Mid-Wake in part returned to the surface—most of the current residents of Hawaii were descendants of the men and women of Mid-Wake.

"It's like coming home every time I come here, like being some kind of space traveler in a movie or a book and returning to my home planet," Emma Shaw whispered.

John Rourke squeezed her hand. It was, of course, unmilitary that they should walk hand-in-hand here, she in uniform, but he was a general in the United States Forces, appointed to the rank more than a century ago here at Mid-Wake. Although he didn't take the rank as more than honorary, at times like this he was glad that rank, however unearned, had its privileges.

They ascended the steps, armed Marine Corps guards in camouflage BDUs—rather than dress blues—manning guard posts at the doors.

John Rourke and his party were allowed entrance, the sailors who had escorted them thus far, falling back.

Inside the main doors there was a vast hall. On the floor at its center, as a mosaic, was the Great Seal of the United States. Beyond its boundaries was a large desk, manned by three marines, two women and one man, all in dress blues, but all with sidearms.

Rourke stopped before the desk, the marines saluting him, Rourke returning their salutes, then taking the identity badges for all in his party, passing them to the appropriate persons whose faces and names appeared on the badges, then asking directions. "We're here to see Commander James Darkwood."

"I've already called him, sir, when I saw you and your party entering. The Commander will be joining you momentarily, sir."

"Thank you, Corporal."

And, as if on cue, elevator doors within the bank of four just past the desk opened and James Darkwood stepped out. In uniform, when Darkwood neared them at last he stopped, came to attention and saluted. John Rourke smiled, returning the salute and suppressing his laughter.

"If you would accompany me, General," James Darkwood said.

"Certainly, Commander." And Rourke walked toward the elevators, letting Darkwood fall in beside him, Emma dropping back a pace. Under his breath, John Rourke murmured, "Let's cut out this formal crap once we're about our business, all right?"

"Yes, sir."

"Thank you."

The elevator was locked open and they entered, Darkwood using a key to work the controls. He programmed the elevator for the third floor and the doors slapped shut and the machine began moving upward.

Within seconds, the car stopped and the doors opened.

Standing on either side of the elevator banks were two pairs of Marine Corps guards, these men and women in camouflage BDUs and armed with energy rifles and cartridge pistols. They snapped to as Rourke ordered, "As you were, marines," Darkwood still beside him.

They entered a long, grey synth-marble corridor, stopping before the third door on the right.

Two marines, dressed and armed like the last batch, flanked the doorway.

The marines made rifle salutes. Rourke returned the salutes and entered through the doorway.

There was another doorway just inside, two more marines guarding that. The salutes, then Darkwood took a credit-card key and used it on the vaultlike door which the two marines flanked.

The door opened and James Darkwood said, "After you, sir."

John Rourke looked inside. A little woman with grey hair and wearing a dress which almost matched the color of her hair sat before a bank of computer consoles, her eyes, as she looked up, speaking volumes more than any words could say.

Twenty-five

Professor Dr. Wilhelmina Krause had very beautiful blue eyes, nearly as surreal in their blueness as Natalia's.

And, she was a meticulous woman, with prepared notes (John Rourke was certain that they were written in an admirably neat hand) in several notebooks beside her on the desk into which the consoles were set. There was an exactly appropriate number of chairs set about the room.

John Rourke waited until the women were seated, then seated himself.

Within the room with them was the President of the United States, the ambassador of New Germany, the ambassador of Australia, the ambassador of Lydveldid Island, and the representative of what had been called the Wild Tribes of Europe, now simply known as Gallia, after the Latin term. The Russian ambassador was unable to attend and would be briefed by her counterparts.

Professor Dr. Wilhelmina Krause cleared her throat, then began to speak. "I feel so so very little among you," she began, her voice slightly quavering, her speech heavily accented. "I am but a university professor, and I sit with leaders of the world and the legendary John Rourke."

"It is we who are honored, Fräulein Doctor," Rourke interjected.

She smiled sweetly. "My English is not so good as my command of my native language, especially at the technical

104

level. And so, I apologize in advance." She cleared her throat again and said, "I have reviewed the materials provided me, although it would take many days of study to understand all that is included here I think. My medical specialty is not epidemiology, and such experts must indeed be consulted by you at once. What is represented here is most grave, indeed."

"Could you tell us, Fräulein Doctor," the President of the United States asked, "just what it is which we face?"

"Horror, sir, is what you face, you and all of us. The materials presented to me outline a plan so despicable that I sicken at the very thought of it. Deitrich Zimmer has revived a disease from the distant past and made it more virulent than nature could ever have made it. It would be unstoppable."

"AIDS," Paul Rubenstein said only half aloud.

"Exactly!" Professor Dr. Krause exclaimed, clapping her tiny hands together in her lap. "He has reinvented the disease known as Acquired Immune Deficiency Syndrome, modifying the HIV virus in such a fashion that it can be transmitted in the very air that we breathe, in the very water that we drink. He has modified it in such a way that the virus will almost constantly mutate, therefore be unstoppable. Every disease possible for mankind to contract will be contracted and the body's immune system will not fight back. People will die from diseases which have long since ceased to claim human life.

"The cure for most types of cancer which was developed almost two hundred years ago will no longer be of any effect, because this cure must work in conjunction with the body's own immune system. Common viruses, such as those which affect the upper respiratory system, will become mankillers. Deitrich Zimmer must be the devil incarnate to do this to humanity."

"I've read about AIDS," the President of the United States said, "but I'll confess that was quite some time ago."

John Rourke recited the litany. "In the last part of the twentieth century, a disease which attacked the body's immune system surfaced. It flourished at first within the homosexual population, spreading quickly into the heterosexual population as well. Sexually transmitted. There was a Simeon variant, logically enough called SAIDS. Bodily fluids carried the disease. There were theories running rampant as to the disease's origin, and as to how it vectored. The disease, a virus, could remain dormant within a host body for years before any real symptoms manifested themselves.

"People were dying. Scientists worked, studied. No remedy was forthcoming, it seemed.

"If," Rourke continued, "Deitrich Zimmer has brought back this scourge and discovered a way in which the virus can be transmitted other than by sexual contact, transfusion of blood or the sharing of a needle, he could quite literally kill every human being on the face of the Earth, as well as some of the higher animals.

"We're talking about calculated murder of the human race," John Rourke concluded.

Professor Dr. Krause said, "Deitrich Zimmer has developed a means by which to immunize against the permutations of the virus, and administered this immunization to himself and to Martin Zimmer and to what are referred to as clones of themselves."

"He has perfected the process of human cloning," Natalia said matter-of-factly.

"This man would unleash this horror, then?" Professor Dr. Krause asked, almost as an appeal to be contradicted.

Annie responded. "He is evil, Fräulein Doctor, beyond human imagining. He is obsessed with his own immortality and with his own mastery of the planet. Nothing else matters to him."

Professor Dr. Krause looked on the verge of collapse. John Rourke suggested, "I propose that we briefly adjourn while the Fräulein Doctor rests a bit and we get some epidemiologists in to assist her, if that meets with your approval, Mr. President, ladies and gentlemen."

The President of the United States, his face ashen, stood. "Yes, yes, of course. We should do that. Let's break for dinner, then." And he walked over to Professor Dr. Krause, asking, "Would you join me for dinner, Fraulein Doctor. I promise that we will not discuss this matter. I'll show you the aquarium, or what I call an 'aquarium.' It will relax you. I promise."

"Thank you, Mr. President," she answered, sounding on the verge of collapse.

John Rourke stood up as she stood. He was suddenly more angry than he had ever been in his entire life, and more committed to a single purpose than any since he had set out across a nuclear wasteland six centuries ago in the immediate aftermath of the Night of the War to find his wife and children. He would take the life of Deitrich Zimmer or die in the attempt.

Twenty-six

Mid-Wake was a full-fledged community, even more now than it had been when John Rourke first came here over a century ago in the belly of Jason Darkwood's submarine, near death after being captured by the Communist forces beneath the sea.

There were fine restaurants, and John Rourke picked what James Darkwood had told him was the very finest.

Despite the fact that he was dressed in rough clothes and Emma Shaw in her flight suit and even the waiters wore tuxedos, John Rourke and Emma were seated immediately. He was, of course, John Rourke; the thought at once amused and bothered him.

Seafood was an obvious specialty, but John Rourke was not terribly hungry and Emma seemed even less so, so he ordered the fettucine Alfredo and a house salad for each of them.

"He's insane," Emma Shaw said as he lit her cigarette, only their coffee on the table.

"Obviously."

"Can he do this? I mean, really do it?"

"Yes, he can; more to the point, Zimmer will."

"We have to stop him."

"Again, obviously."

"How, John?"

"Kill him before he can release the virus, if he hasn't

already released it. In either event, kill him and rid the world of him forever. In the twentieth century, there was considerable debate over the morality of a death penalty for capital crimes. I was always firmly convinced that the death penalty was not a deterrent to crime, merely a cure of sorts.

"Fear of death," he told her, lighting a cigarette for himself now, too, "would not stop a murderer from taking the life of his victim. The only demonstrable benefit inherent to capital punishment was that the murderer or other capital criminal could never be released onto the streets, could never commit such a crime again. Death was the only way to make certain of that; lifetime incarceration was not only impractical, but could prove impermanent.

"Deitrich Zimmer has stepped outside the human community to such a degree that in murdering him there would be no more moral import than in shooting at a paper target."

"You can't get near enough to kill him, John, without—" Emma Shaw let the sentence hang.

"Without getting killed myself?"

"Yes."

"I'm going to contact Wolfgang Mann and see if the divorce papers which Sarah had filed have been cleared yet. If they have, or the moment that they have, be my wife, for as long as that is and then afterward if there is an afterward."

"Yes."

"Thank you," John Rourke told her, smiling, reaching out and touching her hand.

Their salads arrived and he told the waiter," The lady had the house dressing and I had the Thousand Island."

"Very good, sir."

John Rourke waited until Emma lifted the first forkful of salad to her lips.

He loved this woman very dearly, more than he had ever loved before. He began to eat his salad, savoring the moment more than the taste.

Twenty-seven

If the synthesized virus were to be released by radio signal alone, Natalia realized, there would at least be a realistic chance of foiling Deitrich Zimmer's intentions. But, Zimmer had, in the best tradition of John Rourke, planned ahead.

That was the one thing which John Thomas Rourke and Deitrich Zimmer held in common, aside from medical degrees and being of the same sex: both men were the embodiment of genius, but opposite sides of the coin. Whereas John's superior intelligence had always been directed toward the good, Zimmer's was directed toward doing evil.

Zimmer's plan, as Professor Dr. Wilhelmina Krause outlined it from the data revealed through raiding Zimmer's computer network, was—as Croenberg might have described it—convoluted.

The canisters of compressed air, containing the airborne virus, were secreted over the course of five years, not twenty. They were placed in strategic locations throughout the civilized world. Whether or not each of these locations was pinpointed deeper within the data remained to be seen; and, if so, were these locations encrypted in such a manner that they might not be easily identified? The personnel who had placed the canisters were murdered, following much the same plan as had been utilized in the burial rites of the pharaohs of ancient Egypt. Dead men, as the expression in English went, tell no tales.

A corps of trusted SS-trained fifth columnists, perhaps very much like the man who had nearly killed John through use of a cyanide gas pistol, was enlisted to activate radio signals when given circumstances occurred, these still to be discerned as well. Blind after double blind, Deitrich Zimmer's system was all but fail-safe, perhaps unable to be defeated.

To jam every radio frequency possible would be impossible. Even the very stars emitted radio signals, of course.

To locate and terminate or otherwise disable each and every one of the saboteurs might be equally impossible. All that was needed was for the contents of one canister to successfully be released and Deitrich Zimmer's plan, if slightly slowed, would nonetheless succeed. If the data so far gleaned from Dr. Zimmer's computer network included the identities of each and every one of these saboteurs, and how they could be located, it would be sufficiently miraculous that her own indecision about the existence of God—Natalia truly wanted to believe, as did the Rourkes—would instantly be washed away.

Assuming that all of the saboteurs were somehow located and prevented from releasing the contents of their assigned canisters, it was equally far-fetched to believe that each of these personnel would willingly cooperate afterward, assuming each of them lived. Unless the location of each canister was correctly discerned, the canisters would eventually release their evil into the world, without any help from Zimmer. The canisters were made from a type of stainless steel. The air inside the canisters would, perforce, be moist. The environment surrounding the canisters would have moisture in it as well, if only ordinary humidity.

No stainless steel was truly 100% rustproof in the long term. Stainless steels of various types were merely rust-resistant, some more than others. Eventually, at least one canister's integrity would be compromised and the contents would release. Again, Zimmer would have won and mankind would have lost.

Professor Dr. Wilhelmina Krause, who had fallen silent for a few minutes in order to consult her notes, thus allowing

Natalia's reverie, resumed speaking. "It is unclear at this point whether or not the nature of the inoculant Herr Dr. Zimmer had administered to himself and his son—" Natalia glanced at John, saw the pain in John's eyes, "—is revealed in these materials. It may become necessary to invade Dr. Zimmer's computer network again."

"If we do and he catches us," James Darkwood said, "he might order the instantaneous release of the virus just to destroy us, gambling on the suboceanic vent not destroying the planet. And, anyway, we wouldn't all die instantly. We'd keep trying to produce a biological means by which to defeat the virus and, in the hopes of success, keep working to stop the spread of the suboceanic rift."

"Commander Darkwood's point is well taken," John agreed.

Michael, his voice little more than a whisper, suggested, "It seems that whatever action we might take, Zimmer has already countered it. We have to think of something that Zimmer has somehow overlooked. Otherwise, he'll win this one and there won't be any other ones to win or lose."

"His own thoroughness," Paul interjected, "might be the key to defeating him. There's a difference between meticulous, conscientious attention to detail and obsession. We know, from our own observations and from Croenberg's analysis of Zimmer, that obsessiveness is there, with Zimmer's unrelenting passion for immortality. If we try to analyze Zimmer's methods from a standpoint of his being obsessive rather than being a genius, maybe we can indeed discern something that he's overlooked, perhaps by his very nature of paying such inordinate attention to detail."

"I'm not trying to sound naive," Annie said, "but is there no way at all to either reason with him or threaten him?"

The President of the United States smiled indulgently—a little too indulgently, Natalia thought—when he told Annie, "My dear Mrs. Rubenstein, how can we threaten him when he holds the world virtually at bay?"

Then John spoke. "Perhaps we can turn his obsession against him, as Annie was getting at." Natalia smiled. Annie merely folded her hands in her lap and listened. "Even now,

112

Zimmer is, in the interests of humanity, surrendering his tactical nuclear warheads in order to assist in the attempt to divert the volcanic vent which might destroy us all. What if we threaten him in the only way that he can understand?"

James Darkwood said, "How?"

John Rourke smiled. "I've never been good at telling funny stories, so indulge me while I attempt to illustrate with one. There was this American Indian lad walking about a train station in the southwestern United States, likely in the 1950s or earlier when train travel over great distance was popular because air travel was still in its infancy. At any event, the lad walks up to various female tourists, one after the other, raising his right hand palm outward and saying, 'Chance.' Well, after saying this to a variety of different women, one of the women at last said to him, 'I thought Indians said, How.' The Indian replied—and here's the point, of course—'Me know how; me want chance.' This an obvious sexual reference. The point I'm making is that I think we have the perfect mechanism, that we know how. What we need is the chance."

"What sort of 'mechanism,' Dr. Rourke," the President asked him.

"Well, Mr. President, everyone's been talking about it; and, it is the obvious thing. He donated his warheads not out of any love of humanity, obviously, but because we can do something about the vent, possibly, and he cannot. Eden has a comparatively minuscule navy, virtually no sea power and has never been interested in undersea exploration. The Nazis have nothing at all.

"We, on the other hand, command the greatest naval force the world has ever known, spaceships as it were, but capable of traveling within the sea. No one on Earth has the power to stop the volcanic rift, except us. What if we choose not to?"

"That would be suicidal, Dr. Rourke!" the President insisted.

"Suicidal? What's better? All of us die in a fiery blast, instantly, or we linger for weeks and months and years, dying a little bit at a time while we work to combat a constantly mutating virus, just so that we can leave a perfect planet in the hands of a madman who would corrupt the entire human race?

"I think the former, sir, or certainly that we convince Deitrich Zimmer that it is the former option we select. While our scientists work to discern and hopefully duplicate the inoculant Zimmer has administered to himself and to Martin, we attack on a second front. We call Deitrich Zimmer's bluff. And, we offer him a deal."

"What sort of deal?" James Darkwood asked.

"His life, with his Nazi comrades, in his own country. He can live forever there, rule forever there if he wishes, over the men and women within his group and within Eden who chose to live with him. He would be eternal master of his own part of the world; either that, he dies with the rest of us," John concluded.

"We would rue such a bargain, Doctor," the President suggested.

"Indeed we would. But, after we get the canisters secured, after we know that we have the means by which to combat the disease, then I will kill him. To do so would be totally irrational, so he'd never suspect that I would do it. I'll kill him because he must die; whatever guilt there might be associated with the act will be mine alone. He would never expect me to break a promise; I'll deal with the consequences of my actions, with my own conscience. We offer him life or death."

"What if Deitrich Zimmer chooses death, John?" Natalia asked.

John Rourke smiled at her, saying, "We'll still be working to combat him on other fronts. Should those efforts fail, and we cannot defeat him, then I'll kill him anyway. It would be the ultimate moral sophistry to allow Deitrich Zimmer to live, to sacrifice future generations, should there be any, just to spare my conscience, or to allow him the satisfaction of knowing that even in some very small way he had triumphed. I've predicated my life on the concept that good always triumphs and evil always fails. I'm sure, over the years, that some people have thought me foolish, or naive for believing

114

what I believe. To let Zimmer taste even a moment's victory would be the abdication of everything I've always believed in. It's a battle for the future of the world on the grander scale, but on a personal level it's a battle of his ego versus mine. From the very beginning of this, from the moment he shot Sarah and kidnapped our baby, he's made this a personal thing between himself and the Family. Well, he's got a personal thing."

And John stopped talking for a moment and looked at President Arthur Hooks. "In the twentieth century and in the centuries before, there was a unique and bloody concept, whereby a man would swear an oath of revenge, and nothing other than death or the achievement of his objective would dissuade him from following through on his oath. It was called a vendetta. That's what this has finally devolved to. Zimmer will die."

Natalia remembered another vendetta.

Twenty-eight

John Rourke stood in the corridor, beside an ashtray, his pulse rate something that he could feel. There was only one other time when he had committed himself to killing someone, although he had killed far too many men in the course of his life. Even when he stood atop the mountain and fired at Rozhdestvenskiy in the helicopter, on the morning of the Great Conflagration, it had been for other reasons than the deep, personal need to end a human life.

The only other time was over a century ago on an island in the Pacific; and the man whose life he had sworn to himself to take was Natalia's husband, the architect of thermal nuclear war, as much the living embodiment of evil as Deitrich Zimmer. The man was Vladmir Karamatsov.

John Rourke lit one of his thin, dark tobacco cigars in the blue-yellow flame of his battered Zippo, then closed his eyes, remembering . . . Serovski shouted, "My Hero Marshal—it is a trap!"

John Rourke released the cord that he held about his wrists and with his left hand drew the Crain Life Support System X knife and rammed it forward, his right hand going for one of the twin stainless Detonics .45s beneath the borrowed winter coat, the point of the knife gouging into Serovski's back as the Russian started to move, severing the spinal column, the body flopping to the sand at John Rourke's feet, his hand

116

letting go of the knife as his right fist stabbed forward with the little Detonics and he fired.

But Vladmir Karamatsov was already moving, dodging left, Rourke's bullet striking one of the KGB Elite Corpsmen who had been surrounding him, Natalia's pistols in Karamatsov's fists now, spitting fire, John Rourke stepping forward, Natalia about to fire and also to be hit, he knew, the left side of Rourke's body shouldering Natalia away. Darkwood fired and so did Stanhope, two more of the Elite Corpsmen down, John Rourke felt a tongue of fire kiss across his left biceps and he dropped to his knees and fired again, a double tap, chunks of rock near where Karamatsov's head had been exploding.

And Karamatsov was running up into the rocks.

John Rourke had the second little Detonics out now and fired, Karamatsov's left leg buckling under him, Karamatsov falling, lurching forward and out of sight into the rocks. Sand spurted up into Rourke's face. Natalia was firing now. Rourke's right sleeve wiped across his eyes and he blinked. He was up, running, Darkwood and Stanhope at his right, Natalia at his left. He looked back once—the three marines had fanned out to right and left into the rocks by the lapping surf, their Soviet assault rifles firing, Elite Corpsmen going down. Rourke emptied both pistols into his adversaries.

He reached the rocks, pistol-whipping one of the Russians aside as he started up the path in a dead run, the abdominal surgery hurting him now, running.

"John!" It was Natalia's voice, behind him. He shoved one of the little Detonics pistols into his belt and buttoned out the magazine from the other one, pocketing the empty, grabbing a fresh one from the Sparks Six-Pak on his belt beneath the coat, ramming it up the well, his right thumb working down the stop, the slide slamming forward. There was no time to reload the second one.

There was gunfire still behind him.

Ahead of him—he raised the little Detonics in both fists and fired, Karamatsov lurching forward, stumbling, then running on. Rourke fired again and missed. He kept running, Natalia almost passing him, real pain in his abdomen now

117

from the surgery, his breath coming hard. He kept running, shouldering past Natalia, shouting, "I want you—Karamatsov!"

"I want him more, John!"

Natalia was even with him again, and in her right fist she held the American pistol, in her left the blood-dripping knife he had used to kill Serovski.

The helicopters—their rotors were turning, Karamatsov running toward the nearest of them, Rourke stabbing the little Detonics toward him, firing it out. Karamatsov's body lurched once again and he stumbled to his knees, was up, ran on. John Rourke's body screamed at him to stop. He kept running, Karamatsov just twenty yards ahead, limping badly.

Karamatsov wheeled, Natalia's pistols in his fists, firing them out, Natalia screaming, Rourke lurching forward as one of the .357 Magnum rounds ripped his left leg from under him. He looked at Natalia, her right arm limp at her side, her body thrown back against the rocks, her left fist still clutching the knife. "Get him!"

Rourke drew himself to his feet, throwing himself into the run, his left leg dragging, Karamatsov kept using the pistols, but they were empty now and he flung the one in his right hand, then the one in his left, Rourke dodging the guns as they sailed toward the nearest chopper.

The distance was less than ten yards, Rourke's abdomen on fire with pain, his left leg numbing. Karamatsov stumbled, fell, spilled into the dirt and snow, pushed himself up. John Rourke hurled himself toward Karamatsov, his hands grasping for the shoulders, Karamatsov lurching forward, Rourke tearing the vest from Karamatsov's back, Karamatsov crawling across the ground, Rourke throwing his body against the man. Rourke had him, his hands closing over Karamatsov's neck. Karamatsov's left fist hammered up and Rourke sagged away to his knees now, as Karamatsov rose to his feet.

Gunfire ripped into the ground beside him from the open helicopter door. Rourke pushed himself up and ran. More gunfire, but from along the path in the black rocks, Rourke saw the body of the Elite Corpsman in the open fuselage door stitched across the chest in red.

Karamatsov threw himself into the fuselage doorway, reaching for the fallen Elite Corpsman's assault rifle. John Rourke's hands closed on Karamatsov's waist and he threw his weight back, tearing Karamatsov away from the helicopter, the gunship going airborne, the *Reagan*'s deck guns opening up in the distance, shells landing around them everywhere as they rolled across the ground, Karamatsov's fist hammering at Rourke's face and neck and head.

Dirt and rocks rained around them, John Rourke's left elbow snapping back into Karamatsov's jaw, the Russian's mouth suddenly washed with red, Rourke's right fist impacting Karamatsov's left temple.

Karamatsov fell back.

Rourke was to his knees. Karamatsov threw his body toward Rourke and Rourke fell back. Karamatsov's right fist crossed Rourke's jaw.

Karamatsov was up, running, Rourke lurched forward, to his knees, to his feet.

More shells were falling from the *Reagan*'s deck guns, helicopters exploding in the air and on the ground, their fiery skeletons falling from the sky. As Rourke ran, he dodged chunks of burning debris.

"Karamatsov!" The Hero Marshal was running for the last of his helicopters, the machine already hovering three feet from the ground, two Elite Corpsmen in the open fuselage doorway, firing, as Rourke was throwing himself to the ground behind the still-burning tail section of one of the downed Soviet choppers. From over the rise behind the last chopper, he could see Aldridge and his marines, their assault rifles blazing. Aldridge fired a grenade from the tube beneath the barrel of his rifle. The last Soviet helicopter seemed to hesitate in midair, and then there was a burst of flames and a fireball of black and yellow and orange belched skyward.

"Karamatsov!" Rourke had a fresh magazine up the butt of one of his pistols as he pushed to his feet, running forward. "Karamatsov!"

And Rourke stopped. He saw him. Karamatsov had reached the edge of the promontory on which the chopper had landed. He stood there. Rourke ran toward him.

Karamatsov's right hand moved to his shoulder holster and John Rourke dodged left and fired. Karamatsov fired, Rourke fired, Karamatsov fired. Rourke fired again, throwing himself to the ground, rolling, Karamatsov's pistol discharging still, the slugs furrowing the ground, Rourke firing blindly, emptying the little Detonics toward him.

Karamatsov's gun was empty and Rourke pushed to his feet as the hero marshal started to ram a fresh magazine up the butt of his Model 59. Rourke had no time to reload. He launched his body toward Karamatsov and impacted, Karamatsov's pistol flying from his hand over the edge of the precipice and gone, Rourke's hands going for Karamatsov's throat as they fell, Rourke's body taking the impact, Karamatsov's right fist slamming into Rourke's left cheek, Rourke's right knee smashing upward into Karamatsov's groin.

Karamatsov fell back.

Rourke was up as Karamatsov stood. They charged at each other, John Rourke's left snapping out, catching Karamatsov across the chin, the Russian's head snapping back, Rourke's right impacting Karamatsov's left ear, Rourke's left hammering Karamatsov's nose to pulp.

Karamatsov's body wheeled left, his right foot snapping up and out, John Rourke's body feeling as if it were exploding as the hero marshal's jackbooted foot struck into his abdomen. Rourke staggered. Karamatsov closed, fists flying, Rourke's hands and arms going up to protect his face.

Rourke was falling back, the pain in his abdomen washing over him, consciousness starting to go.

Rourke wheeled half right and lashed back with his left elbow, striking bone, Rourke's right fist hammering forward, Karamatsov's head snapping back hard, his body rocking back.

John Rourke's hands gripped at his abdomen and he sagged forward on his knees, coughing blood.

Karamatsov was on his knees, his right hammering forward, John Rourke lurching against him, Rourke's own right impacting the center of the hero marshal's face.

Karamatsov's body weaved, fell. John Rourke tried to stand.

Vladmir Karamatsov was crawling away from him. Rourke got to his feet, lurched after him.

Karamatsov crawled to his feet, staggered back, by the edge of the precipice over the sea.

Karamatsov's right hand shot forward and in his fist was the little snub-nosed Smith & Wesson revolver he had carried five centuries ago. "You are dead, John Rourke!"

John Rourke stood there, hands clutching to his abdomen, about to throw himself against Karamatsov and hurl them both over the edge and into the sea on the rocks below.

And then he heard Natalia's voice. "No, Vladmir!" And she rose up beside Karamatsov and Karamatsov turned to look at her and in both her tiny fists she held the short-sword-sized Life Support System X and the steel moved in her hands over her head and around in an arc to her right and then—

The Crain knife stopped moving.

Karamatsov's body swayed.

The little revolver fell from his limp right hand.

His head separated from his neck and sailed outward into the void.

Blood sprayed geyserlike into the air around Karamatsov like a corona of light.

The headless torso of her husband rocked backwards and was gone over the edge.

Natalia screamed.

John Rourke closed his eyes.

This time death was forever . . .

The next time, death would be forever as well.

The fire had gone out in Rourke's cigar, and he rolled the cigar into the left side of his mouth as he returned to the briefing room.

Twenty-nine

Sarah Rourke could not sleep this night.

Fully recovered from her debilitated physical condition, aware fully too that she bore memories within her brain which were not her own, one feeling within her would never change, that she had been violated as surely as if she had been raped.

To be a woman was hellish at times.

She was expected to let the man from whom she was in the process of being divorced avenge what had happened to her, while she sat helplessly by, waiting.

She sat, in the equivalent of a solarium, bright lights, plants growing in greenhouselike conditions, the perfect facsimile of a real hospital solarium where patients, too long confined, could be exposed to sunlight without being exposed to the elements.

But this was not real sunlight, only pretend. And, she was aboard a submersible aircraft carrier somewhere in the Pacific Ocean, the vessel on a war footing.

Sarah Rourke wondered, at times, what had brought her to this?

Before the Night of the War, she had illustrated—and eventually written, too—children's books, with all sorts of nice jungle animals as characters. Then, in one night, she found herself consigned to a jungle for all of eternity, her little boy killing a man who was sexually assaulting her, her little girl never knowing a real home throughout the years of childhood.

And, her husband.

She was married to a living legend, not a man. Soon, she would not be married to him, but married to the most sensitive man she had ever met, Wolfgang Mann. And, he was a German general, for God's sake. A professional soldier! Life was madness, when life wasn't terror.

John would go on forever being the hero, or at least until he died.

She was just too tired to be a hero's wife anymore, too tired of the fighting and the danger and all of it. She had tried, tried to be the heroine in the play and done rather well at it, despite insufficient preparation for the role.

Then a lie was implanted in her brain by a madman and she discovered, only too late, that she could not trust her own mind. She was reduced to murdering a human being she had never met in a vain attempt to engineer the death of her husband, who had loved her with perfect fidelity for half a millennium. Sarah Rourke was ashamed of what she had done, despite the fact that she was neither legally nor morally responsible. The fault was clearly not her own.

She remembered the words of William Shakespeare in *Julius Caesar,* "The fault, dear Brutus, is not in our stars, but in ourselves. . . ."

The fault was hers, regardless of the circumstances.

And now, with happiness perhaps just within her grasp, the world might end. If it did, her world would end in the arms of a man she wished she had met in the twentieth century rather than the twenty-fifth century, a man she wished she had married in the twentieth century instead of being about to marry in what was the twenty-sixth.

She loved John Rourke, and he loved her, but marriage between them was insanity.

She did not love Wolfgang Mann as much, rather differently.

Sarah Rourke looked up, as Wolfgang Mann and the naval equivalent of an attorney entered the solarium and approached her. The naval officer was younger than either of her children, although she was biologically just in her middle thirties. And the naval officer was an adult. Another of John's master strokes, letting the children age into adulthood while she did not age, all through the use of cryogenics.

The naval officer said, "Ma'am, I have the papers for the divorce. Once you've signed them, they can be sent by facsimile to Dr. Rourke." And then the young man's throat seemed to catch. "None of my business, Mrs. Rourke, but are you and your husband sure, really sure about this?"

She reached out her hand and Wolfgang Mann took her hand in his. Sarah Rourke told the young man—whom she felt sorry for—"I know that a lot of people, most people, think of us as like George and Martha Washington, or Garibaldi and his wife, or whatever historical couple you could imagine. But we aren't anything special, John and me. We're only people. He'd be the first one to tell you that. And, people make mistakes. The wise people attempt to correct them. That's what we're doing now, correcting a long overdue error in judgment. So, don't feel badly for us, son."

Michael and Annie had not been a mistake. They were the finest people that she knew, as were Natalia and Paul, their mates. And, so was John. This girl, Emma Shaw, would be good for John.

Sarah Rourke bit her lower lip as she took the papers and the pen from the young naval officer's hands.

As she signed the name Sarah Rourke for the very last time, tears began to fill her eyes and she let them come, hoping they would wash some things away, knowing they would not.

Thirty

Tim Shaw's right arm was stiff, in a way in which it had not been stiff for a very long time. It had "fallen asleep," tingling as he tried to move it, the fingers stiff and thick feeling, and almost seeming to be disconnected from his body.

In the half light, half darkness of the grey morning filtering through the rain and volcanic ash and, at last, almost unnecessarily, through the partially open venetian blinds, he could see Linda's face quite clearly as she lay in the bed beside him.

He hadn't been a "virgin" since the death of his wife, but he hadn't done anything like this, either.

Linda Cunningham was actually two years younger than his daughter, and he hadn't even come close to giving himself a heart attack satisfying her. And, he was certain that he had, in fact, satisfied her as well as he had satisfied himself.

He was an old street cop who'd been around maybe too long—otherwise he would have thought he was falling in love, or had already fallen. But, the only reason they were together was because the Earth was shaking beneath them, and not in the romantic sense of the "earth moving," just really shaking. Twice during the night he had been awakened by mild earth tremors, but hadn't bothered to awaken the girl sleeping beside him.

When she awoke, the magic would probably be over. She'd

look at his overnight growth of beard, seeing all the white which vastly outnumbered the black that formed his stubble beard, realizing the horror of being in bed with a guy his age and all that went with it. She'd be polite, get out of the apartment early on the excuse that she had to get clothes or something, and try her damnedest never to see him again.

Tim Shaw would have lit a cigarette, except for two reasons—he'd promised Emma he wouldn't smoke in bed, because it terrified her that he'd fall asleep and burn to death, and if he moved to get a cigarette and an ashtray and everything, the girl would awaken. Tim Shaw wanted the last few minutes or seconds, no matter, but he wanted them.

And, he had to piss.

That could wait, too.

After several minutes—objectively, he knew that—but what seemed like seconds, Linda stirred, rolled over against his shoulder and opened her eyes, still sleepy-looking like a little girl's eyes.

Now, it would happen.

He could read eyes. Reading eyes had helped him to stay alive all those years; and, this morning, he wondered if it had been worth it.

Her eyes opened wide, almost startled. He wanted to look away, but she was so beautiful that he couldn't force himself to do it, or to say something flippant which would save his ego. He waited, letting it happen.

"I love you, Tim. Can I come back tonight, when I'm off duty? And every night? I love you so."

Tim Shaw took the girl into his arms, holding her tight against his chest, feeling her breath against his skin, listening to himself as he said, "I love you, too, kid. I honest to God love you."

Thirty-one

All through the night, they had gone over every scrap of data contained within the pirated computer records taken from Deitrich Zimmer's network, and John Rourke's resolve to do what must be done, even should he compromise his soul by promising Deitrich Zimmer life, then giving him death, had deepened.

As he left the chamber in which they had conferred until well past dawn, Emma—yawning, looking young and perfect and beautiful—beside him, a young, ordinary seaman approached him. "General Rourke, sir! This facsimile message has just arrived for you, sir!"

"Very good, son. Hang loose a minute."

"What is it, John?"

John Rourke saw the first line.

"I'm afraid I'm without a proper pen," he told Emma and the young sailor. "Does anyone, ah—" He closed his eyes, sniffed. "A pen, please. Please."

Emma handed him a pen. "What is it, John?"

John Rourke took the pen, placed the papers against the wall, initialed as instructed on the first page—he had insisted that Sarah receive half of everything he owned, which was a considerable amount because of the century and a quarter of brigadier general's pay which had been accruing for him ever since the rank was bestowed upon him here.

Sarah insisted that she required nothing, that Wolfgang

Mann would provide for her, that what he wished to give to her he should give to the children instead, or otherwise do what he thought best.

That was initialed.

And, he signed at the bottom of the last sheet. "I need a witness, sailor, and it wouldn't be appropriate for Commander Shaw to fulfill that function under the circumstances."

"Aye, sir."

John Rourke handed the young sailor Emma's pen. The sailor signed the divorce decree, returning the pen. "Please fax that to point of origin."

"Aye, sir—ah—"

"Yes?"

"Ah—"

"I know, sailor," John Rourke told the boy.

As the sailor left, John Rourke looked at Emma Shaw. "If we were to step aboard one of the submarines in port, and the captain of the vessel were aboard her, would that be—"

"Are you asking me to marry you this morning?"

"I guess it's legal, or would be, even though we don't have a license. And, anyway, I always thought that marriage was in the heart."

"If I don't tell your children and Paul and Natalia, they'd never forgive us."

"You need a wedding dress, too. I'm not crazy about you getting married in a flight suit you haven't been out of in two days."

Emma laughed. "I'd look like an idiot in a wedding dress, John!"

"No, you wouldn't, but we can wait until tomorrow, if you like. Would that be enough time?"

"You're serious."

"Yes, I am."

"Yes, it would."

"Take Annie and Natalia with you when you pick out a wedding dress; that's something neither of them would forgive if you didn't."

"I love you, and I swear to God I'll make you the best wife I can be."

John Rourke took Emma Shaw into his arms, kissing her lightly on the forehead. "You know what you're getting yourself into? What if we live through this? Have you thought about that?"

"In every dream since you asked me, John Rourke, and before that, too. I never fell in love before."

He wanted to do something, to crowd out of his mind what he had just done by signing that piece of paper. And, very suddenly, with a sick feeling in the pit of his stomach, John Rourke wondered if he would ever see Sarah again. She had started all of this for him. Not the Night of the War, of course, but all which had transpired since then had stemmed from his search for her and their then two young children, little more than babies.

As he looked to his right, he saw Annie and Michael, and Paul and Natalia, too. "The hour's late, or early, depending on one's perspective," John Rourke said, looking at all of them in turn, then his eyes finally settling on Annie and Michael. "I'm sorry."

"You signed the papers," Annie said, almost too calmly.

"I signed the papers, yes," John Rourke told them. And, suddenly, it seemed so damned stupid to him, that signing something was necessary to end something which had gone on so long between them. Signing something didn't end a marriage; the marriage ended of its own force, or lack of it. Signing something was just to make other people—lawyers and judges and accountants (if they still had accountants)— feel better, have something to look at and touch and read and file away for no one ever to bother reading again.

Michael said, "We both love you, Dad," and he walked over to stand beside him. And Michael put his arms around John Rourke and kissed his father's cheek.

Annie came to stand at his other side, holding him.

Paul and Natalia stood side by side, his best friends in the world. Natalia nodded, that everything was all right. Paul would always be Paul, the truest and finest man John Rourke had ever known.

And John Rourke reached out, taking Emma's hand. Annie embraced her. Michael kissed her cheek. Natalia joined them, embraced Emma. Paul took Emma into his arms and kissed her lightly on the lips, then smiled. "Well, you already asked me if you thought it would be okay to have two best men instead of one."

John Rourke turned away.

He was, after all, an anachronism in the truest sense, he realized. He loved his family and he loved them so deeply that their expression of love for him brought tears to his eyes.

He let them come; in truth, he could not have stopped them.

Thirty-two

Deitrich Zimmer's favorite computer model of the effect of the virus was playing on screen before him. It was neither the most optimistic, nor the most pessimistic; but, instead, the most realistic.

Only eight percent of the canisters would actually be released and function properly, disgorging into the air their entire contents.

Fewer than three hundred thousand people would be infected by this direct method.

Each of these people would infect no more than three people (although, according to other models, more than five times that number would be infected within the first ten days). That would mean slightly fewer than one million people would be dying from the virus and, at the same time, spreading it—but long before they knew it. These people would infect at least three people each; and, again, those numbers were grossly underestimated.

Within three weeks, three million people would be infected, already dying, but fewer than ten percent of this number would realize that their lives were at all altered, let alone in mortal jeopardy.

Within sixteen weeks, better than ninety percent of the entire human population of the planet would be dying, fewer than twenty percent realizing it.

Before six months had passed, over ninety-six percent of

all human beings, regardless of where they lived, no matter how remote the location, would be dying. Many of the higher animals would be affected as well.

Within nine months, over fifteen percent of the initially infected persons would be dead. Within twelve months, better than seventy-five percent of those initially infected would be dead.

Within two years, better than ninety-three percent of all humankind would be dead, as well as millions of the higher animals. The human race, as it was called, would be in its last throes.

Within five years, no human being would remain alive, except for himself, his son and the clones he had made of them both. It would be difficult, making do without assistants, without servants, but the two would somehow manage for the good of the greater purpose. And, after ten years had passed and the virus had run its course and died—that was part of the beauty of the thing, that the virus would, in a decade, destroy itself—conditions would be safe for the first few of the subspecies to be released, slaves to perform the necessary manual labor, to prepare for the coming of the Master Race.

Within a century, by manipulating the breeding process, the population of the Earth would be stabilized at acceptable levels and all would be in order.

Order, nearly as much as life, was his fondest desire.

Yet, all his planning might be for naught if the racial inferiors who postured as governors of the Trans-Global Alliance were unable to stop the spread of the suboceanic rift, divert the energy within the vent without destroying the entire planet in the process.

The potential irony of such a situation did not escape him, that he had successfully laid the groundwork from which humanity's brightest hour would emerge, and his plans might never come to fruition because of the very humanity he was trying to uplift.

The mongrelization of the human species was what had brought about all of this, from the Night of the War forward. It was only fitting that the genetic stock which comprised the Rourke Family would become the basis for his new world order, that the raw abilities lying dormant within their genes would, at last, be brought to the surface, all inferior qualities excised.

And the Jew, Rubenstein, he would serve in part as the basis for the slave race, creatures in whom the ability to think beyond the most basic concepts, even the ability to talk would gradually be bred out.

It would be a perfect world. And, any attempt to breed with these creatures, should some degenerate member of the new race of true men be found attempting to do so, would be at once fruitless and punishable by the most severe means possible. The slave race would be reproduced as clones only, their ability for sexual reproduction removed. Mankind would be forever pure.

In future centuries, with the Earth reformed and technology exultant, he and Martin would lead the new race to the stars and beyond, to master the universe as they had mastered the Earth. The human species would have attained its ultimate destiny of perfection, because of his sacrifice. Whatever Deitrich Zimmer might have to endure in the years to come was as nothing when compared to that . . .

When he thought of what he had finally done to the girl, Mary, and what Elder Watts and his Land Pirates would have put her through before they let her die (or she died of her own accord), Martin Zimmer came in his own hand.

Thirty-three

John Rourke was being fitted for a general's dress blue uniform which he would wear at the wedding. The wedding was to be at four o'clock and would be performed by a Protestant navy chaplain rather than a ship's captain; and rather than aboard a submarine, in Mid-Wake's central park area fronting the government buildings. Rourke reviewed transcriptions of the discussions with Professor Dr. Wilhelmina Krause. He was trying to understand the specific nature of the virus which Deitrich Zimmer planned to unleash upon the world, the more knowledge he acquired the more potential he would have for succeeding in his ploy against Zimmer.

"Must you wear these two handguns and this little knife, Doctor Rourke?" The civilian tailor was a large-boned, skinny man of average height, pleasant enough. This was the third time that he had asked about the double Alessi shoulder rig and the twin stainless Detonics CombatMasters which John Rourke habitually wore.

"Fine," Rourke told the man. "Will you settle for this gun and the knife?" He picked up the Hip-Gripped Centennial from the desk. With the little .38 and the A. G. Russell Sting IA Black Chrome, at least he would be armed.

"It's a deal, Dr. Rourke."

Rourke placed the Centennial in his waistband, crossdraw behind the left hip bone. Leaving the knife sheathed at the small of his back, he shrugged out of the double Alessi rig, setting guns and holsters onto the desk top.

The tailor resumed tailoring and John Rourke resumed reading whenever he could. This wedding business was getting out of hand, Natalia and Annie off with Emma doing all sorts of things John Rourke couldn't even imagine in preparation.

After a few hours' sleep, the day had started in earnest at about 10:00 A.M. It was now nearly two.

Paul and Michael were nowhere to be seen either, evidently getting fitted for dress clothes; uniforms or tuxedos, Rourke wondered? Neither of them held military rank of any sort, so probably the latter. He would have preferred a tuxedo himself. After all, Emma didn't have to wear her dress uniform.

But she had insisted that he wear a military uniform, so he acquiesced.

"Have you ever considered the concept of uniforms?" Rourke asked the tailor; the fellow's name was Cleveland.

"I don't follow you sir. Now—just stand right like that."

It was impossible to read, and this was a waste of time. "The whole concept of people dressing the same to imply that they'll somehow act the same. During the 1960s, with the hippie movement, it was the same idea. Hippies—they were called by various names—wore their hair long and liked tie-dyed T-shirts and wore love beads and things like that— uniforms. Mankind's fascination with conformity has always amazed me."

"I just make them, sir; I don't decree that people wear them."

"Oh, I know, but the whole idea of business suits and the like. Why should everyone look the same? Before the Night of the War, I wore a tuxedo maybe ten times in my entire life. I owned two three-piece suits—you know, with a vest— and both of them were dark blue and I almost never wore them. I had a couple of nice tweed sportcoats. They were pretty comfortable and you could wear one with jeans if you needed to, without looking dumb. But all these people, they'd spend fortunes on clothes just so they could look the way someone thought they were supposed to look.

"I was getting my teeth cleaned and I remember waiting in the oral hygienist's office and looking for a magazine. I'd just finished the book I'd been reading and hadn't brought an extra book in the car. Whoever purchased the magazine subscriptions had somewhat different tastes from mine. I liked *Guns & Ammo Handguns,* the thinking man's gun magazine. I knew the editor quite well, a marvelously erudite fellow named Jan Libourel, and a fine staff too, with men like Dave Arnold and Garry James. I enjoyed *National Geographic,* too. Now, there was a magazine! At any event, there were just a bunch of fashion magazines, women's and men's.

"To make my point," Rourke continued, "there were men's suits modeled in this magazine which looked like something no man in his right mind would want to wear. And the prices! I remember seeing a blue suit which fit the fellow wearing it like a cross between a casket and a tent, and it had these cheap-looking white plastic buttons. The price was about two thousand dollars!"

"Was that a lot in those days, sir?"

John Rourke merely answered, "Well, to me it was. And, it was an ugly suit."

"Yes, sir; well, as they say, beauty is in the eye of the beholder. This is going to work much better without those two guns. You'll really like it, Doctor."

And, John Rourke thought, a full-dress military uniform with general's rank that he was convinced he hadn't earned was something he'd not get much use out of, either . . .

It was no surprise when John called her on the radio telephone, asking how she was feeling, asking about Wolfgang, asking if there were anything at all she needed. And, telling her that he was marrying Emma Shaw. She had already given their union her blessing, as John had given his blessing to her forthcoming marriage to Wolfgang Mann.

"Would you like to come? I can arrange transportation for you from the *Paladin* to here. I'd really like it if you could, Sarah, unless you don't feel up to it."

John had been looking for a way of doing nothing behind

her back, being perfectly open and above board; and this was always his way.

She started to give the classic answer, "Well, I don't have anything to wear," but decided against that.

She loved him still, the failure of their marriage incidental. She respected him, loved and respected her two children. For the children, for John's sake, she told him, "Nothing could keep me away, John give Emma my best, too."

And she called Wolfgang Mann to get her out of the damned hospital . . .

Tim Shaw had finally gotten to go to the bathroom, as Linda was making them breakfast while he showered (it was wiser to shower quickly lest the next tremor should break a water main and suddenly there wouldn't be anymore water). When he stepped out of the shower, Linda knocked on the half-open door. "It's your daughter, by telephone from Mid-Wake."

He thought there was something wrong. And, what was Emma doing at Mid-Wake, anyway?

Wrapping a towel around his waist, still dripping wet, he took the cordless telephone, sat down on the stool and asked, "You all right, kid?"

Linda brought him a cup of coffee and planted a kiss on his forehead.

He ran his fingers back through his wet hair as Emma told him, "John and I are getting married this afternoon. We can have transportation for you. Can you and Eddie come?"

"You sure about this, kid? Real sure?"

"I love him, Daddy."

"That's sure enough. Yeah, I don't know how, but Eddie and I'll get the time off and be there."

"Who's the girl? You been keeping secrets on me?"

"Tommy Cunningham's kid, Linda, all grown up and a cop."

"You two, uh—"

"MInd your manners, kid. And yeah."

"Oh, Daddy!"

"Shut up," he told his daughter, good-naturedly . . .

Natalia seemed to know everything. Emma Shaw just let her take over, Annie helping her.

The dress. Even the underwear. The flowers.

Nails and hair.

Emma Shaw found herself thinking that it would have been so much simpler if they'd found the captain of one of the submarines and just done it . . .

John Rourke would not let another man shine his shoes, unless that were the way in which a man earned his income. Just because he had arbitrary military rank didn't mean he needed an orderly to wait on him.

A good shine on a pair of shoes was not just for looks. With shoes or boots, careful care preserved the structural integrity of the leather, guarded against scuffing and helped to keep one's feet dry. A spit shine, in the military context, was absurd, on the other hand. The process of spit shining could actually damage the leather. And, John Rourke might wear the uniform for a few hours, but the black navy oxfords he would wear with it would be perfectly serviceable shoes on other occasions, with the tweed sportcoat that he owned, for example. There was no sense having anything more than a good, honest shine.

He set down his new shoes.

The world was possibly ending—either by vulcanism on a scale unprecedented in the history of the universe perhaps, or by the whim of a mad genius—and he was wasting precious hours getting fitted for a uniform he'd never wear again, in all likelihood, and shining a pair of shoes when his combat boots were already perfectly well shined.

Wasting time.

Then he opened his wallet and looked at the picture of Emma that he'd begun carrying recently.

Rethinking things, John Rourke realized that he wasn't wasting time at all.

Thirty-four

James Darkwood buttoned the tunic of his dress whites. The latest data in from the *Dauntless,* where Dr. Thorn Rolvaag was headquartered, was not promising. The speed at which the suboceanic rift was driving eastward toward the North American Plate was accelerating.

The combined arsenal of tactical nuclear warheads from Eden and Eden's Nazi allies was already en route to a rendezvous with Rolvaag's ship. The tactical nuclear arsenals of New Germany and the United States, including every nuclear warhead in the United States submarine fleet, were en route to the location as well.

Rolvaag was finalizing plans for implanting the devices, already working out the finishing touches for a detonation schedule. Because of its importance, although Rolvaag would have final approval, his calculations would be reviewed by the leading scientists of the United States, New Germany, China and elsewhere. One miscalculation might not only neutralize the potential benefit of the detonations, but might, in fact, speed disaster further along.

And there was to be a wedding.

He did not find this frivolous, nor even incongruous. Weddings and births were the celebration of life. The entire purpose of Rolvaag's work over the volcanic rift was the perpetuation of life. Without life's celebration, its perpetuation would be meaningless.

And, should Rolvaag's work fail, or should Deitrich Zimmer's doomsday virus be disseminated, there would be little time left for humanity in the celebration of life. Time was, in the final analysis, the most precious commodity of all . . .

Annie Rubenstein knotted her husband's tie for the umpteenth time, at last getting it just perfect. "You look great, Paul. My handsome husband!" And she leaned up and kissed him lightly on the lips.

Paul took a step closer and embraced her. He had told her that he clearly did not look forward to this thing, and, he repeated that now. "Getting everybody together for this wedding; I don't know. But, I do know I'll be glad when it's over."

He took his battered old Browning High Power from the dresser top and shoved it into the waistband of his tuxedo, the butt of the pistol sticking outside his vest.

Annie turned toward the mirror, to give herself one final inspection. There had been no time to find matching bridesmaids' dresses and have them fitted. If there'd really been time, she would have made the dresses for herself and Natalia, even made Emma's dress.

Instead, Emma wore a perfectly beautiful long white bridal gown bought off the rack and altered on the spot. There wasn't even time to make a proper headpiece, so Emma bought a veil. She and Natalia, on the other hand, their tastes in clothing wildly divergent—Annie liked frilly things, Natalia liked tailored clothes—had agreed with Emma on just getting long dresses of no particular style or color (except neither dress would be white, of course).

Annie wore pale pink, the bodice low-cut but plain, sleeveless and strapless, the skirt, packed beneath with petticoats and ankle-length, full and multi-tiered. Her hair was piled atop her head, interwoven with garlands of pink flowers.

She had seen Natalia's dress, champagne-colored and probably the most perfect dress to be had at Mid-Wake . . .

* * *

140

Michael Rourke watched Natalia as she checked herself in the mirror. If she was hiding a gun or knife—and certainly she would be—he couldn't figure out where. He'd asked the color of her dress, thinking it was a shade of khaki. He was told that it was called champagne. He'd had champagne, but didn't remember it being quite that color at all.

It was almost sleeveless, except for little sleevelike things just below her shoulders and over her biceps. Even though Natalia was strong for a woman, her biceps didn't look like anything at all.

The front of the dress stopped so that the cleavage between her breasts was visible, forming a kind of heart-shaped look. The back was even lower, he observed, as she turned around. The bottom part of the dress—nothing fancy about it—came all the way to her ankles. She wore high-heeled shoes, which made her nearly as tall as he was.

Her jewelry was nothing special, just gold earrings (they were tiny balls about the size of pellets of #4 buckshot, or just a little smaller) and her regular watch, a ladies' Rolex with a gold and stainless-steel jubilee band.

Her hair was caught up at the nape of her neck, but not with anything, just sort of woven together, but not braided.

"How do I look?"

Michael stood up, pulling on the jacket for his tuxedo as he answered her, "Like the most beautiful woman in the world. But you always look that way."

"You're sweet," she told him, her voice a soft, warm alto. And, even though she stood nearly to his height with the shoes she wore, somehow she was able to lean up in order to kiss him on the cheek.

Michael picked up one of the Berettas and stuffed it inside the waistband of his pants. He didn't like vests and a cummerbund reminded him of a sash on a pirate in a video movie.

Natalia picked up her purse, a really small one that wouldn't have been practical to hold anything much larger than a .25 automatic or a mini-revolver. It was the same color as the dress, so he supposed that she was stuck with it. Rather than commenting on the impractical size of her purse, he said, "You all set?"

141

"Um-hm. But, let me fix your tie, Michael."

Michael stood there while she untied the knot, then retied it. Her nails, he noticed, were painted the same color as the dress. She had a good eye for detail, but women generally did.

"There! You look so handsome."

"Why don't we get around to doing this the first chance we get?"

"Getting married?"

"Yeah."

And she kissed him again.

Thirty-five

The dress Emma Shaw wore was simple but gorgeous. White, of course. Natalia had always felt that the two terms were mutually dependant. Annie, who was always dressed very nicely, had opted for Emma's dress to be dripping with lace, with puffed sleeves and high buttoned cuffs and high neck.

The dress Natalia had helped Emma to settle upon was off the shoulder—Emma had a nice little bustline and a very pretty back and should take full advantage of it—and had three-quarter-length lace sleeves (as a concession to Annie). The skirt was draped on both sides and very full, the train not too exaggerated.

Emma looked beautiful.

Natalia Anastasia Tiemerovna's eyes scanned the crowd assembled in the park as, beside Annie, her hands clasped round a small bouquet, she and Annie walked in Emma Shaw's train. But, beneath the skirt of her dress she had a pistol, in case the wedding turned out to be more than anyone had planned. She had occasionally used thigh holsters Before the Night of the War, liking those from Galco. What she wore now was a Lancer duplicate of that Galco holster, the gun within it a Lancer duplicate of the Seecamp DA .32.

Natalia was looking for familiar faces at which she would smile, and she was looking for faces which might somehow seem out of place. At these, she might have to shoot. Security at Mid-Wake was at its highest level because of the man who, along with his bride, was to be the center of attention here.

If the forces of Eden or their Nazi allies could assassinate John Rourke, the event would demoralize the Trans-Global Alliance, because John had become its very symbol, although he would have rejected the idea had Natalia or anyone else mentioned it to him. He had survived since Before the Night of the War, led the United States to victory over her own native land, was leading the Trans-Global Alliance, whether he was aware of it or not.

Perhaps, like the American general, he would attempt to retire to his Mount Vernon, only eventually to be convinced to assume the mantle of leadership, as Washington had. Perhaps John would simply retire when this was all over. Or, perhaps, he would find some new call to adventure.

But, despite the fact that the "guests"—virtually everyone who could pack into the park—included a significant number of Naval Intelligence and SEAL personnel in plain clothes or ordinary uniforms, all of them armed, the best security was that which one provided for oneself—or was provided by those who loved.

She loved John Rourke and she always would. It was not that she loved Michael more, nor did she love him any less. Just differently.

The irony of being bridesmaid to the woman who was marrying John Rourke did not escape her either.

Nor did the fact escape her that even though she saw no bulges, the tuxedoed man beside Emma Shaw, her father, Inspector Tim Shaw, who would be giving her away—how barbaric, as if a woman were a slave or an inanimate object—would certainly be armed.

Probably the only persons not armed, from within the wedding party, at least, were the bride and the minister.

Clasped within her hands, surrounded by the trailing ribbon from the bouquet of wildflowers was her knife.

She saw Sarah Rourke, hair in a chignon, wearing a nice-looking two-piece beige dress with full skirt, standing beside Generaloberst Wolfgang Mann, Wolf in a very conservative dark grey business suit and striped tie.

Natalia walked ahead. As her eyes met Sarah's, Sarah smiled, quite warmly and Natalia smiled back. Sarah, quite obviously, equally appreciated the irony of Natalia's being Emma's bridesmaid as well. By the same token, Sarah might have seen the irony as somehow fitting. Natalia was not sure.

They stopped at the altar table erected there at the center of the park.

John, flanked by Paul and Michael, stepped forward.

Tim Shaw lifted his daughter's veil and kissed her on the lips, smiled, then went off to the folding chair which had been left for him. A very pretty young girl, in an inexpensive-looking but very tasteful blue dress, was sitting there and took his hand as he joined her.

Emma took John's arm and they turned to face the minister.

Natalia took her place beside Annie, listening but not hearing the words of the minister, her eyes alternating between scanning the crowd for trouble and watching John's and Emma's faces.

She very much wanted them to be happy.

Soon, if the world survived that long and they survived with it, she would be the one wearing white—as a concession to Annie, again—and taking vows beside Michael.

Very oddly for her, she realized, she somehow longed to be pregnant with Michael's child. Perhaps becoming a mother would serve as the emotional break between her past and her present. She hoped that it would.

But there was still work to do.

John and Emma would have a honeymoon—what a silly English word—of exactly one night. Tomorrow, John would join Thorn Rolvaag aboard the *Dauntless,* where they all would work with him in assisting to plant the nuclear charges beneath the sea. Hawaii, Australia and the few scattered islands where there was human population were all reporting earth tremors of growing magnitude and frequency.

As soon as the warheads were in place, John would leave—he insisted alone—to meet with Deitrich Zimmer and try his desperate gambit.

If John did not succeed, the world would die.

145

He might die even if he did succeed, leaving his pretty young bride—the minister said, "I now pronounce you man and wife"—a widow.

But, Emma was part of the Family now, and would always be.

Sarah still was, even though officially and legally she was no longer, she always would be, always would be one of the most heroic women ever to have lived.

And John was killing Deitrich Zimmer not only in order to save the world, but also to avenge Sarah. While exterminating the man who had so cruelly used his first wife, he would be trying desperately to save the life of his second wife.

John kissed the bride.

Annie cried.

Natalia wanted to but would not.

Thirty-six

The President of the United States, Arthur Hooks, pro-
posed the toast: "To the Rourke Family, past and present and
future, and to John Rourke in particular. The nation and its
people, the world and all future generations owe to this man
a debt which can never be repaid. To the Rourkes," Hooks
concluded.

All who sat around the table in the Presidential dining
room raised their glasses.

Emma felt tears coming to her eyes.

She saw Sarah Rourke, and when their eyes met, Sarah
took a second sip from her champagne glass and nodded her
head toward her. Emma Shaw smiled.

The President of the United States was handed a large,
flat wooden box, the box itself engraved on the lid with the
Great Seal of the United States.

John got up from his chair beside her and stood beside
the President. The President opened the box lid and tilted
the box toward John Rourke and the cameras.

Inside the box were two revolvers, the most ornately beautiful handguns she had ever seen, engraving covering every
fraction of an inch of the richly blued metal surfaces, tasteful
gold embellishment at the muzzles and on the frames. The
grips were of richly figured wood, inset within them gold
renditions of the Great Seal.

"These are Lancer copies, faithful to the last detail, of the

Colt Single Action Army .45, with original barrel lengths of seven and one-half inches. The guns have been painstakingly tuned by Lancer's finest gunsmiths. The wood in the grips was carefully taken from a limb in the first hardwood tree—a black walnut—which was planted after the return of the people of the United States to the land more than a century ago. Without your efforts, that would never have happened, Dr. Rourke. The gold embellishments were mined here, beneath the sea. We felt that the combination was only fitting." As President Hooks handed the cased revolvers to John, he added, "And the Lancer people tell me the guns shoot great, too."

John smiled as he took the presentation box, then set it on the table and removed both revolvers, holding them in his hands. He merely said, "I will treasure these for as long as I live, and if we succeed in those endeavors which still lie before us, these revolvers will be handed down through the generations of my family for as long as the Rourke Family exists. If they are ever fired in anger, may that only be in the defense of human freedom. Thank you."

John sat down. Everyone else—she did it, too—stood up and applauded . . .

They were in an apartment in the married officers' quarters for their wedding night, the formal reception long since over, the informal gathering afterward with the Family just concluded.

John had embraced Sarah. Sarah had kissed him, then kissed Emma, telling her, "I wish that every moment for you both will be filled with happiness."

Emma, still wearing her wedding dress, stood in front of the long bedroom mirror, looking at herself.

There were a few wrinkles in the fabric and a few hairs were out of place.

This was the prettiest she had ever looked, would ever look, she knew. It was the prettiest she would ever feel.

And, because of that, Emma was reluctant to undress; that

was stupid, she knew on a rational basis, but it was the way she felt.

Throughout her life, she'd always considered herself pretty enough but nothing special. There were more important things to do than look for the perfect shade of lipstick or the perfect shade of makeup. Most of the time, she wore neither. In the last year, she had curled her hair exactly twice, neither time convinced that she had done a decent job of it.

Like every woman, she guessed, she had a few "killer" items in her wardrobe. She almost never wore them.

And, here she was, wearing the prettiest dress she had ever owned and looking the best she would ever look (Natalia and Annie had done her makeup and her hair, helped her dress, too).

John, whether he was planning to or not, would take these clothes from her body.

She could not bring herself to do so.

John entered the bedroom.

He had evidently stopped to remove his jacket and to check his guns. The double shoulder-holster rig which John normally wore was in one hand, a case with his other pistols in the other.

He set them down.

He walked across the room toward her. "You're the most beautiful woman in the world."

"Yeah, right," Emma responded, smiling, looking down at her hands and the unfamiliar-feeling wedding ring. John had always worn a wedding ring. Tonight, he wore a different wedding ring.

"I love you, Emma Rourke," John Rourke told her.

Her arms limp, her hands in front of her, resting over her skirt, she told her husband, "Undress me."

He kissed her first.

Thirty-seven

Within the data pirated from Deitrich Zimmer's computer network there was no map or anything like it showing the locations of the various canisters of the viral agent. There would be no way of locating and, subsequently, interdicting their use, without the cooperation of Deitrich Zimmer. And that could only be gained by John's being able to outwit the man.

Michael said, "Talk about living on the edge. There are so many variables and if only one thing goes wrong, the entire human race is destroyed. Except for Zimmer and my wonderful brother, Martin."

Paul Rubenstein smiled, saying nothing. Michael's thoughts echoed, more or less, his own.

Following the private Family reception, he and Michael had changed to more comfortable clothing and left their wives—Paul found himself already thinking of Natalia as Michael's wife—and retired to one of the small conference rooms, referring to the printouts of the data gleaned from Deitrich Zimmer's computer network, and of the conference with Professor Dr. Wilhelmina Krause and the medical and intelligence assessments.

The comparatively few medical experts consulted—largely epidemiologists—were of like mind except for a detail here and there. To a man or woman they believed that Deitrich Zimmer's plan would work even if only one of the canisters were allowed to discharge its lethal contents into the atmosphere of even a small-sized population center. The only major divergences of opinion among the epidemiologists concerned how long it would actually take for the end of humanity to come.

Some gave it five years, some gave it a little less.

As Paul poured through the data, he reached a frustration point where he was about to stand up, leave the room and find someplace where he could purchase a package of cigarettes. Many of the old brands from Before the Night of the War were back, although, according to Natalia, few tasted quite the same.

What was he saving himself from?

Cancer was essentially conquered, tobacco was non-carcinogenic and the only way to get sick from smoking was to smoke so much as to damage the lungs to the point where emphysema was incurred or to damage the heart.

"Nuts," Paul said, starting to get up. As he did, his eyes caught something in one of the medical reports. "Holy shit!'

"What?"

Paul Rubenstein leaned back and started to laugh.

"What's wrong, Paul?"

"We've got him! We've got the bastard!" And Paul Rubenstein stood up, in the next second almost doubling over with laughter. "He was so damned smart! Zimmer outwitted himself! Ha!"

Michael was standing up too, now, demanding, "What are you talking about?"

"Think about how fast John was able to recover from the heart transplant. When was the last time you had a cut? How long did it take to heal by comparison to how long it would have taken to heal six centuries ago?"

"I still don't get it, Paul."

"Fine. Think about this, Michael. It says in every one of these analyses of Zimmer's virus that Zimmer's own data shows how the virus mutates. The problem is that it would be impossible to inoculate against every possible mutation and the one or dozen or whatever that you didn't inoculate against would get you. And the virus mutates very rapidly.

I've got a gut feeling about this. I know it could be done. I know it. What if we—hell, let's go wake up Professor Dr. Krause. She can tell us, I bet."

"Tell us what?" Michael demanded.

"If I'm right. And, if I'm right, Zimmer's out of the genocide business! Come on, Michael!" And Paul Rubenstein grabbed his notes—the printouts were too dangerous to be taken from the room. With Michael behind him, he ran out of the room . . .

Professor Dr. Wilhelmina Krause stood in her doorway, looking at them very oddly. "Do you two young men realize the hour?"

Paul felt like he was talking to his sixth-grade teacher when he answered, "Yes, ma'am. And we're really sorry to disturb you. I mean, I am. Well, we're both sorry, but it was my idea. I needed your input. If I'm wrong, you can shoot me down—"

"Shoot you down?!"

"I mean, if my idea's all wet—a dumb idea—you'll be able to tell me in a split second, I'm sure. But, if I'm right, I think we've got the way to defeat Deitrich Zimmer's virus, his Omega Option."

"Come in, young men."

"Thank you, ma'am." And Paul entered her small suite of rooms, Michael beside him.

She wore the kind of old flannel bathrobe he would have thought nobody made anymore and her hair was up in curlers, covered with a hairnet. She sat down on the overstuffed chair, just perching on the edge of it, her hands neatly folded, palms upward, in her lap. With a nod, she gestured them to the couch and Paul closed his eyes for a moment, organizing his thoughts.

He opened his eyes. Her pretty eyes went wide as he started to explain. "I think Fräulein Doctor, that the way to defeat Deitrich Zimmer is right at hand. There wouldn't be time to make up inoculants which would defeat one fatal mutation after another, let alone disseminate them to every

152

human being on the planet. And, even if John Rourke succeeds in getting Zimmer to divulge the locations of the canisters containing the virus, what if Zimmer were intentionally to leave out even one of them? We'd all be just as dead.

"All of us except Zimmer and Martin, that is, and their clones."

Her voice was low, soft, musical, yet filled with emotion. "Because they have been inoculated against the virus in all its possible mutations!"

"That's right, and unless Zimmer made up an antiviral cocktail over the course of a decade or so—most of the epidemiologists think the virus will die out within about eight years. Zimmer's own computer models proclaim that it will take ten years for the virus to mutate itself out of existence. So, how did he get the means to make the inoculation which will keep him and Martin Zimmer and their clones safe? He had to have found a way to accelerate the mutation process in the laboratory, right?"

Professor Dr. Krause's extraordinarily pretty blue eyes sparkled. "If we could obtain a sample of the virus, it might be possible for our scientists to devise exactly the same inoculant in as short a period of time or even less. We would have the same advantage which Dr. Zimmer had, knowing the exact nature of the virus. And, instead of frantically developing the means by which to defeat each and every manifestation of the virus, we could inoculate against the virus in all its forms at once!"

"And, there's another possible thing," Paul told her, rising from where he sat and crouching before her. She didn't draw back. "And it's so obvious. That's why we didn't think of it. Because it was right there in front of our eyes! If we could grab, kidnap, snatch, shanghai Deitrich Zimmer or Martin Zimmer or even one of their clones, their blood could be used to synthesize a serum against the disease, couldn't it Fräulein Doctor? Hm?"

And then the Fräulein Doctor positively smiled. "With even a small sample of Dr. Zimmer's blood, we could save days or weeks or months of research. We would have the serum almost instantly. It would be possible, by utilizing

153

every available facility within the Trans-Global Alliance to produce a sufficient amount of the serum so that everyone in the world could be inoculated against the disease. We would start with the most densely populated areas first, of course, and move out into the more rural areas where there was less danger. We could defeat the Herr Doctor!"

Defeat was a much more polite word than the one Paul Rubenstein had in mind, but it captured the spirit of the thing well enough.

Thirty-eight

It was as if a great weight had been lifted from his shoulders, and John Rourke embraced his friend, then took a step back, clasped Paul's hand and quietly said, "President Hooks should have given *you* those pistols."

The younger man grinned, saying, "All in a day's work for a faithful Jewish companion, or a night's work, I should say."

The observation deck overlooking one of the sea walls of the dome was an exceptionally beautiful place, sea life of every possible description flourished above and below and in front of them, as in an enormous aquarium, but instead of the sea life looking out and the humans looking in, the situation was reversed. The men and women of Mid-Wake lived within what amounted to a gigantic terrarium, maintaining a surface environment beneath the sea.

Emma, hair pinned up loosely, wearing what looked like an enormous white T-shirt, a near ankle-length full skirt of blue denim and sandals, leaned up and kissed Paul. "I guess I can do that now," she said.

"You're the prettiest stepmother-in-law a man could ask for, and the nicest, too," Paul told her.

John Rourke dug his hands deep into the pockets of his black BDU pants. "The whole perspective of this thing is changed," he told them, the three of them slowly starting to walk the observation deck's length. He lit one of his thin, dark tobacco cigars as he talked, then turning the battered old Zippo windlighter over in his hand. "We don't need Zimmer's cooperation on a willing basis. We can grab Zimmer and Martin, we can get the blood samples we need. If we have Zimmer, it probably won't be possible for the virus to be released. Through hypnosis or whatever means necessary, we can extract the information. And, we'll have the time to do so because we'll have a serum which can combat the disease. We'll still have to find the canisters, because eventually they'll leak as we discussed, and it'd be nice not to have to inoculate the next ten generations against it. Although we can if we have to, if there's no way of getting Zimmer to divulge the information.

"What we'll need," Rourke went on, "is as much time as we can to get to develop the serum. I propose this. The clones of Zimmer and Martin—those which survived—have been inoculated, as the data obtained from Zimmer's computer network tells us. If we can get to the clones and make it look as though we were after something else besides a blood sample—taking samples from at least one of each type of clone, Zimmer's and Martin's would be the safe thing—we might be able to get the jump on Zimmer and have the serum in preparation, possibly even disseminated on a limited basis before he realized what was happening.

"It's dangerous that way, but if the release system—keep in mind, Zimmer's for all intents and purposes immortal—has to be something to which he constantly attends, say in order to keep the virus from releasing, which would make good sense on his part, as a fail-safe against his own destruction, then the virus might be released automatically. So, we have to gamble that Zimmer won't release the virus while Thorn Rolvaag's project is underway. But, probably, immediately after Thorn succeeds—which we all hope he does. So, if Thorn is hard at work planting the charges and readying them to detonate, we could use that same time to create a serum."

"We'll need to locate the clones, get in on some pretext, get the samples and get out in such a way that he doesn't suspect our real purpose," Paul said, echoing Rourke's own thoughts.

"Yes, indeed. How? Have to think about that one." And John Rourke dropped his lighter into his pocket, rolled the cigar into the corner of his mouth and clapped his hands together. "So! We join Thorn Rolvaag on his research vessel, help him however we can. Meanwhile, we're working to locate the clones which still survive and come up with a way of getting at them. As unobtrusively as possible, we recruit laboratory research facilities and the best-qualified people we can find to use them. I think Professor Dr. Krause would be the logical person to head up that latter effort, wouldn't you agree?"

"Perfect for it," Paul told him.

Rourke looked at his wife. Emma nodded agreement.

"Fine," Rourke announced. "We should make the most of every moment. Paul, get Michael to coordinate with Darkwood, and Emma's dad, too. He's still at Mid-Wake?"

"Yeah, I think so."

"He was going to take a shuttle after lunch today," Emma supplied.

"Great. He's got a good tactical head. Put together as versatile a team of personnel as we can muster so we'll have all the right people for whatever type of tactical situation we can expect to encounter once we locate the clones. Get Darkwood and his people on that right away. Get Annie to stick with him and keep him moving on it, help however she can with that. Have her also start marshaling any kind of equipment she can think of that we'll need.

"She can liaise between Darkwood and the Intell people and you and Natalia. I want you and Natalia," Rourke went on, "to work out scenarios we can employ once we get the location, and then work out an outline of the tactical requirements for the operation.

"Emma," he told his bride, "start coming up with all the air-support options we might require, figure the equipment, line it up and have it waiting so we can take the equipment and personnel we'll need—whatever those requirements turn out to be—at essentially a moment's notice. If there are any major aircraft-related aspects to the operation, beyond basic transportation, I'd like you taking personal charge of that. I can get you whatever authorization you'll need. Just let me know. We'll need air cover, possibly, or diversionary actions, perhaps specialized types of aircraft. So, get on that.

"We're going to do this," John Rourke announced.

He started walking back toward their borrowed apartment. In a few hours, along with his new bride and the rest of the Family—what remained—he would be en route to join Thorn Rolvaag. By that time, the operation against Deitrich Zimmer should already be taking some initial shape, however crudely defined.

He rarely used profanity, but as he thought of Deitrich Zimmer's plans for the destruction of the human race, John Rourke rasped under his breath, "Omega Option my ass!"

Thirty-nine

Emma had simply said, "You take the controls on three," never asking him if he wanted the yoke. And, he took it. They were a mere few hundred yards out of the carrierlike docking bay at Mid-Wake—these air-sea docking bays had been installed at Mid-Wake less than two decades before—when Rourke had the controls.

He had watched Emma, studied how the controls worked, convinced himself that flying a dual-environment craft through water wasn't much different from flying a single-environment craft through the air. That was a little overly optimistic, he realized, but as he aimed the V-Stol's nose toward the water surface above, he knew that he had it.

He wasn't as smooth as Emma was with it, and doubted that he ever would be, but he was doing it. They broke surface, the sun bright and Rourke's eyes squinting against it despite the windshield's self-adjusting light transference.

The feeling of freedom was magnificent.

The V-Stol's controls were the most responsive of any aircraft he had ever flown.

Piloting the aircraft was, to John Rourke's thinking, perhaps the closest man could come to flying, actually flying unaided.

"You're doing great, John."

"You're too kind. Can I keep the controls for a while?"

"As long as you want," she answered through his headset.

Flying. Beneath his hands, the V-Stol tore over the surface

of the water, sucking up into the craft's contrail a wake of magnificent proportions as he glanced behind them.

"You need to fly one of the new Blackbirds," she told him. "If this gets you, that would be better."

"Faster, I know, but as responsive?"

"Oh, yes. Once they make them so they're capable of both environments, like these babies, flying one would be the next best thing to sex."

John Rourke laughed, telling his bride of less than twenty-four hours, "That would be impossible."

"I only said 'the next best thing' remember?" And she laughed.

"What's our course, Commander?"

"Already laid in, General; just follow the headsup and watch those banking maneuvers. I just had lunch."

"Aye, aye," he laughed.

John Rourke felt invigorated. Despite what lay ahead, a final confrontation with Deitrich Zimmer, perhaps the final confrontation forever, he felt alive.

He had just begun life again, no matter how little of life might remain to him, and the essence of life is to be aware of living.

He was that.

He told Emma, "I love you."

"Why did you say that, John? I'm glad you did, and I like it when you say it. But, why did you say it right now, at this instant?"

"This is why," he told her, pulling back gently on the yoke, the V-Stol's nose rising. "And I know we're off course, but I had to do this." And he started the V-Stol toward the sun. In a few seconds he would turn back on course, but only after a few seconds.

"I understand you, John Rourke; I think I really understand you."

He knew that . . .

As the sun began setting and the ocean water beneath began darkening, he could, in places where the water was

160

clearer, occasionally, see just the faintest glow. That would be the trench and the volcanic activity within it where the depth of the trench was less than the average.

Fire, burning within the water, like a living organism of indeterminate yet malevolent nature, but beautiful. He was aware that he was looking at death, too, but only if mankind failed and nature won. In the closing years of the twentieth century, many people spoke of man learning to live in harmony with nature. That the planet should be cared for, protected, was only logical. But man had never lived in harmony with nature. He conquered nature or nature conquered him. Man could not live in harmony with elements which, by their very essence, were inharmonious with human existence.

Nature brought rain and cold and darkness; man found shelter and heat and light. Hurricanes and tornadoes assaulted man's structures; man built stronger and more wisely and, when nature won, man rebuilt.

Harmony was a fallacy.

He could see the death and beauty in the suboceanic vent, finding nothing contradictory in either.

They were nearing the *Dauntless,* Rolvaag's research vessel from which all efforts against the vent were now coordinated.

Aircraft and ships—hydrofoils capable of genuine speed—even now ferried the world's tactical nuclear warheads to aid in the effort.

Soon, the battle between man and nature would be joined.

To live in harmony with nature now would mean to accept death.

"Take the controls, please; landing a V-Stol with my limited experience might be a little dangerous for all concerned, more than a little dangerous."

Emma laughed, "All right, but you could do it if you had to."

"Probably, but it wouldn't be prudent to set out to prove that at this very moment."

Ahead, he could see the *Dauntless,* the largest ship within the flotilla assembled here for the assault on the vent. "On three," Emma said, starting the count.

161

On three, John Rourke released the controls, his eyes going toward the flotilla again. The *Dauntless* was as large as a twentieth century oil tanker, but utilized the hydrofoil principle and, comparatively speaking, could start and stop on a dime.

The dime over which it had stopped was surrounded by various other vessels, some of them clearly deep-dive submersibles, tethered to the *Dauntless* itself, others surface-going warships; and, there was one submersible carrier vessel, only partially surfaced.

"That's the *Paladin,* John. The *Paladin*'ll be our home base. We'll land there, then transfer to the *Dauntless* by helicopter or submersible whaleboat, whatever's handiest and available."

"You've got me on that one," Rourke said into his helmet radio. "What's a submersible whaleboat?"

"Minisub, fully surface capable, hydrofoil type. Kind of fun to pilot one, really. And yes, I'll let you try it."

John Rourke laughed.

Forty

When he had delegated tasks to the Family, he had left one task for himself. That was to make a prearranged contact with Otto Croenberg. He told Croenberg simply, "If you want to rule your people—both those within the Nazi movement and the people of Eden—meet me at these coordinates however you can. If you'll require transport, let me know." And Rourke gave the coordinates for the *Dauntless*.

Croenberg, as Rourke knew he would, recognized the longitude and latitude immediately. "I would be broadcasting my complicity with you."

"Hopefully not, but if it means that, so be it. This is your chance, not only to live but to rule, if you play it right."

Croenberg agreed, and would rendezvous with them at the *Dauntless*—John Rourke consulted the face of his black-faced Rolex Oyster Perpetual Submariner—in less than one hour if all had gone well.

Rourke climbed into what would correspond to a copilot's seat within the whaleboat, Emma in the pilot's seat.

It was like a ride at an amusement park (something John Rourke had avoided whenever possible). One sat in the whaleboat, the boat in a narrow channel of water, on either side of the channel heavy bumpers to protect the exterior of the whaleboat. Then, the upper portion of the whaleboat was closed, cocoonlike, and the whaleboat started ahead along the channel. When it reached a certain point, it began to

163

descend, within seconds fully submerged in a pool with an enclosed top. The whaleboat then moved toward various ports at the far side of the pool, passing one of these and entering the open sea.

The *Dauntless* was not a submersible, nor was it equipped for below-waterline ingress or egress, so Emma began surfacing the whaleboat. As the tiny craft broke surface, she announced, "Watch this, John! Look to one side or the other."

John Rourke looked to port, the vessel rising over the surface as the framework for a hydrofoil unfolded from the whaleboat's hull. He quickly turned his head to the right, looking over the starboard side, the framework unfolded there as well, the craft rising, then rocketing ahead, nearly flying over the water. "Generally, the smaller the vessel, the more the effect when you go up."

"I wish this were open-topped," Rourke told his bride.

"Your wish is my command! Look out! It's a rush!" The craft's cocoon began to disappear into itself, the spray and the cold sea air were washing over them. It was, indeed, invigorating. "Don't worry, John, these things are made to run with the cockpit open or closed. If we had high seas, the craft would automatically bail itself, but we'd be soaked. Just enjoy the ride!"

He was enjoying the ride, literally and figuratively . . .

The *Dauntless* loomed above them as John Rourke looked up, stepping from the cockpit of the whaleboat, turning back to help Emma, but she was already out. Together, they started up the companion ladder leading to the main deck above. John Rourke glanced downward once, toward the whaleboat. If all of this—life—were to end, it would be the ultimate madness.

His hair and face and hands and clothes were damp, but not soaked, and he wasn't sorry.

Forty-one

Otto Croenberg looked down at the sea.

It looked hard and flat and grey black in the gathering twilight.

And he looked forward, toward the cockpit. The pilot and the copilot were carefully chosen. Although officially under his command, he had known for months that these men were in the employ of Dr. Deitrich Zimmer, spies and potential saboteurs and assassins, should their master bid them to be. That was why he had chosen them to crew his personal aircraft for "a secret mission on behalf of the Führer." These two men were wholly expendable.

Secreted on Otto Croenberg's person was a waterproof miniaturized radio transmitter, preset to a distress channel which would be monitored by the *Dauntless* and all vessels in the area (at Dr. Rourke's request).

Croenberg reviewed the contents of his pockets. A waterproof bag for his pistol and spare magazines, a second waterproof bag for his personal belongings—cigarette case, etc. Each of these bags was fitted with a shoulder strap. They were standard equipment items and were packed within his attaché case. He would have only seconds to fill the bags before he had to leave the aircraft.

As usual, there was a parachute, but he'd made arrangements for his chauffeur, Max, to check that the parachute was properly packed—Max was airborne-qualified and good at his craft. And, integral with the parachute pack was a life preserver. In one of his pockets was a canister of shark repellent. Supposedly, it worked. He hoped that he would not need to find out how well.

He was arranging his apparent death, to be lost at sea in such a fashion that, should the need arise, he could miraculously reappear within a few days, discovered floating adrift, recovered by a rescue craft, the usual thing.

The evidence of what he planned to do to his traitorous crew would be buried deep beneath the waves, failing an explosion on impact, which would make impossible any chance of reconstructing what had really happened—or was about to.

Croenberg glanced at his wristwatch. Waterproof and shockproof.

He wore casual clothes, lightweight slacks and a windbreaker and track shoes (he had no desire for heavier shoes). Beneath the windbreaker was his pistol. Croenberg reached for it now. Although he had little time for entertainment, he always found it amusing when, in old vid-movies, someone drew an automatic pistol from a shoulder holster or what-have-you and then drew back the slide. If one's gun was so unsafe as to demand a chamber-empty carry, one needed a different gun; if one was so stupid as to carry a gun chamber-empty for any other reason, one needed a different brain.

With his thumb, he felt the loaded chamber indicator, confirming what he already knew. He thumbed up the safety on the Walther P-38 and released his seat belt. Glancing at his watch again, he confirmed the time. In five minutes, he should be bailing out, in less than twenty find himself in warm clothes.

But first, Croenberg had two traitors to dispose of . . .

John was looking at his watch quite a bit. As they stepped into the elevator which would take them three decks below, Emma asked her husband, "Are you waiting for something to happen?"

"Yes, to be alone with you."

"Get serious."

John laughed. "Actually, I'm expecting someone to drop by, a fellow who might be of some help to us; in fact, I'm almost certain that he'll be a great deal of help."

"Drop by?"

"Drop in might be the better way of phrasing it," John told her, kissing her cheek the moment the elevator doors closed and they were alone. "Trust me. We could be hearing from him in as little time as seven or eight minutes, depending on wind velocity and altitude."

"Wind velocity and altitude?"

"Trust me," John smiled again. The elevator stopped and they stepped out into Thorn Rolvaag's computer lab . . .

Otto Croenberg's right fist closed tightly around the butt of the Walther. That the pistol was totally reliable was extremely comforting to him at this precise moment. Under some circumstances, he might have felt handicapped with only an eight-round magazine and one round extra in the chamber, but nine 9mms should be perfectly adequate for the task at hand.

He opened the cockpit door and stepped inside. He checked his watch, glanced at the instrument panel in order to read the compass heading and, satisfied, pointed the muzzle of the pistol toward the neck of the pilot. He pulled the trigger, but firing at a downward angle so that there was no chance that the bullet would overpenetrate and damage any of the instruments or systems.

The copilot started to shout something, started to draw his own gun.

Croenberg shot the copilot through the mouth, then again in the chest. The man's body slumped into the seat.

In the next instant, Croenberg grabbed the yoke, keeping the aircraft level. He licked his lips. He wasn't much of a pilot, not much of a one at all. But, then again, how difficult could it be to crash?

Forty-two

John's eyes kept alternating between the computer monitor screens and his watch.

The computers were playing scenarios—elaborately detailed animations and special-effects generation programs—laying out, as best as any computer model could, the anticipated effects from the chain of nuclear warheads which would be detonated in order to relieve the pressure on the volcanic rift.

The only sounds were the soft hums of the computers, the even softer sound of the climate-control system and Dr. Thorn Rolvaag's voice. "Since we are utilizing nuclear explosives, we must always keep in mind that we will gain nothing if we halt the progress of the rift while at the same time irradiating the Pacific Ocean and eventually killing ourselves, anyway. Therefore, we have not only to achieve the desired explosive effect but also to bury the source of the explosion in order to prevent a radiation incident.

"We'll have monitors going as soon as it's safe to do so and physically inspect each of the detonation sites—that will take some time, of course—and deal with any residual radiation which might be of significant levels. Fortunately, too, the tactical nuclear weapons we'll be using are relatively clean. You see," Rolvaag added, turning away from the screen at which he'd been staring and looking at John, then at her in turn, "even if the size of the warheads from the comparatively few ICBMs in the world's nuclear arsenals hadn't been a problem, the radiation yield would have been. But, sticking to battlefield and theater-sized weapons, we have a safety factor that we couldn't do without."

"You'll have teams of personnel waiting to inspect each of the warheads coming from Eden and the Nazis?"

"Of course, John," Dr. Rolvaag answered, nodding his head. "Not only for sabotage but for compatibility. Many of the nuclear triggers will have to be replaced and the wiring will have to be altered for uniformity with our own warheads. That's why time is so critical. We're talking a lot of intensive detail-oriented work which will have to be accomplished in perfect efficiency in an extremely short period of time."

"Speaking of time," John said, "we should be interrupted in a very short while."

As if John were a mind reader, one of Dr. Rolvaag's assistants—a pretty Eurasian girl with gorgeous straight hair—walked over to them, saying, "Excuse me, Dr. Rourke, but there's an urgent message for you from the *Paladin*'s communications room." She handed John a portable phone and left.

John spoke into the receiver. "This is Dr. Rourke."

He murmured the occasional affirmation, then said, "Thank you, Ensign. We'll be on deck by the time your transport arrives." Then he turned to Emma, saying, "The oddest thing has happened. A Nazi aircraft carrying Lieutenant General Croenberg has crashed in the vicinity, and there's a distress beacon being broadcast. Of course, the *Paladin*'s responding with search planes. Meanwhile, one of the surface ships—the *M. L. King, Jr.*—is sending a chopper to pick us up and assist in picking up survivors should there be any."

And, her husband smiled at her.

Emma Rourke merely said, "Well, dear, then we'd best get topside as quickly as we can, hadn't we?"

"Of course, darling." And John looked at Dr. Rolvaag. "Duty calls, I'm afraid; my sincerest apologies. My wife and I look forward to continuing this."

"Certainly, John, Mrs. Rourke—or do I still say Commander?"

169

Emma told him, "Just Emma will do fine."

She was feeling herself really getting into this, being the great man's wife. And, she so loved that word—*wife*.

Forty-three

The fuselage door was fully open. Strapped in so that they wouldn't fall when the machine would bank, John Rourke and his wife crouched beside the opening, Rourke with his German field glasses to his eyes, scanning for some sign of wreckage, and most importantly a sign of Croenberg in a life raft.

Emma was monitoring a transponder, identical to that in the cockpit, the latter homing them toward the signal. In the distance, skimming over the water, V-Stol fighter bombers from the *Paladin* were streaking through the sky, following the same signal.

In Rourke's ear, the chopper pilot's voice cut in, asking, "General Rourke, sir. Permission to ask a question?"

"Fire away, Lieutenant."

"Well, sir, how did my transponder and that portable unit wind up getting set for the identical frequency this downed aircraft would be broadcasting its distress signal on?"

"Ever heard the expression that in Intelligence work, there's no such thing as a coincidence?"

"No sir."

"Well, you've heard it now."

"Yes sir."

Emma, like the rescue chopper's copilot/navigator, was in continuous radio contact with the leader of the V-Stol squadron, the V-Stols working triangulations off the signal from the downed aircraft, the *Paladin* and the *M. L. King, Jr.,* working triangulations as well. It should only be seconds before there was a fix on the position.

Emma tapped Rourke on the shoulder, "John! We've got him. The pilot and I both have the position, and so does the leader of the search planes from the *Paladin.*"

Before John Rourke could speak, the wind tearing at their hair, a fine spray of seawater soaking their exposed skin and their clothes, the helicopter—flying so close to the whitecaps that it could have been terrain-following, banked hard to starboard, Emma losing her balance a little, Rourke catching her in his right arm. "How close are we?"

"To each other or Croenberg?"

"What do you think?"

"About ninety seconds out from the fix."

Rourke nodded, then picked up the HK-91. The rifle would need a cleaning as soon as they were in quarters aboard the *Paladin,* to keep the salt spray from damaging it. But these were shark waters and the rifle was insurance for Croenberg's survival.

Emma and a corpsman were already getting the winch ready to retrieve Croenberg.

The pilot's voice cut on Rourke's headset. "We've got visual on a man in the water, no raft, about ten degrees to starboard. Looks like he's got some unpleasant company, too."

"Sharks, Lieutenant?"

"Aye sir."

"Make best speed to the man in the water. Is there any armament aboard this craft?"

"Negative, sir. Just individual small arms—cartridge pistols—and one energy rifle in the event we had to ditch."

"Monitor my transmission constantly until we've got the man in the water aboard, Lieutenant. If he's in danger from sharks, you'll have to provide me with as steady a firing platform as possible."

"Aye, General."

Rourke raised the binoculars to his eyes, sweeping them to the right along the horizon. He spotted a man in the water, the flash of a pistol shot in the twilight, then another.

Emma shouted to Rourke, "About twenty seconds, John."

"Don't know if there'll be enough time." He let the binoculars drop to his chest on their neck strap, working the HK's bolt and bringing the rifle to his shoulder. There was a single twenty-round magazine, filled with the German copies of his favorite 7.62 NATO cartridge, Federal's 165-grain Boattail.

Rourke could see shark fins in the water surrounding Croenberg. Whether or not Croenberg had already been struck was uncertain but doubtful. If blood had been drawn, there would be a feeding frenzy and Croenberg would already have been torn to shreds.

John Rourke had hunted since he was a boy, but only game that could be eaten. In the twentieth century—as it would be again once the population of the planet, human and animal, was fully restored—hunting was essential to conservation, regardless of the bleating of the antihunters. Killing an animal for the sake of watching it fall and adding a trophy to the den wall was an obscenity, however. Although John Rourke didn't relish the prospect, these animals—sharks— were attacking a human being (however anyone might argue over Croenberg's validity within that classification) and there was no moral dilemma at all; the sharks would be killed as necessary.

John Rourke told the pilot, "Give me that stable firing platform now, Lieutenant."

"Aye sir!"

The aircraft slowed, hovered; John Rourke told his wife, "Hold your ears!" And, he fired, his first shot hitting the water a yard or so off the nose of one of the sharks. The creatures kept circling the man in the water.

Firing a warning shot was like the police officer shouting 'Halt!' three times before firing; it was morally obligatory. John Rourke triggered his second shot and didn't miss, the shark which he shot bouncing up in the water, in the direction of the bullet's travel, rolling belly up for the merest instant as the others in the pack came at it, the feeding frenzy started by the blood in the water. The shark John Rourke had shot was one of those furthest away from Croenberg.

Rourke ordered the pilot, "Close in, Lieutenant."

"Aye sir!"

Safing his rifle, handing it to Emma, he ordered his wife and the corpsman, "Be ready to get him in quickly!"

As they started the winch, Rourke braced himself as much as he could against the movement of the helicopter and drew the Model 629 from the flap holster at his hip. His old friend Gregg Kramer, the holster maker, made some of his holsters from sharkskin. This wasn't the way to get it.

With the Metalife Custom 629 in Rourke's right hand, loaded with 180-grain JHPs from the old Federal recipe, Rourke followed the movement of the feeding frenzy through the water, lest it come too close to Croenberg.

"He looks okay, General!" It was the pilot's voice in Rourke's ear.

"Keep us as steady as you can in case I'm forced to fire again." At this distance, the pistol would be more practical than the rifle. Years ago with his friend Ron Mahovsky, Mahovsky had used Rourke's 629, targeting an abandoned bus left in a public firing area, not a range but just a place where people would come to shoot for fun. Someone, at some time, had started shooting at the bus. By the time John Rourke saw it, the bus—rusty, falling apart—was as full of bullet holes as the hide of a thriller novel's hero.

Mahovsky wanted to see just what the Federal 180-grain JHPs would do. Standing at the rear of the bus, he fired forward, the bullets entering the rear of the bus, penetrating what remained of some of the seats and exiting through the front of the bus into the embankment.

These bullets would penetrate a shark well enough.

"Steady as she gets, sir!"

"Right, Lieutenant. Emma, lower the winch!"

"Lowering now!"

"How's he doing?"

"So far so good. He looks okay. He's slipping into the harness. We've got him! Pull her up, sailor."

"Aye, aye, ma'am!"

One of the sharks was starting for Croenberg, Croenberg's lower body still in the water. John Rourke couldn't take the chance. "Watch your ears!" Rourke double actioned the 629, nailing the creature with the first shot, the body rolling over. But the other sharks were coming toward the fresh kill, toward the scent of the blood in the water. Too close to Croenberg.

Croenberg's legs were still partially in the water. Rourke fired again, killing another of the sharks, then another.

Croenberg's feet were above the water now, but one of the sharks lunged upward.

John Rourke fired, striking the creature, firing again, then again, the shark spiraling into the water, the others in the pack tearing at its flesh before it was fully down.

Croenberg swung free.

"Get out of here, Lieutenant. Now!"

"Aye, aye, sir!"

John Rourke holstered the empty revolver, closing the flap. Then reached over the side, toward Croenberg's body.

Otto Croenberg, as Rourke and his wife grabbed at the man's shoulders, looked up, gasping for breath a little. Clutched in his right hand, its slide open, was his Walther P-38. Rourke volunteered, "That's going to need a good cleaning, Lieutenant General."

"You saved my life, all of you, but especially you. I could see you here in the doorway."

"It seemed like a good idea at the time," Rourke told him honestly.

Forty-four

Natalia Anastasia Tiemerovna, Major, Committee for State Security of the Soviet, Retired, had seen W-80 warheads Before the Night of the War. These modern-day tactical nuclear weapons were very similar.

As she started to go nearer to the warheads, Michael grabbed her arm, stopping her. She wheeled toward him. "What's wrong, Michael?"

"Hey, maybe I'm old-fashioned or something, what if these things are leaking radiation?"

"We're wearing badges, Michael! We'd know."

"Look, Natalia, there are plenty of other things you can do, just as important if not more so. We're going to be having babies, so don't go near these things."

She struck him—lightly, but so that he would notice—straightarming him in the chest with her open palm. "We are going to have babies, hm? How? And I don't mean that. Are we going to have them in or out of wedlock?"

Everybody on deck had to be staring at them hearing what she said, so she switched to German, which Michael understood quite well. "You order me around like a wife—although there's no reason that a man should order around his wife, or that his wife should take his orders. But a lot do, and I will, too—most of the time. But, I am not your wife, Michael Rourke. I am your mistress and that is a little bit different, I think."

"Well, damn it—"

"German, Michael, unless you want every sailor on board the *Dauntless* to hear us!"

"Fine!" He switched to German, telling her, "There just has not been the time, Natalia!"

"And, what should we wait for, hm? For the world to end and us to die with it? I do not think so. I'm going to sit on one of these damned warheads if I please, and you cannot tell me otherwise, Michael Rourke."

"No, damn it," he shouted in English, pulling her into his arms, kissing her mouth harder than anyone had ever kissed her in her life, so hard that for a split second she thought he would cut her lips or break one of her teeth, her body bending to him, the sailors on deck of the *Dauntless* cheering for them.

At last, he let her go. Involuntarily, she started to slap him, but slowing her hand, letting him catch her wrist.

"You'll do as I say when it comes to these damned warheads. No wife of mine—fine, then we find the captain and we do it tonight! All right?"

"Yes. Kiss me again."

After a beat, Natalia gave some thought to what she had just agreed to. "Let's wait. Only until John and Emma return though. It wouldn't be right, our wedding without them."

He kissed her again and there was more applause.

She had no intention of sitting on these facsimiles of W-80 warheads, despite the fact that she knew they were safe to be near. And, she would make certain that Michael stayed clear of them as well, just because she wanted very much to have his babies, and it took two.

She could always talk him into another ceremony, more elaborate, if they survived. For now, she had some clothes in her things. Not a wedding dress, but something that would do well enough.

Forty-five

They sat at a small conference table, hot coffee and gun cleaning equipment on the table.

John Rourke said to the only other person in the room, "Have you read Milton?"

Otto Croenberg answered, "Yes, oddly enough."

"What would be more your idea of hell? Death or participating in a community of free nations for the betterment of all mankind, you as one of the principal leaders?"

"Well, death, of course. You witnessed today that I am not terribly fond of dying, Dr. Rourke."

"Call me John, Otto."

"Why do I feel something is about to change my life, John?"

"For the better, Otto. You're a Nazi. Calling a spade a spade, and no personal offense, Nazis suck shit. Always have, always will."

Croenberg started from his seat.

"Easy, Otto," Rourke told him. "You don't always have to be a Nazi. Have you ever thought about, oh, say objectivism?"

"Objectivism?"

"The philosophy of Ayn Rand. I'll get you a copy of *Atlas Shrugged*. Be your own person, not a slave to dogma who has to check the code book every time he opens his mouth. Be yourself, Otto. I always strove toward the objectivist ideal, but was too bound by my obligations to others, never quite realizing that by true, enlightened selfishness, I would not only better serve myself but better serve the world and my fellow man. Shakespeare, remember? 'To thine own self be true, and it follows as the night the day thou canst not then be false toward any man.' Notice the ring on Emma's finger?"

"I was too busy being happy to be alive."

"Well, she's my wife now, as of yesterday."

"Congratulations. She is a lovely woman."

"Thank you, Otto," John Rourke told him, sincerely. "Yesterday was an awakening for me, really. And, today can be an awakening for you, Otto. If you'll come over to the side of the good guys, you can rule—whether you consider it heaven or hell—rather than die. I need your help to achieve certain goals, which might otherwise be impossible. I'll see to it that you become the leader of Eden and of your Nazi followers, at least until free elections can be established. If you do well, you'll be elected. If you keep doing well, you can keep being elected. But, no more of this Nazi crap; you know, no more anti-Semitism, no more killing political rivals, no more exaltation of the state over the individual."

"Unless I really want to?" Croenberg asked, almost laughing.

John Rourke did not laugh, rejoining the buttstock of the HK-91 to the receiver, dropping in first one pin, then the other. "Well, you have to come to understand enlightened self-interest a little better, Otto. But, trust me, you could learn to live with it. If you don't, I'll kill you. You can bank on that, because it would be in my self-interest. Trust me. Read, learn, believe. It takes a long while to reach perfection. None of us has yet; it's trying your damnedest that counts."

"You are serious, John."

"Dead serious, Otto. ' . . . rule in Hell . . . '?"

"Do I have a choice?"

"There's always a wide range of choices, but some of them are better than others, Otto."

"Enlighten me," Otto Croenberg told him.

John Rourke set his freshly cleaned rifle aside and began to clean his revolver, choosing the immediate situation over philosophy for the moment.

Forty-six

By late that evening, John Rourke and his wife had again conferred with Thorn Rolvaag and progress was being made with the warheads and their arrangement for their placement along the length of the suboceanic volcanic vent. Michael, Natalia, Annie and Paul, along with Emma's father, Tim Shaw, and her brother, Ed Shaw, were aboard the *Paladin* as well. Sarah and her husband-to-be, Generaloberst Wolfgang Mann had flown out as well, John Rourke considering Wolfgang Mann's tactical expertise vital to whatever operation was planned, and Sarah's logical input vital as well.

This was all turning into something very "civilized" as the term was used in the latter part of the twentieth century, divorced couples interacting for business reasons, etc.

No matter, Rourke thought; the reasons were sound.

Commander Washington, the SEAL Team commander with whom the Rourke Family had worked in the Hawaiian Islands and in the assault on Nazi Headquarters in western Canada, was fully restored and returned to duty.

As Washington joined them in the conference room aboard the *Paladin,* Paul began to applaud, the rest of the company— with the exception of Otto Croenberg—joining in as well.

Commander Washington grinned ear to ear nearly, taking his seat and saying, as the applause ended, "If I'd known I was going to be this popular just by getting injured, well—"

Annie stood up, walked over to where Washington sat and

bent over to kiss him on the cheek. "You're a good man to fight beside."

"Thank you, Mrs. Rubenstein, and that's to all of you."

John Rourke told Washington, "Just think of it this way; when we go against Deitrich Zimmer, you'll have the opportunity of gaining popularity all over again."

"Maybe I should have stayed in sickbay longer."

Everyone laughed, except Croenberg.

John Rourke called the meeting to order as Annie retook her seat beside her husband. "We have arrived at a general, overall scheme, the purpose of this meeting to refine that scheme into a concrete plan. Before you, each of you has the results of the research already performed, initial tactical observations, available equipment and personnel. I think I speak for everyone when I say that I'd like Commander Washington to be the on-the-ground leader of whatever military forces are employed in the actual commando operation. We couldn't have better."

"Hear, hear!" Michael chorused, Paul joining him.

"I'll try my best, Doctor."

"That'll be the best, Commander," Rourke told him. "Now, with the help of Lieutenant General Croenberg, who has detailed knowledge of Deitrich Zimmer's bunker outside Eden City and access to security controls and the like—at least to a point—we should be able to formulate a tactical scenario.

"Our strategic goal is complex, yet basic. We need blood samples from one of the clones of Deitrich Zimmer or Martin Rourke Zimmer. The blood samples must be obtained. At the same time, we need to make the raid appear to be for some other purpose. Should there be an encounter with Deitrich Zimmer, we can't let him get to any computer or communications apparatus whatsoever, even if that means killing him on the spot. I'd surmised as much, but Lieutenant General Croenberg can put things in a little better perspective."

"Thank you, Doctor. I have known Deitrich Zimmer for quite some time. Dr. Rourke told me that he suspected that the Herr Doctor had arranged the release of his virus canisters to be on some sort of timing mechanism, continuously—

or periodically, I should say—updated. In other words, if Dr. Zimmer does not attend to the discharge system for the canisters on a regular basis, the canisters will discharge their contents into the atmosphere at a prearranged time. The only way to prevent them from discharging is for Zimmer to remain alive and cancel the discharge order, obviously computer-linked. So, if Zimmer suspects what we are about, he will release the virus at once. If we are forced to kill him, we could have minutes, hours, days, weeks, months before the canisters would release their contents and the world would begin to die."

"We're gambling on what time period, John?" Paul asked.

"It would seem logical that Zimmer wouldn't set the thing for an hourly basis, or even a daily basis. That would wear very thin and be very dangerous. Especially on a war footing. What if he were unable to link with his computer network for several days? Would he want the virus to be released just because of bad luck? I don't think so. I'm guessing one each month. But, he could just have reset the release system, which would give us nearly a month, if I'm right, or be just about to reset the system, which might only give us days or hours. So, the entire question of how often he has to attend to the release system becomes wholly academic. If we confront Zimmer in such a manner that he realizes we're taking blood samples, the jig is up and he'll know exactly what we're doing, that we discovered the one flaw in his plan, a flaw so obvious not only he didn't notice it but none of us noticed it, except for Paul." And Rourke nodded his head toward his friend.

"So," Rourke went on, "should Zimmer become aware of our true mission when we hit his bunker, we kill him and hope we can find the secret of his system before the virus is released, while every scientist available is working to synthesize a serum from the blood samples we obtain and, once that is achieved—Professor Dr. Krause says that could take as long as two weeks or as little time as seventy-two hours—the production of the serum and its worldwide dissemination is begun at once.

"Our only viable option is to enter Zimmer's command

bunker without his suspecting the real reason, obtain the blood samples and get out."

"That will not be terribly easy, Doctor," Croenberg told them all. "Through my chauffeur, Max, whom I trust with my life, we can obtain uniforms, identity papers, everything we might require, but there will be codes—access codes are changed hourly, not even daily—and we will have no orders actually issued for entering the bunker."

"How well do you know Helmut Anton Griem," Rourke asked, lighting one of Emma's cigarettes as he raised the question.

"The Reichsführer? Well, I suppose as well as anyone knows his overall commander. You are not suggesting—"

"Is Griem a dedicated Nazi first, or a dedicated soldier? Where does his loyalty lie? To Deitrich Zimmer overall, even if it meant every man under his command would be killed?" Paul asked.

Wolfgang Mann spoke for the first time. "I do not know your Reichsführer, Croenberg, but I do know soldiers, good ones. I do not know what kind you are, but a good soldier would not allow the slaughter of his entire command for the sake of fulfilling a madman's ambition. John may have hit on our solution."

Croenberg looked at Mann, eyes cold. "Sir, I should remind you that without my divulging what I had already learned concerning Deitrich Zimmer's plans regarding the Omega Option virus, we would—all of us—merely be biding our time before death. No rational man is willing to sacrifice all of humanity for the whim—as you say—of a madman."

"Then, our solution perhaps lies before us," Natalia observed. "We must, somehow, make contact with Reichsführer Griem and lay before him what we know, relying on his humanity to do the rest."

"The direct approach," Sarah noted. "It may work. Over the years since the Night of the War, I've lost some of my faith in humanity, but in other ways I've developed a greater faith in humanity than I ever had before. For my money, I say try it."

"I agree with Sarah, John," Emma added.

John Rourke looked at Michael, then at Paul, his son and his friend nodding their assent.

Then, Rourke turned his eyes toward Croenberg. "How could we meet your commanding general?"

Croenberg leaned back from the table, a wry smile on his face. "Well, I should think that by now I have been listed as missing. We could fabricate some sort of story, I suppose, that I was taken aboard the *Paladin,* as I was—the truth is usually the best basis for a lie, at any event—and say that I had discovered some sort of plot, perhaps against Deitrich Zimmer's life, or against Martin—perhaps the possibilities of a coup. The Reichsführer would have to believe me, since I would be his principal suspect were a coup discovered at any event. I would think that this might be the way."

"I'll need to see him, too," Rourke stated.

"That further complicates the circumstances, Dr. Rourke. You, I am afraid, will have to put your trust completely in me, as I have in you."

Rourke nodded, his voice almost a whisper as he said, "I know."

"How do we get this going, then?" Paul asked. "And, what do we do if the Reichsführer doesn't believe us, or even if he does and he fails as a human being?"

"Neither of those questions can be answered, Herr Rubenstein, at least not at this juncture."

Paul Rubenstein laughed. "You forgot to use my pet name, Croenberg."

Otto Croenberg laughed.

Forty-seven

The captain of the *Paladin* officially informed Mid-Wake by open transmission that the wreckage of a Nazi aircraft had been discovered and that one passenger, hardly the worse for wear, had been fished out of the Pacific, Gruppenführer Otto Croenberg.

The President of the United States, after consultation with the leaders of the Trans-Global Alliance, transmitted his response, which John Rourke read aloud. "In the new spirit of international cooperation following Eden and the Nazi movement led by Dr. Deitrich Zimmer donating, for the benefit of all mankind in the face of an unprecedented natural disaster the entire stockpile of tactical nuclear warheads, the Trans-Global Alliance wishes to reciprocate in this small way by releasing to his commanding officers or other suitable officials from his government, the subject Gruppenführer Otto Croenberg. It is hoped by all mankind that this is merely a first step in the easing of tensions between our alliances."

Natalia laughed. "Governmental double-talk."

"Agreed," Rourke told her. They were alone with the *Paladin*'s radio-room crew, the other Family members, and Croenberg as well, all involved in various preparations for what was to come.

"I should go with you, and so should Paul," Natalia told him.

"We have to trust Croenberg, to a point at least. It'll be

185

tough enough getting me in to see Griem. No, we do this as planned. If anything happens to me, you and Paul take charge and carry out our plans, such as they are, and do whatever has to be done."

Natalia only nodded . . .

By midmorning, Nazi headquarters had completed arrangements with the Trans-Global Alliance for the return of Otto Croenberg. There were perhaps two dozen flying boats operational in the modern world. Not true amphibians—less numerous as well because of their limited utility—the aircraft, which were only capable of water landings, were used, primarily in the Hawaiian Islands and in Australia. Slow in speed, they were hardly suitable for any sort of air combat.

The United States Navy employed a grand total of six such machines, used almost exclusively for ferrying personnel and equipment back and forth between distant surfaced ships.

One of these waited off the port bow of the *Paladin,* the craft rocking in the swells as, by whaleboat, John Rourke and Otto Croenberg were brought out. Rourke had kissed his wife, Emma, goodbye, grabbed his gear and boarded the whaleboat, seating himself beside Croenberg, with two seamen aboard to operate the whaleboat and to assist in the transfer to the seaplane.

The flying boat was to travel to a rendezvous at approximately forty north and one forty west where one of the Russian trading vessels, in the service of Eden, would be waiting.

There would be Nazi personnel aboard, but for the most part personnel loyal to Otto Croenberg. With their help, the crew of the Russian trader and any Eden or other Nazi personnel aboard her would be subdued, after which Croenberg would send an encoded radio message to his commanding general.

Once aboard the seaplane, John Rourke strapped in and looked out the window.

"What are you doing?" Croenberg asked him.

"Just enjoying the experience. I've flown in almost every kind of aircraft you can name, but never in one of these."

"Do you really think that Reichsführer Griem will come?"

"Do you?"

"He might come with an entire army of SS commandos, too."

"I'm sure he won't come alone," Rourke agreed. "But, the important thing is to get him talking, then go from there."

Croenberg lit a cigarette. "Is blind faith something I must learn as well, in this philosophy of yours?"

John Rourke laughed, lighting a cigar as he spoke. "No. But, calculated risk, as any soldier should know, is inescapable. All life is a calculated risk, isn't it? What if this aircraft malfunctions and we fall into the sea, or blow up before we get airborne? But, would we be better off not traveling by air?"

"I see your point. You have faith, then, and I will be nervous, Doctor."

"Fair enough," Rourke told the man, exhaling smoke as he did. "We have a three-hour flight as best as I can tell. I intend to finish this cigar, then catch some sleep. I'd advise you to do the same when you're done with your cigarette. We may have some long hours ahead of us."

"But, first, a question."

"Okay."

"I was speaking with the Jew—Mr. Rubenstein, I mean. I asked him some rather pointed questions about you, since I'm putting my life into your hands just as you are putting yours into mine."

"And?"

"He said you are a pistolfighter; what does this pistolfighter mean?"

"In what context did Paul say that?" Rourke asked, smiling.

"He recounted the first battle he was ever in, fighting with you against what he called 'Brigand bikers' who had attacked the downed civilian aircraft in which you and he spent the Night of the War. What he told me was amazing. I had asked him why you carry so many handguns. He told me that story by way of explanation. This is actually what happened?"

"I don't know to what extent Paul detailed what took

place; but, yes, we were outnumbered, fought hard and luckily won. We were in the right."

Croenberg laughed. "Your pistols make a difference, but I doubt whether being in the right does."

"Trust me; it does. And, the pistols help."

To paraphrase Paul, it would be a pistol fight, perhaps, when he, Croenberg and Croenberg's men took over the Russian trading vessel. He would need his sleep.

"Perhaps I will get to see this pistolfighting in action, then, hm? I hope not."

"For once," Rourke told Croenberg, "you and I find ourselves in total agreement."

And John Rourke turned his eyes toward the porthole, watching as, the engines firing now, the seaplane started underway. He could see one of the lower-deck companionways where Emma and Annie waited, waved after him.

They wouldn't see if he waved back, but he did anyway.

A pistolfighter was a gunfighter who specialized in close combat with multiple handguns. Some Confederate cavalry during the Civil War had carried the concept to its practical conclusion. Prior to that time, sabers were utilized for close, horse-mounted combat. But certain Confederate commanders preferred pistols up close, encouraging their men to carry at least a brace of revolvers, sometimes more, riding into saber range and, instead of going blade to blade, using the handguns.

It was a sound concept for pitched battle, but not the sort of thing that could be practiced by amateurs.

He had known few true gunfighters in his life, one of them his father. Natalia was another, and Paul was good, too, very good. Michael was showing promise in that direction; but, like any rational man, Rourke wished his son as little practical application of the skill as possible.

Pistolfighters in the strict sense of the term or not, there were some men (and women) who were naturals in a gunfight. He suspected, for example, that Tim Shaw, his father-in-law these days, was such a man. But, as he watched the sea fall away beneath their aircraft, he found himself beginning to smile, the memory of something from long ago.

Forty-eight

Whenever John Rourke would travel near Augusta, Georgia, he would visit with his old friend Steve Fishman. Usually, there was just time for some quick talk in Steve's gunshop, occasionally the chance for lunch. Once in a while, they'd go shooting, as they had that one time in the company of their mutual friend, Hank, a wise-cracking one-eyed sometime mercenary, sometime security specialist.

Occasionally, Steve would come to the farm, bringing his wife and children. Steve's wife (also a writer) would talk children's books with Sarah, while he and Steve would talk guns, politics and everything else.

But, on this occasion, they met neither in Augusta nor at the farm where Rourke and his then-wife Sarah and Michael and Annie had lived. Instead, it was one of the rare occasions when John Rourke was actually at home for a few weeks, not teaching survival techniques, instructing special weapons and tactics, consulting or engaged in any of the other areas of endeavor which kept food on the table and allowed him money—a little bit at a time—to build and stock the Retreat.

John Rourke was, in fact, building two new closets on the second floor of the house, putting some vacant front hallway space to good use.

The closets, a simple enough project (although admittedly simpler had he used prehung doors rather than hung the doors himself), had taken an inordinate amount of time.

It was something he'd start on, spend a few hours on, and then be gone again, leaving the project only partially completed.

He was finishing the framing for the second closet, the ring of his circular saw as he powered off coinciding with the ring of the telephone.

Sarah caught it, shouting up to him from the kitchen, "It's Steve Fishman."

"I'll get it," Rourke called back, catching the upstairs extension. "Yeah, Steve."

"Lucky I caught you. Can't talk about it on the telephone, but I need your help."

Rourke thought for a moment, mentally shrugged. "It'll be almost two hours before I can be there."

"Come ready, okay?"

"Okay," Rourke told his friend, then hung up.

Ready, in those days, meant the twin stainless Detonics CombatMasters, the Metalifed and Mag-na-Ported Colt Python, the little Metalifed Colt Lawman .357 Magnum snubby and his CAR-15. He doubted Steve had meant to bring along the Steyr-Mannlicher SSG, but Rourke threw that into the station wagon, anyway, and told his wife where he was going and that he'd call. She looked less than pleased, but he promised, "I'll finish the closets when I get back."

"All right. Be careful, and if you see Steve's family, say hello for me."

"Sure thing." And he kissed her and climbed into the car. He divided his time on the two-hour drive between listening to tapes of the music of Antonio Carlos Joabim, Anita Baker and language tapes—he was trying to teach himself conversational Japanese.

By the time he reached Augusta, it was nearly one in the afternoon.

Parking in front of Steve's gunshop, Rourke locked the car and went inside.

Steve was sitting behind the counter.

Standing opposite Steve was the one-eyed mercenary, Hank. Hank looked at Rourke, saying, "Good drive?"

"I used my time profitably. Good to see you again, Hank."

"You too, John."

"Steve, what's up?"

Steve grinned and nodded toward Hank. "Tell him."

"This friend of mine, FBI agent."

"Mike?" Rourke said.

"Yeah, that's right. I forgot you met him."

"So, what about Mike?"

Hank tugged at his eyepatch, saying, "He's gotten himself into a little trouble. I asked Steve if he could help out, and Steve figured you might help, us, too."

Rourke looked across the counter at his friend. "Does this mean I should call Sarah and tell her I won't be home for dinner? By the way, she said to say hello to your wife and kids."

"I'll pass it along," Steve replied, dialing a number and handing Rourke the phone.

When Rourke put the telephone to his ear, Sarah was just answering. "I won't make it home for dinner, but I'll call later and explain. Kiss the kids for me, huh?

"What are you doing that you won't be home?"

"I'm not sure yet," Rourke answered.

She hung up.

Rourke handed back the telephone, telling Steve, "Thanks."

Hank started to laugh . . .

Hank's friend, Mike, was the kind of Federal officer that belonged in the stone age, at least according to conventional wisdom, Rourke concluded after Hank started discussing "the problem." "You see, John, Mike's a kind of independent guy. That's why the Galliano Brothers are out to get him. They had an ironclad alibi for the hit on Aldo Franchii up in New York and nobody could touch 'em, right? So, Mike decided that if he could bring them out after him, he could nail them for that. Which started with Mike bracing 'em in their father's restaurant, then following them all the time when he was off duty, all the usual harassment stuff to get them pissed off."

The car they drove in was a midnight blue Ford LTD, 1978

vintage, immaculate on the inside (except for the cigarette smell from the ashtray) and in clean enough shape on the outside. The engine had a nice, reassuring hum to it. "302 V-8?"

"Yeah, really flies," Hank responded.

"So, the Galliano Brothers eventually lost their temper?" Rourke asked, reentering the conversation.

"Here comes the good part," Steve interjected.

"Good part?" Rourke echoed.

"Yeah," Hank resumed. "See, Mike did a few other things. Found a drug lab that belongs to one of the five New York Families, the guys that run the mob."

"I've heard of them," Rourke responded, wondering if somehow he'd fallen into the pages of a cheap crime novel.

"Anyway, he got the DEA to bust the lab, but placed the call from Jimmy Galliano's car phone, then left the phone off the hook long enough for DEA to trace the call. Word got out that Galliano had ratted on the mob. So, by now, as you can well understand, Mike had the full attention of the Galliano Brothers."

"How many Galliano Brothers are there?" Rourke asked as an aside.

"Only two, but they have six or seven other guys with them. See, Mike can't get them busted for anything until they try to kill him, so he set himself up for them to find him and try," Hank told them.

"And he can't get any police or Feds in on the thing," Steve offered, "because no crime has been committed yet and they haven't even threatened him. He found out through an informant—Mike did—that the Galliano Brothers were coming to get him. So, he set himself up in a beach house just south of Savannah. Rental house."

"Insured, I hope," Rourke said.

Hank laughed, "Anyway, I knew what Mike was up to, but only a little bit of it. I did some checking, found out that the Galliano Brothers were coming after—see, he picked the beach house down here because he figured it was nice and remote and the Galliano Brothers would be off their home turf, at a disadvantage."

"And?"

"When I checked with Mike's informant—little guy named Froggie Ledbetter—well—"

Rourke interrupted. "Froggie Ledbetter?"

"He's a bookie."

Rourke decided. He'd definitely fallen into the pages of a crime novel, and he didn't like that sort of reading. "That's how you found out that your friend Mike had bitten off more than he could chew."

"Right. I needed help. The Gallianos and their guys will all be in Savannah by six this evening. I could have gone in to help Mike on my own, but eight or nine guys against two isn't the best situation in the world. I figured to get Steve here to help and Steve suggested you."

"Oh," Rourke nodded. "Thank you, Steve."

"Hey, what are friends for, John? Think of it this way. We'll be assisting a Federal officer in the discharge of his lawful duty."

That wasn't quite the way John Rourke thought of it. By the time the 1978 LTD was on the outskirts of Savannah, Georgia, the three of them had worked out a plan. Hank would go directly to the beach house, joining his friend Mike there and staying inside the house, helping to fortify it, etc.

Rourke and Fishman would rent a second car, then proceed to the beach house, waiting outside for the Galliano Brothers and their crew to arrive. When the Galliano Brothers attacked the house, he and Steve would make their presence known, hopefully forcing the Gallianos and the men with them to lay down their arms, if not, then they would do whatever the situation called for.

By six in the evening, approximately the same time that the last of the Galliano Brothers' crew would have landed, John Rourke and Steve Fishman were parking their rented Chevy behind some sand dunes about two miles from the beach house.

As they took their gear from the car—Hank had waited for them to get the rental set and transfer the weapons, then driven on ahead—John Rourke lit one of his thin, dark tobacco cigars. "Has something occurred to you, Steve?"

193

"That there'll probably be more than eight or nine guys? Yeah. The Gallianos and their New York people probably didn't try shipping firearms legally by air as luggage, so they probably made some local contacts—in Atlanta probably—to meet them and bring the hardware. At least two more guys."

"That makes eleven of them, maybe."

"Yeah."

"Hank is nuts, but not as nuts as his friend Mike."

"That's probably true. Hey, but aren't you glad I called you? Making closets! You can do that anytime, John!"

Fishman placed his ornately engraved, ivory-gripped Beretta 92 SB in a Tri-Speed shoulder holster, on the offside of the rig stringing a second double magazine pouch below the first. From his pocket, he drew a lockblade Al Mar knife, checking the action, closing it, then putting it back in his pocket. There would be a SIG-Sauer P-230 .380 auto in a holster on his ankle and probably one or two other guns as well. He grabbed up a rifle case from the trunk.

"AR-15?" Rourke asked.

"Yeah."

Rourke left his revolvers and his other gear in the old Southwind Sanctions SWAT bag, caught up his own rifle case—under the circumstances, he was glad he'd left the Steyr-Mannlicher SSG in the station wagon parked at Steve's house—and a musette bag. "Ready for a hike?"

And Steve was deadly serious as he answered, "Look, maybe that's all we'll get out of this. I kind of hope so, that the bad guys show up, we fire a few rounds into the air and they fold. Mike busts 'em and we're home free."

"You realize the paperwork we're going to have, regardless? Of course you realize the paperwork. What am I saying!" And they started along the lee side of the dunes toward the beach house . . .

John Rourke looked away from the water below him. His cigar was nearly half smoked. Croenberg had taken his advice literally, finished his cigarette and dozed off.

The copilot of the seaplane came aft, a thermos of coffee

194

and some cups in her hands. "General, would you like some coffee, sir?"

"Thanks, Lieutenant. May as well. Good coffee?"

She smiled. "Made it myself before we left, sir."

"Couldn't ask for a better recommendation. How much air time?"

While he poured his coffee from the thermos, the lieutenant told him, "We have some good tailwinds. About two hours and twenty minutes if they hold up, sir."

"After I finish my coffee, I'm going to try to catch some sleep. Would you mind awakening me about twenty minutes before we're about to touch down?"

"Not at all, General. Will there be anything else, sir?"

He returned the thermos, tasted the coffee and said, "You do make good coffee. Thanks."

The copilot went forward and Rourke, stubbing out his cigar, sipped the coffee. The true test of coffee was to drink it black, of course . . .

Steve's wife had made them a thermos of coffee to take on the drive, and they'd saved it until now. Huddled on the lee side of the dune, able to observe the beach house merely by dodging a few inches to the side and looking at it—about two hundred yards off the windward side of the dunes—Rourke poured coffee from the thermos for himself and his friend. He tasted the coffee. "Cathy makes good coffee."

"Thanks. Cold out here. Good to have something to warm us up."

"Amen to that," Rourke agreed. The wind was picking up, not to the point where it was blowing sand, but to the point where Rourke was grateful he'd brought along his battered old brown leather bomber jacket, its collar turned up now against the night's chill.

According to the luminous black face of the Rolex on his left wrist, it was seven-thirty.

By nine-thirty, the coffee was gone and Rourke was smoking a cigar. It was Steve's turn to watch the beach house and Steve whispered, "I think we've got company."

Rourke rolled the cigar into the left corner of his mouth, twisted around onto his knees and looked toward the house. Four cars were pulling onto the beach. "Eleven or so guys could ride in four cars, Steve."

"Maybe they're all real tall," Steve suggested.

"Maybe," Rourke rasped. "You still licensed to practice law in this state?"

"Yeah, why?"

"Just checking out the possibilities for free legal defense."

Before either of them could say anything else, the cars, which had ringed the house on three sides, the sea itself making the fourth side, stopped, disgorging men onto the sand.

Rourke counted as the men piled out. "Seventeen. How about that!"

"At least we don't have to worry that they're all real tall," Steve remarked.

"Your one-eyed buddy? Remind me to pop him in the mouth."

"I thought Hank was your friend?"

Rourke said nothing, just kept his eyes on the seventeen men who were just hanging around their cars for the moment, taking things—rifles and shotguns—from the trunks of the cars.

"You know, this could turn into one hell of a bust for Mike," Steve remarked.

"Gee, maybe he'll get a commendation," Rourke suggested.

"Maybe even a posthumous one," Steve offered.

Rourke's cigar had gone out. He kept it, unlit, in the left corner of his mouth, clamped tight between his teeth as he buckled on his gunbelt with the Python, then stuck the little Lawman .357 into the small of his back. "If they hit that house," Rourke told his friend, "chances are Hank or Mike will get killed. Too many of them for us to handle this way."

"What are you suggesting, John?"

"They probably cut the telephone lines leading out to the beach."

"Oh, probably."

"No reinforcements possible, at least for our side, until somebody notices the shooting. That might not be for a while. If this turns into a protracted firefight, the numbers are all on their side."

"And?" Steve inquired.

"How about we go down there?"

"Just walk right up to them? You're crazy."

"We stay here, they'll nail us at this distance. Check out the rifles." He should have brought the Steyr-Mannlicher SSG, he realized tardily. "They can outdistance us. And, they've got cars, we don't. Figure they're planning on a bonfire, too. Check out those red things they're taking out of the trunks of their cars. Look like gasoline cans to me."

"Look like that, don't they," Steve agreed.

"On the other hand, they're only about sixty or sixty-five yards from the house. Mike would have some long guns, at least an AR-15 or something. Hank had an AR-15, right? If we get things started toward us then Hank and Mike can back us up."

"Just walk down there, huh? Sure, why not!"

John Rourke smiled. "We shouldn't look too heavily armed. Leave your rifle. I'll do the same. We can pick up what we need down there."

Steve Fishman nodded. Rourke shucked off the gunbelt, sticking the Python into the front of his trouser band, the Lawman .357 still in the small of his back . . .

John Rourke finished his coffee, lighting a cigarette as he looked out the window again. It was a crazy thing that he and his friend had done, going down to brace the Galliano Brothers and their men, but he was younger in those days. And then Rourke found himself smiling; being younger hadn't had anything to do with it. He stubbed out his cigarette, closed his eyes, leaned his head back . . .

Side by side, John Rourke and Steve Fishman walked down toward the beach.

"As soon as the shooting starts, we get to cover by the nearest car, see if we can get the car into action and use it as a weapon, or at least transportation, take the fight to the enemy."

"Right," Steve agreed. The Beretta was still in his shoulder holster, but Rourke had noticed him taking the .380 off his ankle and putting it into his trouser band. As he spoke, Steve's right hand slipped under his jacket, toward the Beretta.

Rourke's bomber jacket was zipped up about two inches, his left hand ready to go for the zipper tab, his right for a gun.

As they neared the closest of the four cars, Steve suggested, "We're crazy."

"I know," Rourke agreed.

The four men nearest to the car turned around almost as one, in their hands a veritable smorgasbord of what were almost certainly stolen military weapons. In a barely audible whisper, Rourke reminded his friend, "Remember, they probably don't know their weapons as well as we know ours."

"I'll remember that."

Rourke nodded.

The distance to the four men who were looking at them was about fifty yards. John Rourke and Steve Fishman kept walking.

One of the four men shouted something and three other men, near to another of the cars, turned around and started to join the first four.

The distance was twenty-five yards now. Rourke wanted twenty-five feet or less, which would make the M-16s less maneuverable. One of the Galliano Brothers' crew had a LAW rocket. "They were gonna torch the house," Steve hissed through his teeth.

"See, we did the right thing," Rourke replied.

"Ask me about that later."

Rourke said nothing.

Twelve yards or so remained between them and the seven men nearest, the only ones so far bothering to pay them any attention. One of the seven called out, "What do you guys want?"

"Just going for a walk," Rourke responded. "You guys cops, with all those guns I mean?" He and Steve Fishman kept walking. "Got some terrorists or like that bottled up in the house? Maybe we could go for help or something, call the local cops?"

One of the men laughed. The man who had spoken before said, "Yeah, we're cops. Now, get the fuck outa here."

"Could I see a badge, officer?" Rourke asked.

"Fuck you," the man snarled.

The distance Rourke and Fishman stood from the seven members of the Galliano crew was about eighteen or twenty feet. Steve suggested, "Now seems good."

Rourke, pulling down the zipper tab on his jacket as he jerked the Python clear of his waistband, replied, "Now it is!" With his right arm fully extended, John Rourke double-actioned the Python into the chest of the man who'd done the talking, bowling the man back into the open trunk of the car. Rourke's left hand was already closed around the butt of the Detonics CombatMaster under his right armpit. He jerked it free of the double Alessi rig as he fired the second shot from the Python, into the throat of the man with the LAW rocket. Steve, the Beretta in his right hand and the little .380 auto in his left, brought down two men with AR-15s.

Rourke fired a double tap from the Detonics into the chest and thorax of the fifth man. Already, at the far edge of his peripheral vision, John Rourke could see some of the other Galliano men starting toward them. The situation would be untenable in about fifteen seconds.

Rourke swung the muzzle of the Python toward the sixth man, the sixth man's M-16 opening up, bullets rippling across the sand toward them. Steve Fishman fired at the same time Rourke did, the man going down.

As Rourke swung the muzzle of the Python toward the seventh man—he was running toward the car—Rourke caught a glimpse of Fishman grabbing two of the M-16s from the sand. Rourke led the seventh man for a split second and fired, killing him.

"Waste not want not," Steve sang out. "Figured these M-16s were just lying around anyway."

"Get the car going!"

As Steve dashed toward the driver's side of the car, Rourke wheeled toward the oncoming Galliano men, emptying the Python and the first CombatMaster toward them, bringing down two more men.

That made nine dead or wounded, eight left, but the element of surprise totally gone.

Gunfire tore into the sand around Rourke's feet as he ran for the car, the vehicle already starting to grind out of the sand, Fishman throwing open the passenger side door.

Rourke half threw himself into the car, stuffing his spent pistols into his belt and grabbing for the Colt Lawman. One of the Galliano men was running toward the car, firing his M-16, bullets ricocheting off the car's hood, spiderwebbing the windshield.

"Can't this go any faster?" Rourke shouted.

"I'm trying already!"

Rourke stabbed the little .357 toward the oncoming Galliano soldier and fired, spiraling downward into the sand, his M-16 firing wildly skyward.

There was gunfire coming from near the house now, semi-auto only, but without special licensing, private citizens couldn't own automatic weapons. Bad guys could steal what they wanted from an overseas-bound arms shipment or a National Guard armory, as was evidently the case here.

Steve was holding the wheel with his right hand, firing the Beretta with his left.

Rourke caught up one of the contraband M-16s, thrusting it through the open passenger side window, firing.

In the end, three of the Galliano men—one of the brothers, one of the New York hired help and one of the local guys from Atlanta—were still standing and able to surrender.

Mike, wielding a long-barreled .44 Magnum revolver, shouted something like, "FBI! You're all under arrest, damn it."

Rourke remembered looking at Steve Fishman and re-marking, "How terribly unprofessional."

Hank was helping Mike handcuff the three men while Rourke and Fishman checked the fallen. Three of them were still alive. The others wouldn't have to worry about a trial, prison, any of that.

When it was safe to do so, John Rourke walked back to the sand dune and retrieved the thermos of coffee, pouring himself a cup . . .

When the copilot awakened him, she brought back the coffee, "Could you use a cup, sir?"

John Rourke looked away from her, out the porthole at the sea below. Then he looked toward her and said, "Twenty minutes?"

"Just about, sir."

"The last time I tasted black coffee this good was a long time ago. I'd love some."

Forty-nine

Rourke awakened Otto Croenberg. Croenberg immediately lit a cigarette.

Rourke was half of a mind to tell him what a pistolfighter really was, but he doubted that Otto Croenberg would understand a Jewish ex-Special Forces man with a law degree who just happened to run a gun shop in the deep South. Instead, Rourke said, "We're about fifteen minutes out. When we land, do you think your men will come out for us?"

"Almost certainly Max will be one of them, but there may be one or two of the Russian sailors, and they'll be loyal to Eden, hence to Deitrich Zimmer and Martin."

"Let's try to get along without any shooting if we can. No sense killing when we don't have to and it wouldn't be good for the inside of the airplane."

"Agreed, Doctor."

John Rourke stood up, grabbing his luggage case from the overhead cargo net and taking out his gunbelt. He buckled on the 629 and the Crain LS-X knife, then, after press-checking the two ScoreMasters, thrusting them into his belt. He already wore the twin stainless Detonics CombatMaster miniguns and the little Centennial .38 Special. He took the two SIG-Sauer 228 9mms from the bag as well, thrusting them into the empty Professional Gear belt holsters which were already threaded onto his trouser belt.

From a second bag, he pulled out two Lancer copies of SIG-Sauer P-226 9mms, requisitioned from the *Paladin*'s arms locker. He handed these to Croenberg. "That P-38's fine, but not enough firepower for what we might have to do. Use these."

"Of course." Croenberg checked both pistols' loaded condition, then thrust them into his belt as he stood up. Rourke handed Croenberg two spare magazines, loaded as well. "I see what Mr. Rubenstein meant."

John Rourke ignored the comment.

The copilot stepped back into the cabin, saying, "We'll touch down shortly, General, Lieutenant General Croenberg. Now's a good time to strap yourselves in."

"Thanks, Lieutenant," Rourke nodded. "Remember, stay in the cockpit until we say it's okay."

"Aye, sir."

Rourke sat down as the copilot disappeared into the cockpit.

Croenberg sat down and buckled up.

John Rourke turned his eyes toward the sea.

Croenberg asked, "What are you doing, Doctor?"

"Trying to enjoy the landing," Rourke told him . . .

A standard, surface-only motorized launch lay to alongside the flying boat, two men in Nazi field uniforms and three Russian traders—which usually meant pirates—in the craft. "The tall man is Max, my chauffeur and bodyguard," Croenberg supplied, ducking back from the porthole. Rourke did the same. "The other one is one of Deitrich Zimmer's men; I don't remember his name."

"So, Max is the only one on our side."

"I am afraid so."

"Hopefully the odds will be a little better once we're aboard the trading vessel."

"Max would not let us down, Dr. Rourke."

John Rourke smiled, telling Croenberg, "See, you do have faith." As he spoke, Rourke moved to stand just beside the cabin door, Croenberg making ready to open it.

There was a porthole in the door. Croenberg said, "Max will be last, Zimmer's man first."

"Good. Be ready," Rourke advised as he pulled both ScoreMasters from his belt.

Croenberg moved well away from the doorway, deeper into the cabin, in order, Rourke knew, to draw the attention of Zimmer's man and however many of the Russian sailors came aboard. From where Rourke stood, he could divide his attention between the doorway and the porthole nearest him, through which he could view most of the launch.

Zimmer's man was moving forward in the launch, one of the Russian sailors clambering onto the pontoon. He helped the Nazi onto the pontoon and a second Russian sailor started coming forward. Max and the last Russian sailor were still in the boat.

If Max could be counted upon to take care of the third sailor, things might go relatively smoothly yet, Rourke thought. Maybe.

Rourke's eyes came back to the doorway, Zimmer's man stepping inside, coming to attention and rendering the classic National Socialist salute. "Heil Zimmer! Gruppenführer Croenberg, I am—"

The two Russian sailors were through the door behind the Nazi.

Rourke stepped away from the bulkhead, cocking the hammers of the two ScoreMasters to full stand, "Move and you die!"

Croenberg's right hand gripped his P-38. In English, apparently so the Russian sailors would understand as well, Croenberg snapped, "Raise your hands above your heads now!"

Rourke glanced into the launch.

Max was still with the third sailor. Rourke told Croenberg. "I've got these guys; tell Max in German to take care of the last sailor as quietly as he can."

"Of course."

Rourke ordered the Nazi and the two Russian sailors, "Against the bulkhead! Now!"

Croenberg worked his way past the three men, staying out

of Rourke's line of fire, leaning his head out of the doorway, saying in German, "Quietly! Get him, Max!"

Croenberg was back inside, gun trained on the three men. Rourke shot a glance through the porthole. Whatever Max had done was efficient enough for the circumstances—the third sailor was lying face down in the launch, Max just sitting there quite placidly.

John Rourke ordered, "The three of you, hands over your heads, not clasped behind your necks. Move to do anything else and you die. I mean it."

Zimmer's Nazi was the first to raise his hands, the others following suit. There was much to do and very little time for doing it . . .

Max was babysitting the Nazi officer who was loyal to Zimmer, the dead man—his neck was snapped—covered over by a tarp in the bottom of the launch and the two Russian sailors cuffed and sedated aboard the flying boat, under the eyes of the pilot and copilot. Max, it appeared, didn't do things by half. It was a needless killing—something Rourke disliked intensely.

The launch moved away from the flying boat, Rourke at its controls. With Croenberg—if Croenberg played it straight—to bellow orders as the launch came alongside and the Nazi officer who was loyal to Zimmer under threat of death from Max, there was a chance they could get aboard the Russian trading/pirate ship without incident. Getting from the launch to the main deck would be the only truly dicey part.

The seas were only moderate, and aside from the occasional swell, the ride to the trader was smooth.

Croenberg said, "I will board first, and this fellow will be behind me, with Max behind him. I suggest that you should be last."

"How well is Max armed?"

"He is always well armed; that is why he is Max."

Rourke nodded.

About a half-dozen personnel were on the main deck of

the trader, peering over the side as Rourke brought the launch alongside the ladder. There was a helicopter landed on the aft section of the main deck, apparently the means by which the Nazi personnel had come to the vessel and the means by which Croenberg was to be returned to the mainland. There would be a pilot for the aircraft, a loose end needing relatively immediate attention before the fellow could get airborne or get on the radio.

John Rourke brought the launch to rest alongside a crudely made float dock. Max tied off, stepping out onto the dock and grabbing hold of the ladder, ostensibly helping the Nazi officer with him to get onto the dock, but Rourke was watching the way Max gripped the man's arm. Had the man moved, Max could have thrown him into the water instantly, and probably broken his arm at the same time.

Croenberg stepped out onto the dock, immediately starting up the ladder.

Rourke climbed out, exchanged a glance with Max, then shifted the weight of the two special musette bags he carried with them, each loaded with disposable syringes, each of these in turn containing enough sedative to put a man out for several hours. Max let the Nazi officer start toward the ladder, Rourke hissing through his teeth in German, "Remember. You would die first."

The Nazi took to the ladder, Max following him just far enough below that it would be impossible for the Nazi officer to kick him in the face.

Rourke glanced back at the flying boat, then toward the main deck above, then started climbing.

As Rourke reached the rail, looking over, he saw Croenberg, Max and the Nazi officer, all in conversation with the apparent captain and first mate of the trader.

When Rourke stepped aboard, all eyes turned toward him. If Croenberg had betrayed him, Rourke would bring Croenberg down with him.

Instead, Croenberg said in English, "Here is the man who assisted me in discovering the plot."

This was not in the script. Rourke said nothing.

"It was he—as you can see, he is the clone of John Rourke

206

who was kidnapped from Dr. Zimmer's facility in the Himalayas—but unbeknownst to the enemies of the Reich, this clone, a physically identical duplicate of Dr. John Thomas Rourke, the notorious terrorist and enemy of the Reich, carries within him the identical memories of Herr Dr. Deitrich Zimmer. They think as one. So, in a sense, you are, Captain Turgenov, you and your men, in the presence of the Führer!"

And Croenberg raised his right hand in salute, shouting, "Heil Zimmer!"

John Rourke smiled.

Fifty

"Where the hell did you get that crazy idea?" Rourke asked through clenched teeth as they moved along a narrow companionway toward the radio room, Max still keeping the Nazi officer beside him.

"When I detected that more than two dozen Russian sailors were on the main deck and heavily armed, Doctor."

"And they bought; that's miraculous."

"They are simple men, and news of what transpired at the secret base in the Himalayas was widely broadcast; I merely informed them of what a clone was."

They were nearing the radio room, the captain of the trader SS *Archangelsk* was the first to enter, followed by Rourke and Croenberg, then Max and the Nazi officer after.

Rourke had little faith in Croenberg's charade holding up for much longer. As soon as they were all in the radio room and the door was closed, Rourke stepped back and drew the ScoreMasters from under his jacket. "Gentlemen, hands up!"

Croenberg drew his P-38. "Why do we do this?"

"Safer this way," Rourke advised. "Tell Max to find the pilot of the helicopter and neutralize him; he doesn't necessarily have to kill him."

"Do as Dr. Rourke says, Max."

"Yes, Herr Gruppenführer!"

The captain of the trader took a step forward, Rourke

swinging the muzzle of one of his .45s at the man's head. "Don't!"

"He called you Dr. Rourke!" The captain's English was heavily accented, but otherwise quite good.

"Sit down on the floor and shut up, hands on top of your head," Rourke ordered. "Croenberg, do your thing."

Croenberg nodded, shoved the operator from his seat and took control of the radio, flicking the dials to a different frequency and amplification. "This is a Condor Level Code Broadcast. I repeat, a Condor Level Code Broadcast."

Fifty-one

After sedating the captain of the *Archangelsk*, the radio operator and the original Nazi officer, Rourke and Croenberg found the first mate and Rourke put a gun to the man's head, telling him to get everyone to report to sickbay on the double for the administration of a special inoculation, that it was discovered that the captain had cholera.

In the ship's sickbay, Rourke had the pharmacist's mate administer a shot to each member of the crew from the supply of drugs Rourke had brought aboard in two musette bags.

The men were ordered to sit down and rest in the event they should have a reaction to the shot. Within minutes, thirty-three crew members were passed out or nearly so. Rourke administered a shot to the pharmacist's mate, then with Croenberg and Max—Max had broken the neck of the helicopter pilot, Max's enthusiasm for neck-breaking something Rourke didn't care for—Rourke went about the ship finding the remaining personnel on watch.

Eventually, all were sedated. Max, enjoined not to kill anyone, was sent about the ship to lock the sickbay, get the unconscious men out of the radio room and locked away into a cabin, then otherwise secure the vessel. Rourke and Croenberg returned to the radio room.

Croenberg had broadcast a Reich-Level Security Alert. There was no return message recorded while they were absent from the radio room.

210

Rourke contacted the flying boat, getting the copilot on the limited range frequency. All was well and there was nothing inordinate coming in as they monitored enemy radio.

Rourke and Croenberg waited.

"What will happen when the sedation wears off?"

"We'll have a bunch of angry Russian seaman on our hands."

"What if the Reichsführer should want to talk with the captain of this vessel?"

Rourke, in his best Russian accent, answered, "There will not be any problems with that, I think." Slipping back into his own voice he added, "And I speak Russian, probably better than the captain does, really. So long as I avoided any colloquialisms which might date my Russian out of the present day, I'd pass."

"Perhaps we should have arranged this differently."

"Perhaps," Rourke agreed. "But this vessel seems an ideally neutral meeting spot, ready and waiting. We must remember that our greatest enemy is time, isn't it?"

Croenberg nodded, lighting a cigarette, offering one to Rourke. Rourke accepted, accepting the light as well.

Pacing the companionway outside the radio-room door, Rourke passed nearly an hour.

Croenberg, standing in the open doorway, smoking his fifth cigarette in that hour, suggested, "I should call to the Reichsführer again."

"No. We don't want to push it."

Another half hour passed.

And, at last, a message came in over the frequency Croenberg had set.

It was Griem himself.

On speaker, Rourke could hear both ends of the conversation. Croenberg told his story, that he had discovered something of the greatest importance which could only be confided to the Reichsführer personally. Griem seemed less than enthused about the prospects of a meeting. Croenberg insisted.

Finally, Griem agreed.

Rourke lit a cigar, wondering whether his troubles were coming to an end or just beginning.

Fifty-two

Three Nazi helicopter gunships, rigged with pontoons for water landings, arrived almost exactly two hours later, small rubber motorized launches dropped from the gunships before they landed and men—SS commandos—rappelling down to the launches. Heavily armed, the launches approached the Russian trading vessel, circling it as if they were in some sort of race, then taking up positions on all sides of the vessel.

Ten minutes passed, two more helicopters coming in, circling over the vessel for a period of several minutes, one of them finally landing.

"He would have flown by high speed transport from Eden City to some coastal location, then helicoptered the rest of the way," Croenberg informed Rourke as they watched from the pilothouse.

Rourke said nothing.

He watched as the helicopter which had just landed set out another of the inflatable launches and four men in black SS commando gear, all visibly armed, exited the helicopter. A fifth man, in black BDUs as well, but wearing only a pistol at his belt, clambered down into the inflatable launch. The launch started toward the *Archangelsk*.

Rourke watched the face of this fifth man, recognizing him from Allied Intelligence files. It was Griem.

"Now we know whether we live or die," Croenberg said, standing beside Rourke.

"Let's move onto the main deck," Rourke suggested. As he spoke, he unbuckled his gunbelt, setting it inside one of the empty musette bags in which he had carried the sedative shots.

They started down to the main deck, Rourke's jacket closed to cover the ScoreMasters in his trouser band and the SIG-Sauer 228s at his sides. He set the musette bag down beside him as he stopped at the approximate center of the open area on the forward section of the main deck.

SS commandos swarmed up both sides of the vessel, brandishing assault rifles and shouting orders.

Croenberg cautioned them to stay back.

Rourke merely stood, hands relaxed at his sides, waiting, ignoring the orders from the SS commandos to raise his hands over his head.

Croenberg again ordered the men to stay back, not to interfere.

In another moment, one of the commando leaders would demand cooperation and decide to back it up and the shooting would start.

John Rourke rolled his unlit cigar in his teeth, clamping it into the left side of his mouth.

Two SS commandos came up from the ladder, assault rifles at the ready.

Stepping up the ladder just behind them came Griem.

Croenberg came to attention, but not in uniform, he did not salute. "Herr Reichsführer! Thank you for coming."

"What is this?"

Croenberg said nothing for a moment.

Griem insisted. "What is this!? That man is Dr. Rourke!"

"Yes, Herr Reichsführer."

"Arrest him!" Griem shouted.

As Griem's men started to move, John Rourke, the cigar still clamped into his teeth, shouted, "Hear us out first or there will be bloodshed, and you'll die, too, General!"

Croenberg took a step forward. Rourke noticed Croenberg's hands were shaking, but the man's voice was firm. "Herr Reichsführer, I beseech you! Listen to us!"

213

"You are with Rourke? I always knew that your loyalties were not as they should be, Croenberg, but this!"

"Maybe his loyalties are just fine, General. Or are you so uncertain of your own loyalties that you can't risk listening to what we have to say?"

Griem's face read like a book for the visually impaired. This was a test of his courage and his honor. He could not ignore the challenge. "Speak, then. And quickly before I lose all patience."

John Rourke simply said, "Let us tell you about Dr. Zimmer's Omega Option."

"What is this?"

"His plan for the death of all mankind, including you, your men here, every human being on the face of the earth except himself, Martin Zimmer and their surviving clones at the bunker outside Eden City. It's an airborne virus, constantly mutating, attacking the body's own immune system and rendering it powerless. Within a relatively short period of time after its release, every human being on the planet will be infected and dying. You, your men, your entire army, everyone who has sworn allegiance to Deitrich Zimmer, all of his enemies too. Everyone. You have a wife, a son and two daughters. They'll die. Everyone will die unless you help us to prevent it."

One of the SS commandos started toward Rourke.

Rourke wheeled toward him, Rourke's coat still zipped closed a few inches about the waistband, but his hands near to the butts of the pistols.

Griem shouted, "Wait!"

Otto Croenberg audibly sighed . . .

They stood there on the deck, under the afternoon sun, surrounded by SS commandos, Griem, Croenberg and John Rourke. Croenberg spoke, Rourke spoke. Griem listened. Griem would not, at first, believe. Rourke produced from the pocket of his bomber jacket a waterproof packet, within it a letter signed by Arthur Hooks, President of the United States, countersigned by the leaders or ambassadors from the other free world nations. Accompanying it was a letter signed by Professor Dr. Wilhelmina Krause, outlining the danger represented by the virus, this letter countersigned by other medical authorities from around the world, the letters flown by trans-atmospheric insertion flights in order to be physically signed rather than bear facsimile signatures.

Griem ordered chairs brought out on deck for them, and ordered his commandos back to the rail.

Croenberg said, at last, "This is real, Helmut. Deitrich Zimmer intends to destroy the entire human race, replacing it with his own race. He wishes to make himself a god, and to build his future on the corpses of not only his enemies, but also those who have served him."

Griem's face was grey, ashen, his eyes dead-seeming, the color drained from them.

"What are we to do, Otto?"

Croenberg answered. "Dr. Rourke has formulated a plan, with several options, depending on how much help you can be to us."

"There are those," Griem told them, "who will follow Deitrich Zimmer even into this madness. They will have to be dealt with. I will help to prevent this, fight to prevent this with the last breath in my body."

John Thomas Rourke was reminded of an oft-heard phrase, to the effect that there was a little bad in the best of mankind, and a little good in the worst. The spark of decency which had lain dormant in Reichsführer Helmut Griem, a Nazi, despicable by any moral standard, had been discovered, had ignited into flame.

Fifty-three

The officers from among the SS unit—all but one of them—accompanying Griem were summoned into the radio room, Griem personally informing them concerning the Omega Option virus. After receiving their pledges of loyalty, Griem dispatched them to their men, to deal with those who could not be trusted, placing them and the one remaining officer—fanatically loyal to Deitrich Zimmer—under arrest.

Griem contacted his own headquarters, instructing his immediate subordinates that he would be delayed in his return to Eden City because of unforeseen ramifications arising from Otto Croenberg's information. By encrypted transmission, Griem ordered his second-in-command to stand by, keeping all officers on unofficial alert.

The arrests made, eight men and one officer under guard, Griem, Croenberg and Rourke returned to the main deck. Already, the men Griem trusted were taking charge of the helicopters.

Rourke, in contact with the crew of the flying boat, ordered the craft airborne.

The *Paladin* was long underway toward a rendezvous with the *Archangelsk* and would arrive within the hour.

Using a note pad taken from the radio room, Griem began laying out details concerning security at Deitrich Zimmer's command bunker, force deployment, those units which could be counted upon with Eden Defense Forces and from among the SS to remain loyal to Zimmer, those whose commanders could be counted upon to listen to reason.

And, gradually, John Rourke's perception of what lay ahead altered.

As he had originally planned, they would find the clones, obtain the blood samples and go forward from there in order to combat the Omega Option virus. But, there would never be another chance like this to stop Deitrich Zimmer forever, taking him alive. Alive, somehow Zimmer could be forced through drugs or hypnosis into revealing how the contents of the Omega Option canisters would be released into the air. Rourke desperately wanted to believe that.

Because he had no choice . . .

Fully surfaced, the *Paladin,* seawater draining from her main deck, from the sail as well, gleaming bright in the setting sun, was incredible to behold. Vast in size beyond anything John Rourke had ever seen, the *Paladin,* surfaced, seemed larger, vastly larger, than she had ever seemed when he approached from underwater.

Waiting on her main deck, accompanied by John Rourke's Family, was the President of the United States.

When Helmut Griem stepped aboard the main deck, the President strode forward to meet him. They shook hands.

Otto Croenberg murmured, "Is this a nightmare or a dream?"

"I'll let you know later," Rourke told him.

Arthur Hooks said, "All of our past differences, sir, are behind us. We are united for the common cause of humanity."

"It is agreed, Herr President. For the common cause of humanity."

"There is much to do, sir," Hooks said.

"And, little time," Griem added.

The President of the United States looked at John Rourke. "I believe that you are in charge from here, Doctor."

Fifty-four

Commander Washington would lead the Trans-Global Alliance Commando Force. Lieutenant General Thomas Wilson, Commandant of the United States Marine Corps, would lead the main body of U.S. ground forces. Wolfgang Mann would, for the moment, rejoin the Armed Forces of New Germany, resuming his rank of Generaloberst.

Naval Forces of the United States Atlantic Fleet were standing by to move into position off what Before the Night of the War had been the Georgia coast and was now the heart of Eden.

A small contingent of commandos from Australia, and Defense Force personnel from Lydveldid Island would be assigned to Lieutenant General Thomas Wilson's Marines. There would also be a small contingent of personnel from the Russian Defense Forces. Airborne troops from the Chinese Second City, the current-day Republic of China, would jump with Marine Airborne personnel.

No invasion force such as this had ever been so hastily assembled.

At the moment that the general assault began, Griem and Croenberg would go on television and radio, quickly outlining the nature of Deitrich Zimmer's Omega Option, the threat posed by the virus and ordering all Nazi divisions to stand down, except for those under the personal command of Croenberg and Griem, which could be counted upon to seize

Nazi strongholds throughout North and South America. Via various means of communication, certain key commanders trusted by both Griem and Croenberg were being enlisted to seize control of certain strategic sites and to arrest certain commanders loyal to Deitrich Zimmer, all just prior to the actual invasion.

Word from the *Dauntless,* where Thorn Rolvaag worked round the clock supervising the placement of the nuclear charges along the course of the suboceanic rift, was that all would be in readiness within forty-eight hours. The schedule was being accelerated because the speed at which the rift was moving toward the North American Plate was increasing with every hour.

In seven days, the rift would meet the plate if it had not been stopped.

The results, according to the latest testing, were no longer even slightly in dispute. If the rift struck the North American Plate, the Ring of Fire surrounding the Pacific Basin would erupt in a chain reaction forming a caldera, destroying the Earth.

As to the results of the explosions which would be used to divert the rift, rob it of energy, even the best computer scenarios were not in agreement. There would be eruptions, there would be tidal waves, there would be disaster. Coastal populations everywhere, especially in the Hawaiian Islands, were being evacuated inland. Earthquakes in Hawaii and elsewhere were increasing in magnitude and frequency.

In light of this, a few hours were set aside aboard the *Paladin* for a wedding ceremony. Emma lent Natalia her dress.

The *Paladin* surfaced once again, the ceremony taking place on her main deck.

"Who will give you away?" Annie asked Natalia.

Natalia said simply, "I am a free woman, and I give myself freely to the man I have chosen."

Paul served as Michael's best man.

Annie served as matron of honor.

Everyone from the *Paladin*'s complement who was not on duty attended.

John Rourke, flanked by Emma and Sarah, stood, watching as the *Paladin*'s chaplain performed the ceremony. When, at last, the chaplain declared, "I now pronounce you man and wife," Michael took Natalia into his arms, turning back her veil (which had remained down throughout the ceremony because no one had given her away) and kissed her.

A cheer went up from the ship's company.

Sarah began to cry.

John Rourke put his arm around her shoulders, while Emma held his hand . . .

There would be very little night this night. Before dawn, a small fleet of V-Stol fighter bombers would depart the *Paladin* for the staging area near the southern boundary of the Midwest Glacier near the site of what, Before the Great Conflagration, had been Chicago.

Annie Rubenstein turned back the covers as Paul got into bed beside her, then covered them both as he took her into his arms. "Are you sure you want us to do this now, Annie? And anyway, what about—"

She inclined her head toward the nightstand beside the bed. On the stand was the little plastic case, like a large compact, but for her diaphragm.

Paul smiled.

"If we're all going to die," Annie told him, "maybe it's bad to start a child, maybe it's wrong. But I want your baby, Paul, our baby. And maybe we'll all live. Hold me?"

"I want our baby, too," Paul whispered, drawing her closer to him. Her fingers splayed over his chest, feeling the strength in him as he held her, as he moved on top of her and slipped between her thighs.

And, if they died, Annie Rourke Rubenstein would take the memory of this night, however short, with her, in her soul forever.

Fifty-five

The V-Stol bombers would fly from the surface flight deck.

The moon was still up, seen fitfully only because of the heavy cloud cover. Volcanic ash, some of it, Rourke knew.

He climbed up onto the wing stem, stashing his gear aft of the second seat. Emma climbed up after him, settling herself in the pilot's seat.

His gear stowed—rifle, other equipment—he looked across the flight deck. Annie and Paul, Michael and Natalia, all of them moving to their assigned aircraft. Wolfgang Mann and Sarah left immediately after the wedding of Michael and Natalia.

Commander Washington and his men were already at the staging area.

John Rourke looked skyward, wishing that he could see the stars—but they were obscured.

As a boy, he had always wondered what lay out there, waiting to be discovered or to discover. As a young man, he had often wondered if, by some chance, someone were looking down from those stars, could the folly of mankind be seen? As a husband and father, as a man forced to fight for his Family's survival, John Rourke had longed for the stars; they were the physical embodiment of his hope, that there was something more than destruction and death in the universe.

But, still well before dawn, the stars were hidden from him.

They would terrain-follow in order to avoid enemy sensing devices such as radar, so they would not fly above the clouds and the stars would remain obscured.

After all these years, when he needed them most, they were not there.

John Rourke closed his eyes for a moment. " 'The fault lies not in our stars . . .' " Rourke murmured, then opened his eyes again and started settling himself into the copilot's seat . . .

Deitrich Zimmer sipped his breakfast coffee. Within the heart of the bunker, night and day were discernable only by the changing of the digits on a clock. As Martin entered the room, Zimmer ordered Martin, "Sit down, my son."

"What is it, father?"

Zimmer poured a cup of coffee for his son. "I wanted to inform you of my plans for us."

"What plans, Father?"

"You have heard me mention that if my attempts to control your natural father should fail that I had a contingency plan which would assure our success. Do you recall?"

"Yes, father."

Zimmer, rarely impressed by Martin's retentive powers, felt mildly happy. "Good. I shall tell you what it is. We shall be alone for a very long time, you and I, a good time for us to become better friends, for you to learn, to grow in wisdom."

"Alone? Are we going someplace again?"

"No. We'll remain here, at least for a while. For just the two of us, there is enough to sustain us for a very long time here."

"Just the two of us?" Martin repeated.

"Yes, Martin. I have decided that once our enemies have activated their explosives in the hope of deterring the volcanic rift, whether or not they succeed, I shall initiate a project of my own. Should the efforts of our enemies fail in preventing the explosion of the Ring of Fire, and the planet itself dies, we shall still have struck the final blow. Should their efforts prevail, you and I will rule the Earth together. We will not be alone always. Within ten years, we can begin the repopulation process. We shall live through many of these bodies," he told Martin, gesturing to himself, then to his son. "We have clones waiting to take our memories, through which we will live forever. In a lifetime or two, Martin, a race of men will walk the Earth like no men ever before. And we will be their sovereign lords, you and I."

Martin said, "What do you mean?"

"Mankind is inferior, but the seeds of greatness are in my hands. We control the future. And, if the world should end, then we will die knowing that there is a God and He engineered this destruction of the Earth in order to prevent me from becoming His equal. What is a god, after all, but an all-powerful immortal? If the planet lives, all of mankind save ourselves and our clones and the raw genetic material I have preserved shall die and I will be the architect of the new Genesis. I will create life; it will flow from my hands. Is that not being a god, Martin?"

"I, I guess."

Zimmer smiled at his son. "The concept is overwhelming, I know, but you will be a god as well. And the race of men we put upon the face of the planet will serve us."

"Yes, Father."

Deitrich Zimmer sipped his coffee.

Fifty-six

On the icefield, there was perfect whiteness and the sky above, relatively cloudless, was a deep, piercing blue.

The skins of the aircraft gleamed dully. The weapons in the hands of the men and women of the Allied Commando Force smelled of lubricant as they passed. The cold made the skin tingle. He held Emma's hand as they walked across the glacier.

This was life.

Soon, it might all end forever.

When they reached the thermal-insulated command tent, the guards at the airlock came to attention, rendering rifle salutes.

John Rourke, tired of fighting it, returned their salutes as he and Emma entered.

Inside, Commander Washington started calling the assembled personnel—some three dozen commandos from all Allied Nations—to attention, but Rourke shouted, "As you were, please."

Commander Washington nodded, smiling slightly (knowing John Rourke's indisposition toward deference being paid to his unwilling rank as general), said, "As I was saying, ladies and gentlemen, ours is the first prong of the attack. Until we have gained entrance to the bunker and reached the clones and secured the blood samples so that the serum can be made, no other action will be taken. Once the signal is given that the blood samples are secure, everything happens fast. There will be amphibious landings on the coast, Marine and Chinese airborne elements will attack Eden City, fighter aircraft will strike Eden's air defenses and the Nazi armies should be up for grabs. As it looks now, certain Nazi units under the personal command of officers trusted by Reichsführer Griem and Gruppenführer Croenberg can be counted on, at the very least, to stand down. Others of these units will actively assist our personnel. At least, that's the plan. If we get enough people on the ground fast we'll have control of Eden City and other major population centers within Eden within twenty-four hours or less. Other Allied units will be hitting major Nazi outposts in North and South America and, we are told, should be able to count on assistance from elements loyal to Reichsführer Griem and Gruppenführer Croenberg as well. Commander Darkwood."

James Darkwood stood up, stepped forward and took the microphone from Commander Washington. Darkwood said, "Now the briefing on the command bunker outside Eden City, where we're going. You've all been given copies of the layout of the bunker as provided for us by Reichsführer Griem. The bunker is designed to withstand anything short of a direct nuclear hit, its defenses against conventional attack quite formidable. But, thanks to the help offered by Reichsführer Griem, if all goes as planned, we'll be let in by the back door. That's a tunnel that is used to service the facility with such things as generator parts and other heavy equipment. The tunnel entrance is secret, but still well-defended. Personnel loyal to Reichsführer Griem—and, more importantly to us, disloyal to Deitrich Zimmer in the light of his plans with the Omega Option virus—will allow us entrance and possibly assist in neutralizing forces loyal to Zimmer. Again, at least that's the plan.

"Once inside," Darkwood continued, "we will break up into two elements. Commander Washington will lead the bulk of the force against the main portion of the command bunker, Dr. Rourke the smaller of these two elements against the genetics laboratory and actual command center, where Zimmer himself should be found.

"We need to control the command bunker entirely. Deitrich Zimmer has some means by which he can control the release of the Omega Option virus. We can't let any equipment get touched by Zimmer or his son Martin, nor can we let any equipment be destroyed. We have to seize control as rapidly as possible, with as little damage to the real estate as possible. Otherwise, if we fail, we could well give Zimmer the win, allowing the release of the Omega Option virus before Allied scientists can distill a serum from the blood samples we'll be taking and before they can begin to disseminate the serum."

John Rourke said, "Excuse me a moment."

"Certainly, sir."

All faces turned toward his. Rourke recognized many of them—Navy SEALS, German Long Range Mountain Patrol Commandos, his wife's father and brother, his son and daughter, Natalia and Paul. "There's only one point I want to make," Rourke began.

"As we all know, within about thirty hours—a little less, actually," he said as he looked at the black-faced Rolex on his wrist, "Dr. Rolvaag will be detonating the charges beneath the Pacific. Even the greatest experts in computer modeling can't agree on just what will happen. The explosions should begin just about the time we'll be entering that tunnel. Whether the explosions stop the progress of the volcanic rift under the Pacific or precipitate the immediate destruction of the planet, our mission doesn't change. If God exists—and I've always believed in Him—then we have the moral obligation to do our best to destroy evil in order to perpetuate the good. That doesn't change just because we all might die within minutes or hours or days of the moment. If there is a life beyond this one, an awareness of self of any type or kind, we have to do our best to stand for what we believe is right against what we know is wrong. Otherwise, we'd be as morally bankrupt as Deitrich Zimmer himself. This sounds like a speech before a football game or something, I know, and I've never been good at this kind of thing. But, in the final analysis, although we'll fight to the last breath to win, what really matters is how we play the game,

226

why we fight. If we go down together in death, we'll at least know that we tried, that we did our best, that we gave it our all. And, even if we're all gone, all of humanity, that'll still count. I can't tell you how, but I know it'll count. That's all I've got to say, except may God bless us all."

No faces looked away. No one spoke.

John Rourke said nothing more.

Fifty-seven

At twilight, their aircraft were underway. Not V-Stols, the Trans-Global Alliance had developed a small fleet of top secret bombers, designed to be sensor invisible because of special materials, construction, paint and sound-dampening equipment.

They had never been tactically employed—until John Rourke, his Family and the Allied commandos boarded the aircraft on the glacier.

In full jump gear, the men and women of the commando force sat huddled together on long benches along either side of the fuselage. Some listened to music through headphones, some read, some few slept. One or two wrote letters they would leave behind aboard the aircraft, to be delivered in the event that they did not return.

Some sharpened their knives, some made last-minute checks of their firearms.

All, except those who slept, periodically consulted their watches. Twenty-three hours remained before the nuclear warheads along the volcanic rift would be detonated, the same amount of time which remained before they would be inside the tunnel, the tunnel leading them to their fate with Deitrich Zimmer.

John Rourke did not sleep.

He thought of Emma; she piloted a V-Stol fighter bomber

that would not be airborne until just prior to the attack. She would lead the first-wave aerial assault against the bunker.

He thought of Sarah; she would assist at Allied Headquarters for the Invasion, liaising between the forces of New Germany, in part commanded by her husband-to-be, and the United States Marine Corps ground forces.

He thought of Annie; she would be stationed outside the bunker with a small force of Allied commandos, poised to utilize that singular power which she alone possessed, her ability to tell if any of the members of the Family, with whom she had her empathic bond, were in mortal danger. If she "sensed" that the attack within the bunker was going badly, she alone had the authority to order in additional personnel. Hers was a tremendous and frightening responsibility.

He thought of Natalia; she would be part of the attack on the bunker, her skills indispensable beside him as they always had been.

He thought of Michael; his son would be with Commander Washington, co-leading the main assault force within the bunker, charged with the Herculean task of subduing all resistance without allowing destruction of computers, electronic equipment, records.

He thought of Paul; Paul would be with him, as always, and had as his primary responsibility the task of getting the blood samples, taken from the clones, into Allied hands as rapidly as possible.

He thought of himself; it was his job to lead the smaller element of the attack force on the bunker, ensuring that the blood samples could be taken from the clones and capturing or otherwise neutralizing Zimmer, and probably Martin as well.

He had never intended to have the fate of mankind rest upon his abilities, abilities everyone around him seemed to regard much more highly than he ever did. John Rourke had never intended any of this. He had studied the art of staying alive, viewed as very real the chance that mankind might well endeavor to destroy itself in the folly of warfare.

All he had ever wanted was to protect his Family.

Six hundred twenty-five years after the Night of the War, he would likely meet death at last.

... positions along the line ... sexes ...

Fifty-eight

The jump was high altitude, high opening, their path
through the night sky guided by passive receptance of satellite signals. Again, he could not see the stars, but manmade
stars guided him and the others from the commando force.

All personnel, with the exception of Tim Shaw and his
son, Ed, were experienced and the landing was without serious incident, one parachutist getting caught up in a stand
of pines, but already having cut himself free before help
arrived. One of the jump canisters—containing food supplies—was partially damaged when it landed on an outcrop-
ping of granite, but the contents were unharmed.

The commando force landed in four elements, regrouping
at a predetermined set of coordinates and moving immediately to the intermediate objective.

This was heavily wooded, a snow-covered area in rolling
hills about ten miles outside of Eden City itself, only seven
miles from the location of the bunker.

With fifteen hours to go before H-hour, human and electronic sentries posted along their encampment's perimeter,
each man and woman, some alone, some in groups, took a
quick, hearty meal, then slept.

John Rourke busied himself for a time with checking sen-
try positions, as did Commander Washington, Paul, Michael,
Natalia and James Darkwood.

Before retiring—if he hurried he'd have six hours worth

of sleep—Rourke conferred with the other leaders of the commando force, reviewing their immediate plans for the morning. After everyone was up, the commando group would move in four separate elements, linking up again approximately one mile from the tunnel service entrance to the bunker, then following an infiltration schedule which would get them on site at the appointed time at the Primary Objective.

Rourke left the informal meeting, rolled out his sleeping bag beside Paul's and James Darkwood's and closed his eyes.

He did not consciously dream, which he had always considered a benefit, derived from his time spent in cryogenic sleep. He awoke once during the night, sat listening to the night for a while, then returned to sleep.

Snow fell overnight, the snow grey-tinged with volcanic ash. Zipping out of the mummy-style bag he'd elected to use, Rourke pulled on his jacket and his boots, grabbed his rifle and went off into the woods. Several slit trenches had been dug the previous night and Rourke selected one over which to relieve himself.

He shaved, washed as well as he could and began gathering his gear. Within another twenty minutes, the rest of the camp was up or getting there. Cold rations were a thing of the past. Modern field rations were packaged in containers which chemically heated the contents without the need of a fire or boiling water. Rourke breakfasted more heavily than usual in light of the long hike ahead of him.

By a half hour after dawn, the camp—with the exception of the disturbed snow—was in order, the slit trenches covered, everything which had been expended policed and buried.

At the head of his own element, Rourke took a last geo-synchronous satellite bearing, which he confirmed with his old-fashioned lensatic compass, and started his people down through the woods, toward the rendezvous . . .

With two hours remaining before H-hour, infiltration toward the service tunnel entrance was already under way, in teams of three persons each. Rourke, Paul and James Darkwood formed their own team, like the others moving through the woods, along the lengths of defiles, avoiding any terrain against which they might be silhouetted.

As night at last came, the sky was heavily overcast, the snow which had fallen lightly overnight returning in full measure, heavy flakes building rapidly into deep accumulation. They paused briefly to don snow smocks in order to blend in with the altered terrain. But the temperature was still mild enough and the snow was not driven on strong winds. The snow, in fact, although it made finding one's footing at times more difficult, almost warmed them as they moved.

Twenty minutes before H-hour, Rourke, Paul and James Darkwood paused once again, consuming a hurried meal, taking care of biological necessities, making their last weapons checks.

In addition to his customary German MP-40 submachine gun, Paul carried a modern cartridge-firing assault rifle, identical to the one carried by Darkwood. In addition to his handguns, John Rourke had the HK-91 rifle.

After finishing their meal, they set out into the last phase of their infiltration route, Rourke closely monitoring their position by satellite and by compass.

Seven minutes before H-hour, they were at the rendezvous, other infiltration teams already in place, a few more still to come.

Few words were exchanged.

One of the commandos ate a candy bar. Another touched up the edge of a knife. One cupped a cigarette in gloved hands. John Rourke had one of the thin, dark tobacco cigars in the left corner of his mouth, unlit.

The digital mission clock built into his satellite positioning receiver reached the hour.

In the Pacific, at this very instant, Thorn Rolvaag would be detonating the first of the suboceanic charges.

Silently, Rourke and the other element leaders signaled the commandos to move out.

Fifty-nine

The tunnel mouth was heavily guarded, a dozen men in SS commando uniforms posted strategically overlooking the driveway off the road toward the service tunnel entrance, more personnel on the driveway itself, at the first and second service gates and on watch beside the deflection barriers. The mouth of the tunnel itself was overset with a canopy of synth-concrete, providing protection from the air as well.

John Rourke glanced at his watch, the mission clock too cumbersome to bother with now.

As the second hand of his black-faced Rolex swept over the inverted triangle in the twelve position, two vanlike trucks emerged from the tunnel entrance, pulling all the way forward to the interior gate.

Two more trucks followed into the driveway about thirty seconds behind the first two, these latter moving one to each side of the drive.

Men exited the trucks. This was the changing of the guard shift; and, if Helmut Anton Griem had carried off what he said he could, these new guards would be the key to Allied penetration of the bunker.

Rourke watched, waited, squinted through the falling snow.

The routine was that the watch detail which was replaced would board the trucks and return to the interior of the bunker.

But, that routine would not be carried out in full this time, if all went well.

The guard changed, the men who had been on duty—a little tired-looking, probably cold—began entering their trucks. The trucks closed up and started back inside the bunker.

Once the trucks had disappeared, John Rourke watched for the signal. A flashlight was turned on, then off, three times in rapid succession.

Flanked by Natalia and Paul, Rourke started up from his position in the snow. Natalia touched his arm, warning him, "This could all be an elaborate trap, John."

"What choice do we have, Natalia?"

She smiled, the surreal blueness of her eyes always had and always would touch him into his soul. She got up, Paul as well. The rest of their unit—six men, SEALs and German Long Range Mountain Commandos—were moving as well.

The remainder of the first wave of the commando force kept in hiding.

Rourke looked at his watch again. By now, the auxiliary commando unit, with which Annie was assigned, was into position outside the main entrance to the bunker, waiting.

Emma's squadron would be airborne, moving into position for the first wave of the aerial bombardment of the bunker.

Washington and the rest of the commando unit here at the bunker's service entrance would be ready either to move into the bunker or to take cover should this be some sort of trap and a firefight were about to ensue.

Rourke, Paul Rubenstein, Natalia Tiemerovna and the six commandos came down along a narrow defile and into the open, a few yards off from the road leading toward the gates. Rourke mentally shrugged, then strode forward, onto the road.

Any normal patrolling formation would have been absurd under the circumstances, all nine of them in full open view of the guard positions and heavily outnumbered.

Rourke, his rifle slung at his side, his right hand on the pistol grip, kept his eyes on the first gate.

It was opening.

"So far, so good," Paul whispered.

Sixty

The officer in charge of the guard detail, bearing the SS rank equivalent of a first lieutenant, introduced himself as Obersturmführer Danzig, saluting—conventionally—as he did so. John Rourke returned the salute. "What happened to the men from the original guard detail, Lieutenant?"

"Harmlessly gassed, Herr General. We will utilize those same trucks as the means of getting your personnel through the tunnel to the main portion of the bunker. If you will accompany me, Herr General."

"Let's drive with the windows open, though, hm?" And Rourke signaled with his flashlight toward the positions occupied by Washington, Michael, Darkwood and the others.

Allied commandos dropped out of trees, slid out from behind rocks and began filling the roadway, their weapons at the ready, starkly black against the white of their snowsmocks.

Danzig, as they walked through the second gate, asked, "May I ask, Herr General, if the detonations beneath the Pacific Ocean have begun yet?"

"I believe that they have, Lieutenant, if they began on schedule."

"If I may say so, Herr General, let us hope that your scientists are successful."

"And that we are successful here tonight as well," Rourke added.

They were walking beneath the synth-concrete lip which lay over the mouth of the tunnel, when the ground began shaking beneath their feet.

Rourke stopped.

Danzig and the three enlisted personnel with him froze.

Natalia murmured, "It is starting."

Paul's face looked ashen beneath the arc lights.

The tremor passed as quickly as it had come.

John Rourke exhaled.

As they started forward again, the ground shook, more violently than it had a second ago, and from above their heads there began a low groaning noise. Rourke looked up. There was an ear-splitting crack as the lip of synth-concrete over them began to separate itself from the tunnel mouth.

"God in Heaven!" Danzig shouted. "It is the end of the world!"

John Rourke wheeled toward Danzig, grabbing the man by his uniform sleeve. "Get us inside! Now! Move!"

The concrete overhang was collapsing around them, the ground beneath them shaking so violently that one of Danzig's men stumbled, fell.

Danzig stammered, "Yes, Herr General! Of course we must!" And Danzig started into a run, toward the tunnel entrance.

Natalia dodged back, tripping over a chunk of concrete, jagged chunks of synth-concrete crashing down around her. Paul grabbed her to her feet, looked at Rourke, nodded, then started propelling her into the tunnel.

Rourke activated the jaw profile radio at the side of his mouth. "This is Rourke! Get back. All bets are off. We're going in, getting what we came for. Meet us out front!" And he ran toward the tunnel mouth, the casing around the tunnel collapsing now, as was the lip above it.

The shaking of the ground was unlike anything John Rourke had ever experienced, could ever have imagined. With each step, it was necessary to fight to keep his balance. And now, as he neared the tunnel mouth, the roadway surface beneath his combat-booted feet was cracking, splitting into massive chunks, debris exploding upward, pieces of the tunnel casing flying everywhere around him. A piece of synth-concrete struck at his left arm, tearing the snow smock. Rourke kept running.

The tunnel mouth was just ahead of him, Natalia and Paul, Danzig and his three men near one of the trucks. There were other SS uniformed personnel around them, but all of them apparently with Danzig, loyal to Helmut Anton Griem and disloyal to Deitrich Zimmer.

As Rourke raced toward them, he shouted, "Zimmer will release the virus if he thinks this is it, the end! Into the trucks!"

Paul swung up into the passenger seat of one of the trucks, Natalia in through the open side door.

The trucks were already starting into motion. Rourke quickened his pace, slabs of synth-concrete from the tunnel ceiling starting to separate, synth-concrete dust everywhere. And the ground still shook, even more violently than before.

There was another ear-splitting crack and the roadbed sheared in half, Rourke jumping to his left, catching onto a chunk of surface material, half vaulting over it.

As he looked up, one of the trucks had overturned.

Paul was leaning out of another one, shouting, but over the noise of the collapsing tunnel Rourke could not hear him. To his feet, John Rourke ran, jumping over a slab of synth-concrete, reaching the truck and throwing himself inside.

Natalia, Lieutenant Danzig, Danzig's three men and two other men were inside. Rourke looked forward. The truck was accelerating, another of the SS men at the wheel.

The truck swerved, nearly impacting the tunnel wall, a massive slab of synth-concrete catapulting outward from the opposite side of the tunnel, swiping at the truck, nearly bowling it over. "Keep driving!" Paul shouted. "Faster!"

John Rourke was up, to his knees. Natalia knelt beside him. "Your face is cut." Rourke touched his face, then looked at his glove. There was some blood there. "Here!" And she daubed at his face with a handkerchief. "Not as bad as it looked."

Rourke nodded, to his feet now, balancing himself as the

truck swerved, his arms outstretched toward the bulkheads as he pitched himself into one of the seats.

And he was now aware of the noise. The noise which before had prevented him from hearing Paul was somehow different, deeper, more intense. "This is the end," Natalia said.

One of Danzig's men made the Sign of the Cross. Rourke wondered where an SS man had learned that, but was glad that the fellow had.

"If it isn't, we have to get the blood so we can—" Before Rourke could finish, his words, all other sounds as well, were drowned out in the roar of an explosion.

Rourke looked through the rear window of the truck.

The tunnel was collapsing behind them, the road surface buckling upward in massive slabs, the walls imploding. "Drive faster, man!" Rourke shouted. And he turned to Danzig. Although they were mere inches apart, Rourke shouted at the top of his voice in order to be heard. "Have your man get us to the bio labs section now! We have to get to Zimmer and we have to get to the clones. Before it's too late. Now!"

And, deep inside his soul, John Rourke wondered if perhaps it was already too late.

Danzig slipped from his seat, crawled forward along the length of the truck, shouting to the man behind the wheel. "Take us to Section Eleven! Go by way of the south tunnel. As rapidly as you can, Rottenführer! Quickly! Quickly!"

Natalia held Rourke's arm . . .

Martin was shrieking, "We must get out of here, Father!"

"When the world is being destroyed, Martin, where else is there to go? Think! But, we will still defy our fate! Come with me." And Deitrich Zimmer grabbed his son's shoulders, hauling Martin up from his knees. Rubble rained down around them, the ceiling of the bunker collapsing, pieces of tile flying from it like missiles.

"I don't want to die!"

"We can die as cowards or we can die defiant! Come with me!" And he dragged Martin in his wake, out of the inner

238

office, into the corridor leading toward the biological sciences laboratory.

His clones, his secret of immortality, lay within. And so, also, did his means to defy his fate . . .

The truck lurched. Natalia grabbed for one of the seat backs, flew forward, crashed against the front passenger seat. Rourke's head slammed against the headliner as he rolled, his body stopping, wedged between one of the seat backs and the roof.

Paul.

Rourke looked forward. His friend was hanging upside down from his seat, shaking his head.

The driver of the van lay half through the windshield, from the attitude of his neck and back, quite obviously dead. Danzig held his left arm. "It is broken, Herr General. But, we can go on."

"You're a brave man, Lieutenant. Help Major Tiemerovna." And Rourke started forward, to free Paul from the seat restraint.

Sixty-one

Paul's left shoulder had dislocated; John Rourke told him, "Bite on your glove, let me have your arm." Rourke rotated the arm and Paul gritted his teeth into the glove. The shoulder turned back into its socket. Paul's face glistened sweat. "Can you make it?"

"What choice do I have?" Paul answered, forcing a smile.

Danzig and his three men leading the way, Rourke, Natalia and Paul Rubenstein followed, running along what remained of the tunnel. Dust choked them, debris still fell on them, but the shaking had stopped.

"Do you think it's over, John?" Natalia called out to him, Paul between them as they ran.

"Honest answer? No. Hurry," Rourke told her. At the very least, there would be aftershocks, and the fabric of the tunnel itself wouldn't withstand much more. Once they reached the bio labs area, assuming they could, and assuming too that the lab had not collapsed, even if they were able to obtain blood samples from the clones of Zimmer and Martin, it was more than likely that the main entrance to the bunker might be sealed, that they would be trapped inside, buried alive. Rourke kept running . . .

Deitrich Zimmer clambered over a mound of collapsed

ceiling material, Martin still in tow. "We can get out of here, Father!"

"To where, boy? To where? The Earth is being destroyed. It is God destroying the Earth in order to cheat me of my power. There is nowhere to run to, Martin! But He will not cheat me now!"

Martin shouted, "We don't know that the world is ending, Father. We can't just stay here! We can't!"

"The plan of Rolvaag and the other Allied scientists did not work, Martin! Instead of halting the progress of the sub-oceanic rift, they have torn the fabric of the planet with their warheads. The Earth is dying and we will die with it, but not before you and I release the Omega Option virus! Hurry, boy!"

"Why, Father? Everyone is dying, you say? Why bother with the virus now?" And Martin pulled away from his father's grasp, half stumbling into a squatting position in a pile of rubble near one of the lab tables.

Deitrich Zimmer turned around, found solid footing, then stared at Martin. "Why? Because I have the power to do so. Come with me, die with me."

Martin closed his eyes . . .

"Only up ahead, Herr General!' Danzig shouted as the tunnel took a sharp bend.

John Rourke's lungs felt alternately cold and on fire, the new heart within his chest beating more wildly than he would have thought possible, his body bathed in cold sweat.

When they came around the bend, John Rourke stopped, leaning against the tunnel wall for an instant, then just stood there, staring ahead. Natalia fell to her knees. Paul swayed, dropped to his knees, leaned his head forward, coughing, perhaps vomiting. That Paul could even walk any great distance, let alone run, after the dislocation of his shoulder, was a tribute to his courage and endurance.

The same held true for Danzig, Danzig's left arm was broken, Rourke having field-splinted it with two sheathed bayonets from the men with Danzig. Danzig and his three men were stopped as well, Danzig swaying, about to collapse.

John Rourke looked past Danzig and Danzig's three men. There was a security entrance, no one guarding it and the door was falling away from its frame.

Rourke walked ahead, slowly. The ground was starting to shake again, but he was incapable of running again for at least a few seconds.

Danzig was starting to collapse. Rourke ordered Danzig's men, "Help your officer there! Get him!"

And Rourke walked on.

There was light from beyond the doorway, the electricity within the structure somehow still operational although many of the overhead light fixtures were down or destroyed. There were piles of rubble, overturned desks and chairs, computer monitors still on, but lying on their side, as if they, like Danzig, had just collapsed from exhaustion.

Rourke looked behind him. Natalia and Paul were coming, Paul's right hand holding his battered old Browning High Power, but pressed tightly to his left shoulder.

The mild movement of the ground beneath them was becoming more violent.

Rourke quickened his pace as much as he could.

Pieces of the tunnel ceiling were beginning to fall free again. He edged closer to the tunnel wall.

At last beside the doorway, John Rourke swung the muzzle of his rifle ahead of him, then began to clamber over the rubble . . .

Deitrich Zimmer righted the chair and sat down.

Martin stood beside him.

The trembling of the earth, which had begun again only seconds ago, had once again subsided.

The computer console before Deitrich Zimmer still functioned.

"After you do this, Father, can we try to leave?" Martin asked.

"Again, son, where would we go?"

242

Martin considered that. And the answer was beyond his reasoning. His two fathers: his natural father, John Rourke, was convinced that evil would perish and right would triumph; his adoptive father, Deitrich Zimmer, believed that there was no good, no evil, only the force of will.

Tonight, both goodness and will would die. Only evil, which was death, would triumph.

"What are you doing?"

Deitrich Zimmer's fingers flew over the keyboard. "I am programming the simultaneous release by radio signal of every single canister of the Omega Option virus. Should any human being survive this night, he will not survive the virus."

"And what will become of us?" Martin asked.

From behind him, he heard a voice very much like his own. "You can leave here, Martin; and, if the Earth survives, you can survive with it."

Martin Rourke Zimmer turned around to stare toward the origin of his voice.

He saw his birth father, John Thomas Rourke.

Deitrich Zimmer's voice was in his left ear. "Stop him while I activate the virus!"

John Rourke stabbed the rifle that was in his right hand toward them. "I want to kill you very much, Zimmer, but don't make me."

Martin Zimmer's eyes shifted from John Rourke to Deitrich Zimmer.

Deitrich Zimmer said, "In the end, John Rourke, you and all that you have ever stood for have lost. The world is ending. I am merely having my moment."

"You won't have your moment."

Deitrich Zimmer started to touch the keyboard.

Martin Zimmer wheeled toward John Rourke. The muzzle of John Rourke's rifle flashed flame and Martin Zimmer's ears rang.

Over the ringing in his ears, Martin heard John Rourke saying, "Come with me and have a chance, son."

Martin Zimmer decided. He turned toward the computer console. The monitor read, "Press OO to initiate program."

Martin reached toward the keyboard, striking the letter O once, about to strike it again. His entire body was seized with pain and his eyes filled with light . . .

Paul Rubenstein looked away from Martin Zimmer and down at the battered old Browning High Power in his right hand. "God forgive me," he whispered, closing his eyes.

The ground was beginning to shake again. Natalia was standing beside him, and he heard her voice as she told John, "We have the blood samples, John."

Paul Rubenstein opened his eyes and looked at his best friend, whose son he had just shot to death. John Rourke's eyes streamed tears, but his head was held erect as he said, "Thank you, Paul, for saving me from doing it. Thank you." And then John started toward the computer console, the shaking of the ground increasing . . .

The CD Rom discs from Zimmer's computer console were secured in the musette bag at John Rourke's side. Together with Paul and Natalia, who carried the blood samples from the clones—she had turned off their life support systems, she told him—and Lieutenant Danzig and Danzig's three men, they ran along the corridor from the bio labs.

As they ran, Danzig, panting, face pale and drawn, shouted to them, "The only way out would be Dr. Zimmer's private escape shaft, if it has not already collapsed. We are more than one hundred meters below the surface here. The escape shaft lead straight up to the surface level of the bunker and a vault door near it."

John Rourke ran alongside Danzig.

"Here! Here it is!" Danzig turned into a partially collapsed doorway, beyond it elaborate double doors, sprung from their hinges.

Beyond these doors was an office, austere by comparison to Zimmer's facility in Western Canada, no black marble, no gold swastika.

The bunker shook even more violently now.

And there was a sound louder than anything John Rourke had ever heard.

He looked back, seeing nothing except more of the bunker collapsing around them. On the far wall of the office was a tapestry, Danzig trying to rip it away, Paul helping him. There was a credenza in front of it, Danzig shouting to his three men to move it aside.

Behind the tapestry lay a steel door, with an electronic combination lock. Danzig dropped to one knee before it, punching the numbered buttons with the first finger of his right hand. Then he told Paul, "Try the handle." Paul twisted at the handle. The door did not open. "Can we detonate the doorway?" Danzig asked.

Natalia shoved past them, handing the blood samples to one of Danzig's men. "Lose these or break them and you won't have to worry about being buried alive here!" Reaching into the black bag at her side and dropping to her knees before the doorway, Natalia set a small charge against the mating point of the door to the frame, where the vertical locking bolts should be.

Rourke moved to help her, taking a similar charge from his second musette bag, laying it across the top of the vault door while Natalia placed still a third charge along the bottom.

The charges had built-in timers and Rourke glanced at the timer on the first charge, setting his to match.

"Back off and take cover!" Rourke ordered. When he turned toward the office doors, he saw water, geysering upward from beneath the bunker floor along the corridor through which they had just passed, in greater volume than would have been possible from any ruptured piping system.

There was ground water here.

And the trembling earth had freed it.

Rourke, Natalia and Paul flanking him, Rourke's left arm around Natalia's shoulders, crouched just beside the doorway through which they'd come, counting the seconds in his head, his eyes looking back toward the water, the floor beneath his feet already puddling, water oozing up through cracks in it.

The explosion came, dust and debris filling the air.

Danzig, barely audible, shouted, "The door is open, Herr General!"

"Up the ladder and as fast as you can," Rourke ordered, shoving Natalia ahead of him, Paul beside him.

Danzig's men were starting through.

The water was rising rapidly now, several inches of it covering the office floor.

Rourke and Natalia were beside the vault door. As he started shoving her through toward the ladder and the shaft beyond, she looked up at him. "Thank you for making what I am, John Rourke." And she kissed him quickly on the lips in the instant she ducked through the doorway.

The water was almost to knee level now.

Paul passed through the doorway, John Rourke after him.

As John Rourke took to the first rung of the ladder, the water was up to his thighs, rising more rapidly now.

Climbing—slowly because of Danzig's broken arm, Paul's dislocated shoulder—Rourke looked down.

The water was filling the escape shaft, rising faster than they were climbing.

John Rourke's foot slipped, his right hand catching onto the rung, Paul's right hand reaching downward, grasping him at the wrist. "I'm all right. Keep going!"

The water roared beneath them now, pushing so violently and so rapidly upward that the air around them was like a wind.

Rourke looked up, seeing Danzig disappear through an opening above. Then Danzig's man with the blood samples, then the other two men. Then Natalia.

Paul was nearly out of the shaft.

The water was gushing upward around them.

The water engulfed them as Paul lurched upward, Rourke's hands grasping for the top rung as the water slammed him against the wall of the shaft. He closed his fist over something solid and pulled. It was the handle at the top of the ladder. The water hammered his body against the roof of the shaft.

There was a door.

The door was closed.

An explosion and blinding light and John Rourke was engulfed, his body hurtling forward into the darkness.

Sixty-two

John Rourke said, "Amen," and his right hand reached for the knife, fisting it firmly as his eyes swept the room. "All right," John asked, his voice barely above a whisper, "who wants a drumstick?"

Everyone at the table started shouting "Me!" in almost perfect unison and Paul Rubenstein started to laugh. He caught the eye of the youngest person in the room, Michael and Natalia's littlest one, Sarah Ann. She was nine and very much the perfect sophisticate, with hair black as a raven's wing and eyes a brilliant blue, just like her mother's. She cocked an eyebrow toward him, as if to say, "Adults are really dumb sometimes, Uncle Paul." He merely shrugged his shoulders, agreeing but enjoying himself nonetheless.

Paul Rubenstein would make an entry about today in his journal, as he did about this day every year. Someday each child in this room would be given a copy of the journal—he had long ago determined that—and know what had gone before and why they were here. To have done otherwise would have been unthinkable.

This was the Rourke Family's personal holiday, the 19th of October. Although the Family got together for every major holiday, which was sometimes challenging, having a day which was all their own was a necessity. The 19th of October was selected for what Paul Rubenstein had always considered a wonderfully logical reason. It was the birthday

248

of Natalia's uncle, General Ishmael Varakov; without Varakov's perfect humanity, none of them would have survived the Great Conflagration, and the general, who had kept his Office Without Walls in a museum in a city which no longer existed, deserved to be remembered and revered.

Paul continued looking about the room as John wielded the knife in heroic battle against the turkey. Emma and John's daughter, Paula, almost sixteen and as beautiful as her mother, was dashing in from the kitchen with a steaming hot dish of something or other in her hands, saying, "Watch out! Hot stuff!"

Timothy, John and Emma's son, was fourteen now and as tall and well built as a full-grown man. And, like all the rest of the men in the Family, just sitting there, waiting for dinner to begin. Beside Timothy sat Paul's and Annie's youngest, John Michael. Jack was a month younger than Timothy and, although more slightly built, matched Tim in height.

"Daddy, you're not passing things!"

Paul turned his head and looked his daughter, Natalie, straight in the eye. "Thank you for reminding me!" And he kissed her cheek, which always embarrassed her; which was, of course, why he did it. He looked past Natalie into his wife's eyes. Although Natalie was sixteen and Annie was in her early forties, the two of them looked enough alike to be twins; or, at least, he thought so. And, his opinion counted better than anyone's when it came to that.

Michael and Natalia's son, John Paul, sat opposite Annie. He was twelve years old, a fine, handsome young man, tall and straight, but soft-spoken and a little shy. Of all the children, he bore the greatest resemblance to John, his grandfather, the resemblance both physical and otherwise. A natural athlete, he seemed to spend all other waking moments reading or working at a computer terminal. His nephew, John Paul, would be interesting to watch growing into manhood, Paul thought . . .

* * *

John Thomas Rourke sat on the porch steps, a thin, dark tobacco cigar clamped in his teeth, his eyes on the stars in the night sky.

From the pocket of his faded blue jeans he took his battered old Zippo windlighter, rolling the striking wheel under his thumb, thrusting the tip of the cigar into the lighter's blue-yellow flame. Before flicking closed the cowling, he held the lighter near the black-faced Rolex on his left wrist. It was nearly nine-thirty in the evening.

Tomorrow, he and Emma would fly to New Germany (Rourke and his wife had agreed to split the piloting, which was the only way John Rourke ever got to do any of it). Wolfgang and Sarah, New Germany's President and First Lady, along with their two daughters, would meet them at the airport. There was a new medical school opening in New Germany, with all the finest in equipment and research facilities and the best staff to be had. Officially being dedicated on the day after tomorrow, try as he had John Rourke was unable to convince the directors of the university that the new medical school should be named after someone besides himself.

He had suggested Professor Dr. Wilhelmina Krause as the logical person to be honored. Once he, Paul, Natalia and Helmut Griem's men had gotten out of Deitrich Zimmer's bunker with the blood samples, it was she who spearheaded the effort to produce the serum which would defeat the Omega Option virus. Indeed, whether or not all the canisters of Zimmer's Omega Option virus would ever be found and disposed of didn't really matter because of her. The serum worked and was now part of the standard immunization battery for every human being on the face of the Earth. An interesting side effect, however, was that since the dissemination of the vaccine against the Omega Option, there had been no outbreaks of influenza on the globe and the common cold was virtually unknown.

Were Deitrich Zimmer alive, it would have been the ultimate ignominy for him to realize that as a result of his efforts to destroy mankind, lives were actually being saved.

The good part about the trip to New Germany, of course,

was that aside from seeing Sarah, Wolf and their daughters, he would get to see his old friend Thorn Rolvaag. Rolvaag lectured in New Germany three months out of every year. Thorn had gambled with the very life of the planet—because he had no other choice—and won. The explosives planted along the suboceanic rift had, indeed, vented the volcanic energy which would otherwise have destroyed the planet. For a time, certain of Rolvaag's less scrupulous colleagues had attempted to blame Rolvaag for the earthquakes and tidal waves which ensued in the immediate aftermath of the suboceanic explosions, saying that his calculations were in error.

But time and unbiased research cleared Rolvaag's name, despite his few, vocal detractors. And today, Rolvaag was accorded the credit he deserved, revered as the world's leading authority on volcanology.

Emma came out onto the porch. Rourke looked at her, smiling. Sweeping her skirt under her, she sat down beside him. "Pondering the imponderable? Or just thinking about Michael?"

"Actually, I wasn't thinking about Michael. If he wants to run for the Presidency, good for him. Politics have never interested me.

"But I'll betchya that the first Tuesday after the first Monday in November next year, you'll be the first man in Hawaii inside a voting booth."

"If he runs. Yeah, I'll vote for him."

"So, what were you thinking about then?" Emma asked him.

"A lot of things."

"Not in a talkative mood, are you John Rourke?" And she laughed softly, leaning her head against his shoulder.

John Rourke heeled out his cigar and put his arm around Emma's shoulders. He kissed her lightly on the lips and said to her, "Why don't we forget we've got a house full of Family and just look up at the stars for a while?"

And, they did.

FOLLOW THE SEVENTH CARRIER

TRIAL OF THE SEVENTH CARRIER (3213, $3.95)
The enemies of freedom are on the verge of dominating the world with oil blackmail and the threat of poison gas attack. *Yonaga's* officers lay desperate plans to strike back. Leading a ragtag fleet of revamped destroyers and a single antique WWII submarine, the great carrier must charge into a sea of blood and death in what becomes the greatest trial of the Seventh Carrier.

REVENGE OF THE SEVENTH CARRIER (3631, $3.99)
With the help of an American carrier, *Yonaga* sails vast distances to launch a desperate surprise attack on the enemy's poison gas works. But a spy is at work. The enemy seems to know too much and a bloody battle is fought. Filled with murderous rage, *Yonaga's* officers exact a terrible revenge.

ORDEAL OF THE SEVENTH CARRIER (3932, $3.99)
Even as the Libyan madman calls for peaceful negotiations, an Arab battle group steams toward the shores of Japan. With good men from all over the world flocking to her colors, *Yonaga* prepares to give battle. The two forces clash off the island of Iwo Jima where it is carrier against carrier in a duel to the death—and *Yonaga,* sustaining severe damage, endures its bloodiest ordeal in the fight for freedom's cause.

*

Other Zebra Books by Peter Albano

THE YOUNG DRAGONS (3904, $4.99)
It is June 25, 1944. American forces attack the island of Saipan. Two young fighting men on opposite sides, Michael Carpelli and Takeo Nakamura, meet in the flaming hell of battle that will inevitably bring them face-to-face in a final fight to the death. Here is the epic battle that decided the war against Japan as told by a man who was there.

HAUTALA'S HORROR—HOLD ON
TO YOUR HEAD!

THE WINGMAN SERIES

#2: THE CIRCLE WAR	(2120, $3.95/$4.95)
#3: THE LUCIFER CRUSADE	(2232, $3.95/$4.95)
#4: THUNDER IN THE EAST	(2453, $3.95/$4.95)
#5: THE TWISTED CROSS	(2553, $3.95/$4.95)
#6: THE FINAL STORM	(2655, $3.95/$4.95)
#7: FREEDOM EXPRESS	(4022, $3.99/$4.99)
#8: SKYFIRE	(3121, $3.99/$4.99)
#9: RETURN FROM THE INFERNO	(3510, $3.99/$4.99)
#10: WAR OF THE SUN	(3773, $3.99/$4.99)